REBLOGS & Hearts

FANGIRL SERIES
BOOK 1

NIKKI RAE

ISBN 979-8-9914741-0-8

Cover design made using Canva (canva.com) by: Nikki Rae.
Graphics designs and character likeness made using Canva (canva.com) and using Imagine AI Art Generator (imagine.art) by: Nikki Rae.
Library of Congress Control Number: 2018675309
Printed in the United States of America

To all the fangirls who pour their love for their favorite fandoms
and celebrities in creating fanfiction, fan art, sharing their
photography, videography, and attending fan conventions.

This one is for you.

GLOSSARY

Common terminology used when writing fanfiction

FANFIC/FANFICTION - stories involving popular fictional characters that are written by fans and often posted on the Internet.

REBLOG - is when you see a post you enjoy and click the reblog button to make the post appear on your blog, too. **OFC** - Original female character

OMC - Original male character

OC - Original character

FANFIC SERIES - One story with multiple parts/chapters.

FANFIC ONE SHOT - One complete story 500 or more words long.

FANFIC DRABBLE - One complete story under 500 words long.

FLUFF - Feel good, lighthearted, happy-ever-after fanfic. **ANGST** - Emotionally wrenching, dramatic, upsetting fanfic.

SMUT - Sexy times

AU - Alternated Universe SHIP - Relationship between characters, usually romantic.

OTP - One True Pairing aka fans favorite relationship between characters.

CANON - Facts about the world and characters that come directly from the source material.

HEADCANON - Idea or theory fans come up with that they prefer to the actual canon of the source material.

RAELYN

Staying up into the early hours of the morning had not been Raelyn Burton's plan. A recent rewatch of her favorite TV show, Red Moon, had inspired a new fanfic series, and she had spent the night trying to purge it from her mind.

Rolling onto her back after turning her alarm off, Raelyn decided there wasn't enough caffeine in the world to get her motivated for her first day back at work.

"Chucks and school polo it is then." She murmured, dragging herself out of bed to get ready, "Hopefully today goes by fast."

Raelyn parked in her assigned staff spot at Collins High School. There were hardly any cars, and she was relieved to see she wasn't the only one having a hard time getting back into the swing of things. Even though exhaustion was clinging to her, she was happy to be back within the halls of teenage drama and academics. This would be her fifth year as a teacher assistant and her first year as the T.A. in the English department.

Waving to the secretaries in the main office, Raelyn headed to her new workspace sharing a classroom with the department chair. Flipping the light on, she chuckled seeing her desk was decorated with streamers and photos of her favorite actor taped everywhere.

She sat down reading the familiar handwriting of her department chair, Maren Gilmore.

"And yet, you're always the one making fun of my obsession with Red Moon." She murmured with a smile.

She stared at the framed photo of her best friend, Maren, and herself during a girls' retreat.

Maren had been trying to convince their principal for the last year that Raelyn was the perfect match for her department. They both received stern lectures about remaining professional during school time and leaving the chit-chatting for after school. They had a lot to prove this year and Raelyn was determined to show everyone that she belonged there.

Another framed picture caught her eye behind the one of her and Maren. Picking it up she gasped seeing the autographed photo of her favorite actor, Austin Jameson, who played Rhys Remington on Red Moon.

"Holy shit…"

"Cost me a small fortune, but worth it to see that look on your face, fangirl."

Raelyn turned to see Maren walking into the classroom, "How in the world did you get this?"

She shrugged, "I searched for autograph photos and found one on eBay."

"Oh lord…" Raelyn closed her eyes, rubbing her forehead, "How much?"

Maren scoffed heading towards her small office, "None of your business. It's a welcome gift so be grateful and move on."

Rolling her eyes, Raelyn looked down at the photo again. Austin's bright emerald eyes stared back at her, and his beautiful smile made her heart skip. She placed the photo next to her other picture and began unpacking her things onto her desk.

Most of Raelyn's day was filled with meetings with the teachers and the other two teacher assistants on what Maren's vision for the

English department was. Maren had assigned her the two hardest groups of students to work with. Freshmen and Seniors.

As the day wound down and everyone began leaving, Raelyn walked into Maren's classroom.

"Either your faith in me is outstanding or you really hate me." She chuckled.

"Might be a little of both," Maren joined her laughing then leaned forward, "but seriously, I know you can make a difference with those students. The freshmen need encouragement and a friendly, trusting face. Our seniors need a swift kick in the ass followed by a reality check with love."

A small spark of confidence ignited in her chest, "Thanks Mare."

"Now if I could get you to stop living in a fantasy world and live in the real world."

Raelyn rolled her eyes, "And that is my cue to exit for the day."

"Raelyn…"

She turned to see Maren's brow pinching together. Her bright blue eyes narrowing on her filled with concern.

"I know the divorce was not easy on you. I'm thankful you found a show that inspired you to not only keep living but to finally finish your associate degree to work alongside me."

Raelyn crossed her arms over her chest, "But? There's a but…"

Maren smiled softly, "However… you can't keep writing about falling in love with your favorite actor and stop living life. You need to get back out there and see that there's someone out there waiting for you."

"I hear you." Maren looked at her skeptically, "Really, I do. I'm not ready to put my heart out there yet. For now, I'm comfortable writing about love and not actually experiencing it. Now, if you'll excuse me, I need to get changed for my night job."

Raelyn took a few steps outside the room before turning around and sticking her head back in, "I love ya sis and thank you for always being there for me."

A wide smile spread across Maren's face, "I love ya right back."

Raelyn walked inside Sanders Markets waving to the manager as she headed to the employee break room. She had been working as a cashier since she was eighteen and loved it. The work was easy, and she loved her regular customers that shopped there.

Tonight was a particularly slow night since a lot of people were taking last minute vacations before the school year began. She found herself helping their grocery stocker fill shelves and rotate product. Thankfully, her favorite manager was on duty and told her to take off early since they were slow. Heading home, she sang along to her favorite playlist happily knowing she could spend the evening with her newest story brewing in her mind.

After a shower, some dinner and snuggles with her big tomcat, Cordy, Raelyn sat down in front of her computer. Stretching her fingers out over the keyboard, she anxiously waited for Rhys Remington's stoic face to appear on the screen. As his handsome face appeared, her phone lit up with a new notification.

Raelyn opened the blogsite on her laptop to see the profile of her new follower. Their blog only had a few reblogs on it of some of the more popular Red Moon fanfic writers. They had reblogged the masterlist page she had created for her new series. Scrolling down, she found their comment.

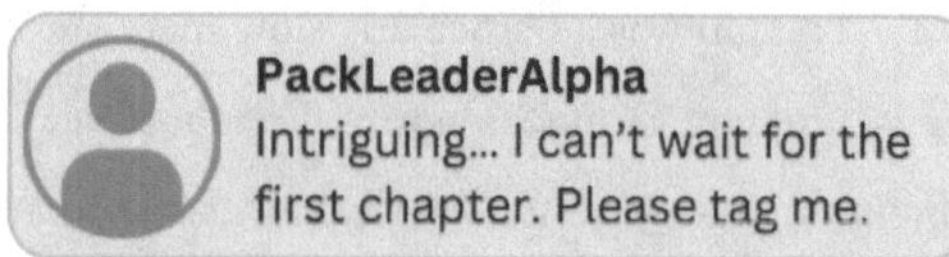

Scrolling back up, she read their blog bio:

She only had a handful of male followers, and it was always surprising to her when they ended up loving her fluffiest, lovey-dovey fanfics. She glanced at his profile picture seeing a recent photo of Austin and Calliope Melton who played Ash Remington on Red Moon.

"Figures he would ship them. Everyone ships Austin and Cali." she chucked.

Raelyn stared at the follow button on his blog for several seconds. An invisible hand hovering hers, pulling mouse cursor over it and pressing her finger down to click on it. Anxiety, fear, doubt pooled in her stomach making it churn. She followed all kinds of blogs, but something about following his made her antsy. Taking a deep breath, she blew out all the negativity in her body.

Closing out of the browser, she pulled up the outline for her series and a blank Google doc. She turned on her favorite Red Moon inspired playlist and let the words flow out of her mind through her fingers onto the screen.

When she finished the first chapter, she continued onto the second then the third. Looking down at the clock, she yawned.

"Perfectly normal for me to function on only four hours of sleep."

Scheduling the first chapter to post the next day, she shut everything down for the night. Climbing into her bed, she was soon dreaming about a certain tall, handsome man coming to rescue her from the boring life she led.

The next day at school was slightly busier than the first. She was helping teachers make copies and answering emails from students or parents about their English classes. Heading to her usual spot in the staff lounge for lunch, Raelyn was able to finally check her phone.

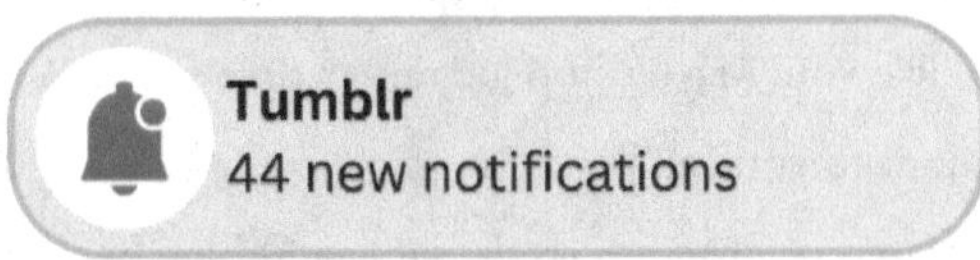

"Jeez…" She murmured opening her app.

There were forty hearts, three reblogs and one comment. The corners of her lips curled upwards. Tapping on the one comment, she was not surprised to see who it was from.

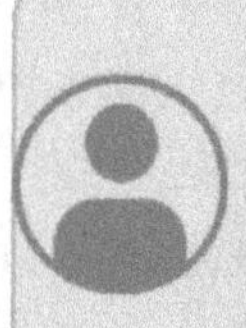

"What are you looking at?"

Raelyn's eyes snapped up seeing Maren smiling like the Cheshire cat. Quickly she locked her phone and slipped back into her pocket.

"Reading a comment on my new fanfic."

Maren's head dropped with a groan, "I thought you were going to cut back on the whole obsessive fangirl thing and be normal about the show."

"Please drop it."

"Not this time." Maren sat across from her, squaring her shoulders back preparing for a fight, "It's not healthy, Raelyn. Spending all your time with people you have no idea who they are and could be deranged serial killers. All because you're obsess with some teen wolf, melodrama TV show."

Heat rushed up Raelyn's neck and face, "Look, we all can't be perfectly healthy and balanced like you. Not everyone is beautiful and successful like you. Maybe stop judging people you don't know and keep your opinions to yourself."

Maren reached across the table grabbing her hand, "I don't give a shit about any of them. The only one I'm worried about is you."

"There's nothing to worry about. I'm happy right where I am." Raelyn pulled her hand out of her friend's grasp, "You're making fun of people I care about and making fun of me. You're the only one hurting me."

She watched Maren's shoulders sag as she looked down at the table, "I wasn't… I wasn't meaning to make fun of anyone, especially you. I…"

"What? You what?"

"I don't want you hiding behind your fanfiction and TV show, so you don't have to deal with your real feelings."

Hearing Maren say her most kept secret was like she was in a nightmare where she's naked in front of a class full of students. The bile rising from her stomach was blocked by the large lump of terrifying emotions lodged in her throat.

"I need to get back to work." Raelyn muttered, walking away before her friend could say anything else.

She avoided Maren for the rest of the day making sure she kept herself busy until it was time for her to go home.

Thankfully, she was not working at the grocery store and could go straight home. Walking inside, she went directly into her living room and flopped down on the couch. Her inner voice getting louder as she processed everything Maren had said.

You know she's right. It's really deranged that a grown ass woman would act a fool over a TV show. I mean, it's not like it's real or anything. Rhys Remington isn't going to come and save you from your pathetic life.

Raelyn sighed, sinking further into the cushions.

While we're at it, this new series is going to flop. You're barely a decent writer with a small, small following that's not worth talking about. Even sparkly vampire fans don't read your crap. Time to move on and grow up.

Her eyes stung with tears as she covered them with her arm. Allowing her inner voice to continue its ranting. When her chest felt like it would cave in from the weight on it, her phone buzzed with a notification. Tapping the screen, she stared at it through bleary eyes.

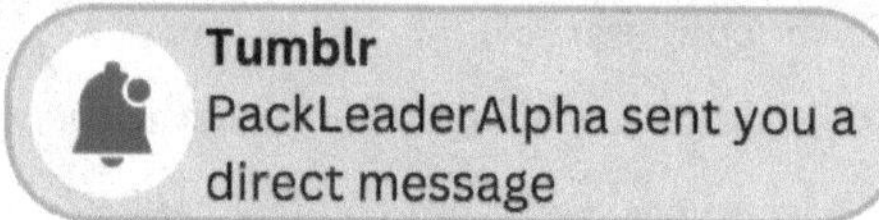

She immediately sat up as the steady rhythm of her heart beating faster drowned out her inner voice. Swiping the notification open, she began to read the simple message that silenced the imposer living in her head.

2

RUNAWAY
PROLOGUE – LIVING HELL
@PACKNERD71

Summary: Hiding in an abandoned house, Noelle remembers the moment everything changed for her.

Pairing: No Pairing / Past-Andrew Clark (OMC) x Noelle Clark (OFC)

Warnings: Angst / Past Abuse

Rating: M - Mature

Word Count: 863

Peeking out over the ledge of the broken window. She held her breath, listening to her surroundings. The leaves rustling from the slight October breeze. An owl in the far-off distance telling a nightly tale for the other animals. No footsteps. No smacking of a belt. No one coming after her.

Noelle Clark crawled over to a dark corner hiding for the moment in the shadows of the night. Letting out a soft sigh in relief, she knew she could not stay long. Noelle needed enough time to catch her breath and rest her aching bare feet. She must have been at least five or six miles away from her house by now. Hopefully that would buy her enough time to get further away from him.

Sitting in the cold, dark abandoned house tears slowly slipped down her cheeks thinking about how things suddenly became a living hell for her. She knew the exact moment everything changed. How could she blame him for being upset? It was her body that rebelled against them. Her body that she could not control. Now, that body was covered in bruises and welts a visual of how her husband was dealing with his emotions.

AUSTIN

Pulling his favorite baseball cap over his head, Austin Jameson headed towards the main entrance of the airport.

There were hardly any people there at this ungodly hour of the morning which was why Austin's manager had booked him the flight. He held onto to his carry-on suitcase and swung his backpack over his shoulders making the all-too-familiar walk to where Clifford would be waiting for him. Seeing the weathered army vet was comforting as he walked out the main entrance doors.

"Austin, looking good."

"Thanks, feels good to be back." He handed Clifford his suitcase and opened the passenger door.

Giggling came from the front seat, "Shotgun." Calliope's smile was from ear to ear having beat him to the car.

"How in the world did you beat me here? Did y'all sleep here overnight?"

Austin closed her door before she could answer and got into the backseat of the SUV. He could hear Clifford chuckling as he put his stuff in the back. When he came around to the driver's side, Austin was surprised when they took off without the third person into their trio.

"Where's Jax?"

Calliope turned in her seat, "We arrived last night, so he's probably still sleeping. I offered to accompany Clifford to get you."

"And here I thought I was arriving early." Austin watched the beautiful Montana scenery past by as the sun started to rise further in the sky.

"We figured you would want to spend an extra day with Birdie."

He smiled thinking of his daughter, Bernadette. His mini me, who had started junior high this year. An ache rippled over his chest thinking about his little girl starting a new school without him there.

"Thanks."

"She'll be fine, Austin. She's an amazing and strong young woman."

He groaned, "Please don't call her that. I like to think she still five wearing pigtails."

Calliope's laughter filled the car briefly, "Keep telling yourself that."

The rest of the car ride to their residence was quiet. As much as he missed his daughter and family back in New Orleans, Austin was excited to be back in Montana filming Red Moon. Every year he looked forward to slipping into his old boots and worn canvas jacket of Rhys Remington.

He always enjoyed his summer hiatus, but there was something nice about not being Austin Jameson, celebrity, for a while. Rhys was a confident, strong, alpha werewolf and there was something freeing for Austin to slip into that persona.

Arriving at their apartments, Calliope headed off to hers while Clifford walked with Austin to his. The apartment was untouched from when he left it at the end of the last season. The only noticeable change was someone coming in to clean it before he arrived.

"Your call time isn't until late tomorrow. Seems like they are taking it easy on you." He scoffed.

Austin rolled his eyes, "Only means it will be a late night wandering the woods somewhere. I'll see you tomorrow."

Clifford nodded before closing the door behind him. Austin looked around briefly before grabbing his suitcase and unpacking what little he had brought with him.

Being on the same show for ten years had small perks to it. He never had to worry about packing a lot of stuff to bring with him since everything was already here for him. Mostly, he had brought a few things from home that his daughter insisted he have and a few items of clothing that were new favorites of his.

His phone buzzed, seeing a text from his other best friend and co-star, Jackson Powell. He was the only other actor to be on Red Moon as long as Austin. They had spent all their thirties on the show and entered their forties together. Though if anyone saw them, they would swear that he and Jackson were immature twenty-somethings.

Austin tossed his phone on the bed and looked out the large window in his bedroom. There were many times over the years that he had considered moving Bernadette and himself up to Montana permanently.

A ripple of guilt rolled over his chest thinking of all the little moments he missed in her life. His mom and dad assured him that it was not that many, but he felt the older she was getting the more he was missing. Suddenly he found himself picking up his phone and facetiming her.

"Daddy?"

"Hey baby, I just wanted to check in." Seeing her face eased the guilt tightening around him, "Are you at school?"

She nodded, "Your timing is perfect. I'm waiting for the first bell to ring for class. You need to get some sleep, daddy. I'm fine."

He smiled, "I know you are. This was more for me than you. I just miss ya."

Her smile mirrored his, "I miss you too."

The bell rang in the background, "Have a good first day, baby. I love you."

"I love you too, daddy. Say hi to Cali and Jax for me. I will call you after school."

She waved goodbye as she walked before ending the call. The guilt and exhaustion hit him hard as he sat his phone down on the side table. Kicking off his sneakers, Austin crawled beneath the covers and sleep took him immediately.

The faint beat of drums was playing in his head. They were getting louder and louder until finally he peeked an eye open. The sun was shining brightly through his window. The pounding he thought was only in his head was louder than before.

That's when Austin realized it was coming from his front door. Rolling out of bed, he made his way to where the pounding continued. Peeking through the peephole, he groaned seeing Jackson's large head.

"Rise and shine, Austin!"

He cracked the door open, "What in the hell are you doing?"

"Come hang out with us before the long grind begins." He pushed on the door only for it to meet Austin's foot.

"I'm gonna be looking at your ugly mug for nine months. I think I'll pass."

Jackson pushed harder on the door only for Austin to let it go free. His laughter filling the room watching Jackson stumble inside his apartment.

"Dude! Not cool." Jackson regained his balance, "Seriously, Cali and I are headed to the trail with lunch."

Austin peaked an eyebrow at him, "Sounds like a date that doesn't need a third wheel."

"You're as bad as the fans." Jackson rolled his eyes, but didn't deny it, "Shut up."

He patted his friend's shoulder, "Tell you what, I'll go out with y'all tonight if you leave me alone for the rest of the day."

"The Rusty Spur?" Jackson asked, his eyes shining with hope.

Austin nodded, "Yes, The Rusty Spur. Now get out of here and enjoy your dat-" He grunted as Jackson elbowed him in the side.

"You meant hang out, right?"

Coughing, he rubbed his ribs, "Yeah… right… hang out with Cali."

Jackson smacked his back heading out the door, "See you at seven o'clock sharp."

"Goodbye Jackson."

Shutting the door, Austin leaned against it for a moment as the familiar ache spread over his heart.

It had been years since he had dated anyone. All last season, he watched his two best friends falling in love as the shadow of loneliness encapsulated his mind and heart.

Between his hectic filming and convention schedule paired with any other free time being spent with his family. Austin could not entertain the idea of having a meaningful relationship.

Trying to take a deep breath in, his chest constricted. The darkness was tightening around him trying to drag him down into a spiral of no return.

In moments like this, which happened more often than he liked to admit, he went get his phone from his room. This is when he was incredibly thankful for their fans.

He opened the Tumblr app and scrolled through his timeline for something to read. Fans would lose their minds if they knew that he read their fanfiction.

What had started out as a lost bet between him and Cali, turned out to be the one thing that could always keep him from spiraling out of control mentally. He looked off to the side where the suggested blogs were listed. One blog caught his eye, clicking on the username *@packnerd71*.

The profile picture was a beautiful woman leaning against a pale-yellow wall. She stood out in her dark pink dress that hugged every curve of her body.

Her shoulder length, bright copper hair framed her heart shape face and her pale blue eyes shined from behind her black rimmed glasses. His eyes scanned over her profile bringing a smile to his face.

"Oh, this sounds promising…" Austin whispered to himself.

He scrolled through her posts seeing that she was engaged with a lot of the Red Moon fandom. Her blog was filled with reblogs of smaller blogs supporting and encouraging them to keep posting. She stood up for the blogs that anonymous asshats would try to tear down.

There were a few personal posts about working two jobs and getting her associate degree at the same time. Finally, Austin checked out her masterlist of fanfics and his jaw dropped.

She had hundreds of stories organized by character and length. Series, one-shots, drabbles, and a few original fiction short stories.

He clicked on the newest series masterlist she had posted reading the summary and instantly loving the premise of it.

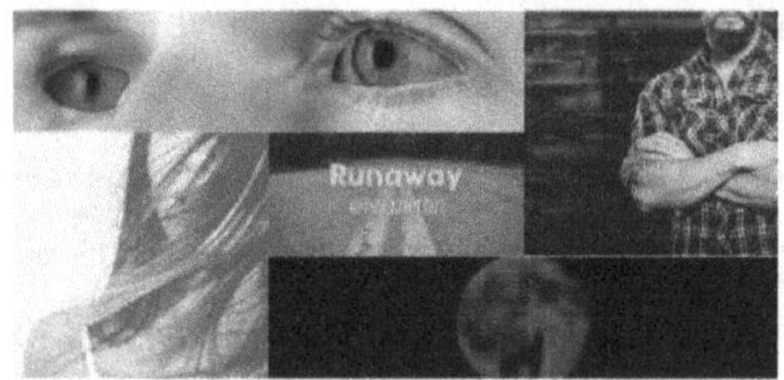

Overall Summary: Noelle thought she had the perfect life until it all ended up going to hell. Now she is on the run from the man she once loved. When she is attacked, a mysterious hero saves her and begins a journey into the world of the supernatural. Will she be able to be free of her past or will it catch up to her in the end?

Characters: Rhys Remington, Tiberius 'Tibs' Greyson, Ash Remington, Red Moon Pack, Andrew Clark (OMC), Noelle Clark (OFC)

Pairing: Rhys Remington x Noelle Clark

Warnings: Fluff/Angst/Mentions of abuse

Total Word Count: TBD

Austin scrolled back to the top of her blog and hit the follow button. He went into his settings and turned on the notifications for her blog.

For a moment, his inner voice tried to knock a strong sense of reality into him.

Be careful about what you do on this blog. You don't want another Britney on your hands.

He shuddered thinking of Bernadette's mom. He knew he should be cautious, but he couldn't rationalize or explain exactly what he was feeling. The only thing he knew was he wanted to read everything by her and be bold. He scrolled back to the 'Runaway' masterlist hitting the comment button.

He was selective about what fanfics he reblogged especially since a few people knew who he was on the site. So far, no one outside his small circle had figured it out. He even used a real photo of him and Cali as his profile picture that she took of them while filming.

A lot of the Austin/Cali shippers followed him figuring that was who he shipped. In reality, Cali, much like Ash is to Rhys, was a little sister to Austin. He loved her and would do anything for her, except date her.

Austin settled in his spot on the couch grabbing his tablet to pull up @packnerd71's blog. For the next several hours, he read every fic he could. Before he knew it, his phone was buzzing with texts from Jackson and Calliope about where he was at.

Cali: Dude! Stop reading fanfiction and get your ass to the bar!

Jax: Austin if you don't call or text back then we'll bring the party to you.

He looked at the clock seeing he was over an hour late to meet them. Quickly he sent a text to Calliope saying he would be there in twenty minutes and changed his clothes to make them think he put in some effort.

The Rusty Spur was in full swing for it being a Thursday night. Austin had on his favorite baseball cap backwards and a nicer looking black hoodie.

The bartender knew who they were and usually was able to get them a spot where they were not the center of attention. Finding Jackson and Calliope in their usual spot, Austin ordered another round for them and a beer for himself.

"About damn time! Please don't tell me you were reading fanfiction this whole time." Jackson down his shot of Tequila wincing slightly.

Austin took a long drink from his bottle, remaining silent. He wasn't ashamed to say he read fanfiction, but on nights like this with Jackson, it was best to not give him ammunition to use against him.

"Jax, leave him be. So, what if he was reading fanfics? I read them too." Calliope bumped her shoulder into Austin's.

Jackson scoffed, "Look we have some talented fans, but sometimes it's best not to support everything they come up with. I mean, look what happened last season."

Austin shuddered remembering the fan chosen episode. Running a competition for charity two fans were able to sit in the writer's room and create the 200th episode.

The episode was filled with long time fans desires including an awkward kiss between his character and the lone wolf character, Brynn. Basically, they had aired an episode that seemed straight out of the world of Red Moon fanfiction.

"Look, everyone has a right to express themselves as they seem fit. Reading fanfiction is no different than what we do every day by putting on make-up, costumes, and a whole different personality. All of entertainment is one big heaping pile of fanfiction."

Austin smiled triumphantly when Jackson had nothing more to say on the subject. Calliope held her glass up knocking it against Austin's bottle nodding in agreement.

As the night went on, fans were starting to recognize them. Most of them were sweet and kind waiting for an appropriate time to ask for a picture with them. Austin always gave those fans a little extra attention to show how he appreciated them treating them like normal human beings.

It was when a group of young women came up during a conversation they were having and hanging all over Jackson and himself. He watched as one woman squeezed Jackson's butt talking about how he had the best ass in the business.

Austin glanced at Calliope who was getting ready to pounce on the poor girl.

"Ladies, ladies, why don't you all make your way to the bar and let me buy you a round." He announced pointing to the bartender for a round on his tab.

The woman with her arms around his neck huffed, "I think you're trying to get rid of us. Is that because your girlfriend doesn't like your fans?"

"Darlin' I don't have a girlfriend."

The woman pointed to Calliope who was heading towards the bathrooms to cool down, "You mean she's not your girlfriend? Which means you're in the market for a good girl to take care of you."

Austin's stomach churned at the thought of what she was implying, "Sorry lovely, I'm not in the market for anything right now. Now, let me buy y'all that drink, and you can go have fun at another table."

"Awe, party pooper." She pouted unwrapping her arms from around him, "I really thought you were into girls, but maybe the rumors are true that you're not."

Jackson snickered as Austin flipped him off leading the group of ladies to the bar. He signaled for his tab to be closed after their drinks.

He glanced over to Jackson, whose eyes were glued in the direction of the bathrooms. Austin pushed his shoulder gently getting his attention.

"Go check on her and make sure she gets back home safe. I'm headed back to my place."

Jackson nodded, taking off. Austin turned his hat around, pulling it down enough to hide some of his face in shadows and headed for the entrance.

Once he was back in his car, he took the hat off and let out a shaky breath. The woman's perfume was permanently embedded into his shirt. He couldn't drive home fast enough to get her stench off of him.

Austin spent the rest of his night reading over his script for the next day. His mind kept wandering to @packnerd71's blog and wanting to continue burning through her masterlist.

Shaking his head, he forced himself to keep reading his script and learning his lines. It was nearly two in the morning before he finally put his script down and fell asleep.

Austin woke up mid-morning the following day. He had a short meeting with his manager and agent over the upcoming season. He received a text from Clifford that his call time had been pushed back due to Calliope being late to hers. He chuckled seeing the text from her almost immediately after Clifford's.

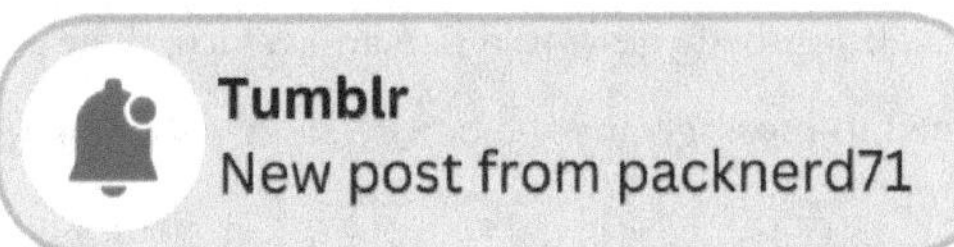

Since he had a few hours to kill, Austin decided to put on his running clothes to run his normal route. Heading outside, he jogged across the street to the park and did a quick warm up.

He headed down the street towards the river that ran through the middle of the city. He was halfway through his route when his phone chimed through his earbuds with a new notification.

Austin stopped at a bench along the river and swiped his screen to open the notification. It was the first chapter of her new series. Not wanting to wait, he sat there reading the chapter.

From all the fics he had read of hers, this seemed to be a little dark for her. An overwhelming sense of pride burned within his chest that he couldn't explain.

He liked her post and then typed out a comment on it. His cheeks started to ache from the smile on his face. He ran his hand over his face before putting his phone away and finishing his run.

Austin had barely made it back in time to take a shower and be ready for Clifford. Night shoots were his least favorite and the next week was filled with them.

Thankfully there were no fight sequences to add to being up all night. When they took their dinner break, Austin headed off to his trailer to relax.

He snapped a first day filming selfie and sent it to his manager to be posted on his social media pages. He sent a text to Bernadette, praying she would not answer it until she woke up.

Then Austin stared at the Tumblr app with his thumb hovering over it. He tapped it and went straight to @packnerd71's blog. The first chapter of her series was getting a lot of likes and reblogs.

Once again, pride swelled in his chest. He was going to tap on her masterlist when the direct message icon caught his attention.

Never had he sent a private message to a fan. A rare comment on a fic or art piece, but mostly he would like and reblog their posts. He had never felt a need to message anyone before since no one knew who he truly was.

In the few short minutes, he had left on his dinner break, Austin hit the icon and began typing a message to her. As if his fingers had a mind of their own, he began typing from the heart as his mind protested.

Hi Raelyn! I wanted to tell you how much I enjoy your fics. You're an amazing writer and I love how you always think outside the box. I also love how you write Rhys. You have a great understanding of him. I hope we can become friends on here since I don't have many. Riley

Say something

AUSTIN

A couple of days turned into a week. One week turned into two. For the first time in his career, Austin had approached a fan and she never responded.

Not a hello, thank you, fuck off creep. Nothing. The disappointment had him moping around the set most days and by the time they started filming episode three embarrassment was crashing into him.

He felt like a stalker constantly checking her blog for a new update on her series or in general.

He couldn't help noticing that her radio silence had come after he had messaged her. Had she figured out that it was him and not a normal, random fan of Red Moon. He double checked everything on his own blog to make sure there was no way of telling it was him.

Everything on there was true except for the use of his middle name. Maybe Raelyn had put all the clues together. The endless cycle of what ifs were trying him crazy. He tried distracting himself by focusing on work or chatting with Bernadette. No matter what he tried to fill his time with his mind would always wander back to Raelyn.

He felt like a crazy person for binging her entire masterlist and yearning for more to read from her. He had tried reading another fanfiction but nothing could compare to hers. He found himself wishing there was someone there he could talk to about what was going on inside his head. That is when the universe sent Calliope to confront him.

"What the hell is going on with you?"

Austin was resting in his trailer during lunch when Calliope came storming inside.

"You're going to have to be more specific." He chuckled.

She sat cross-legged on the couch next to him. Austin did his best not to look right at her. Of all the people in his life, Calliope and Bernadette were the ones who could see through his bullshit.

"You're a mess. Not remembering lines. Careless during stunts. Not to mention not one prank on set in weeks. I'm concerned. What is going on?"

He thought he had been hiding his torment well, but he should have known better. The warmth from his cheeks was spreading up to his ears. Squirming in his seat desperately trying to come up with something to tell her that she would believe.

"It's nothing. Trying to adjust to being back. It was harder this year with Birdie going into junior high."

Austin took a chance glancing over at her. Calliope's piercing green eyes were shooting right through his story, and he knew she would get the truth out of him one way or another.

"You want to try that again?" She folded her arms over her chest.

"You know I really hate that you can see through all my shit."

Finally, her face softened with a smile, "It's also why I'm your favorite. Now tell me what's really going on."

He sighed, "I found a fan blog that I really like online and commented on one of her fics."

Her finger made a circle in the air, "Continue."

"I'm not going to make it out of this with my dignity or pride, am I?"

They both chuckled as she shook her head, "Afraid not, so spit it out before they call us back to set."

Austin gave in telling her all about Raelyn, commenting on her newest series, binging her masterlist and topped it off with the root of his mood lately.

"You messaged her? Did you tell her who you were?"

"Of course not, Cali. I use my middle name on there and so far in the two years I've been on this site no one has figured it out. I'm careful to not post much of anything other than a rare reblog of a fic I like. To anyone who would look at my profile, I'm Riley, a rare male fan of Red Moon. That's it."

He ran his hand through his hair trying to get his stomach to stop flip-flopping. Letting out a long breath he slouched onto the couch covering his face with his hands.

"Wow, this is really bothering you. I haven't seen you like this since Britney."

His eyes shot up narrowing on her, "Don't even bring her up."

Britney Morris was a lesson learned the hard way. She was one of the first fans he had met at a signing event in the mall. He was starring in a young new drama and Britney had done everything in her power to make sure their paths intersected.

Her admiration for the character he played and his insecurities of being good enough at the time were the perfect storm of their dysfunctional relationship. The only silver lining to being with Britney was their daughter being born.

"Hey, earth to Austin." Calliope snapped her fingers bringing him out of his thoughts, "I asked you a question."

"Sorry, what did you ask?" He sat up leaning his elbows on his knees.

She mirrored his position except for her gently rubbing his back, "Do you know this fan? Have you met her before at a con or something?"

The answer to her question is what scared him the most. He had thought the same thing a few days earlier. Maybe they had crossed paths before. Maybe she had been one of the thousands of fans that attended a Red Moon convention or had been in the main panel hall at San Diego. Had he randomly met her on the street and taken a picture with her. The answer was all the same.

"No. I had no idea she existed and now I feel like she is supposed to be a part of my life somehow." He turned towards his best friend, "You're always going on about how the universe rights itself and people being meant to be. Am I fucking crazy or are the gods above trying to send me a message."

Calliope went to speak when there were three knocks on his trailer door, "Austin, they're ready for you on set."

"Coming. Be there in two minutes." He called out.

She took his hands in hers squeezing them, "To answer your question, I think it's a little of both. One thing I do know is the heart makes you do dumb things when it comes to who your soul is tied too. Just be careful."

Austin pulled her into a tight hug, "Thank you for not laughing hysterically in my face and for the love of god don't tell Jax."

Her body shook as her laugh filled the air, "And lose my best piece of blackmail. No way. Your secret is safe with me… for now."

By the end of the week, Austin was feeling almost normal again. Which was good since he was flying out with Jackson and Calliope for a party in Los Angeles thrown by their network executives. A lot of other actors and actresses from the network would be there. All of their managers had made it a point to stress how important it was for the three of them to be there as the stars of the longest running show.

On Saturday night, Austin found himself looking in a hotel mirror making sure he was presentable. He had on his favorite black convention boots that still looked nice but were comfortable to stand in for hours. He decided on a pair of fitted black jeans with an olive button down shirt.

He ran his fingers through his long, unruly hair a few times, taming the strands into place. Running his hand over his copper tinted beard, he sighed seeing more gray appearing in it. Slipping his phone into his pocket, Austin deemed himself presentable.

The Hollywood mansion was owned by the president of the
network. She had always been supportive of Red Moon. Letting them do
what they wanted, as long as, it drew in viewers and didn't get them in
trouble. Mingling with the other actors, Austin hardly recognized any of
them from the other shows. The network had been making changes
within the last year to get a younger audience to watch. Majority of the
actors and actresses were barely of drinking age, not that it mattered.

"Are you Austin Jameson?"

He turned towards the young woman behind him, "Yeah, that's
me. You are?"

"Oh wow… um, I'm Daisy Graham. Wow, I can't believe I'm
meeting you. I grew up watching Red Moon with my dad. He is such a
huge fan."

Austin tried not to flinch, "That's really great. Which show are
you on?"

"I'm on the new teen show, Ravenwood High. We just
started…"

"Hey Austin, we need you for a second."

Looking over, Jackson and Calliope were both wearing amused
grins on their faces. He excused himself, walking quickly over to them.

"Thank you for the rescue."

Jackson swung his arm around his shoulders, "Any time Alpha."

Austin jabbed him in the side, "I told you stop calling me that."

They headed towards the open bar and soon the night was
turning into one big, tequila-fueled blur for Austin. At one point he was in
the middle of a group of young women on the dance floor. With the help
of his liquid courage, he pushed away all the normal boundaries he had in
place to keep him out of the situations he was currently in.

Feeling his phone buzz in his pocket, his heart leaped in his chest. He barely escaped the women who were calling out his name to come back and made his way towards a more open area. Finding a clear spot along a wall, he leaned against it and took his phone out to see a new text notification from Bernadette. His mind began to clear from the tequila induced fog and he typed a reply.

Austin looked around the room in search of an exit and found an open door to a balcony. Thankfully, no one was out on it and the warm night air was comforting. He reread Bernadette's text, silently thanking the universe for her being in his life.

Clicking out of the text thread, Austin looked at his Tumblr app. The disappointment that was slowly easing its way down his veins was now flowing freely as if a dam had been opened.

He wanted it to be a notification from Raelyn, messaging him

back. He wanted to know why she hadn't said anything. He wanted to know why she was ignoring his message. He wanted answers and had enough alcohol in him still to do something about it.

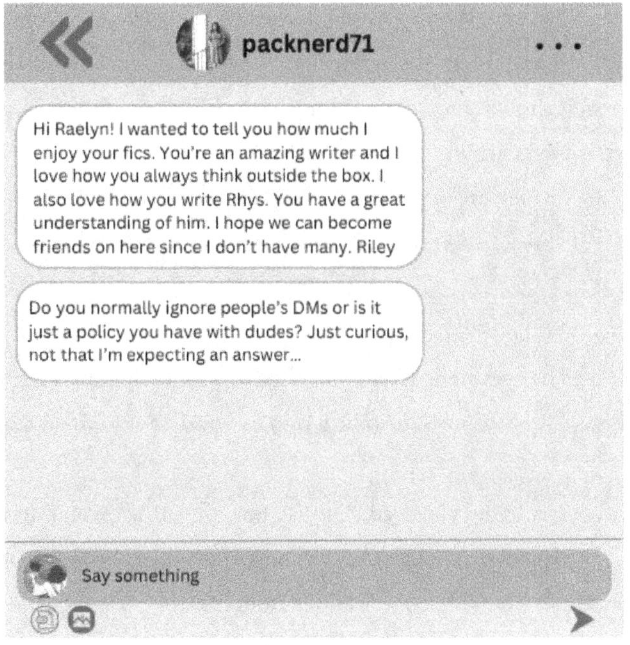

Heading back inside, his stomach started to tighten and churn. The room was starting to spin slowly. He looked for Jackson and Calliope without any luck, but his eyes did land on someone he could trust to get him home.

"Clifford, my hero." He grabbed the man's forearms for balance, "I need out of here."

Austin rolled onto his back with a groan. Every muscle ached and his head was currently the host of the world's longest drum solo. He tried opening his eyes only to shut them tight as the sun blinded him.

"Who's packnerd71?"

His eyes shot open, and his head spun wildly as he sat up too quickly. Fisting the sheets beside him, he shook his head trying to get everything around him to come into focus. Finally, he found Jackson sitting on the chair at the end of his bed.

"There are quite a few notifications from them."

"Fuck." Memories of the night before flooded Austin's mind, "Fuck!"

"Who is it?" Jackson turned around, tossing the phone to him.

His eyes went in and out of focus with each thunderous beat in his head, "Remind me next time we go to a party not to drink tequila or at all."

His friend chuckled, "Noted, but you know I won't do that."

Austin closed his eyes counting to ten then slowly opened them again. There were three notifications from her.

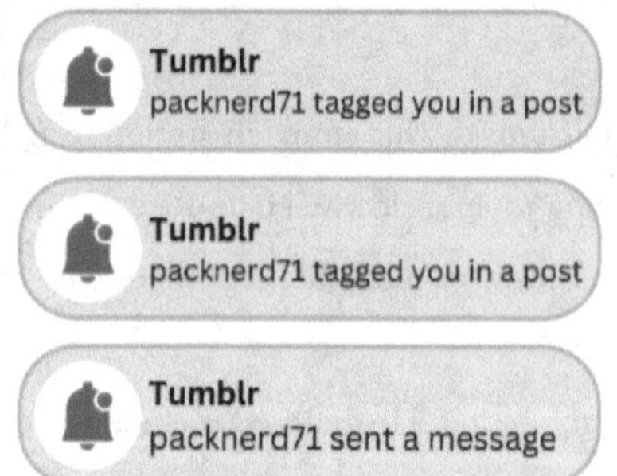

"Fuck me…"

He immediately opened the posts she had tagged him in. The little number one on his inbox taunting him as he ignored it.

Austin's chest ached right over his heart. There was a picture of her surrounded by some of her students. His heart throbbed as the invisible rope of guilt tightened around it. Her smile was bright and beautiful but not quite reaching her eyes. Her fair skin almost shimmering beneath the sun shining down on her.

packnerd71

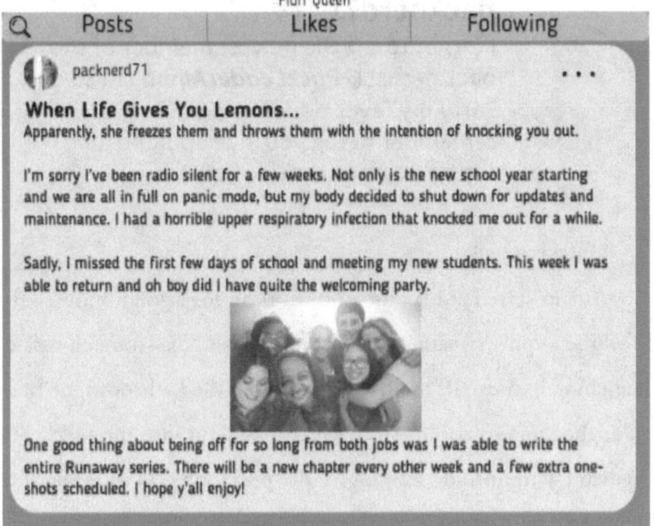

"Fuck." Austin muttered hanging his head low allowing the shame and guilt to blanket over him.

"Dude! What the hell is going on?"

He had completely forgotten about Jackson being there. There would be no way of getting around not telling him everything. He already knew what Jackson would say about it and suddenly Austin felt vulnerable.

"Grab Cali and I will explain everything."

Jackson eyed him suspiciously then nodded heading towards the door. Once Austin heard it click shut, he pulled up the other notification.

The number one on his inbox made his stomach twist as a cool sheet of sweat covered his skin.

He saw it was a reblog of Runaway chapter one that she had tagged him in.

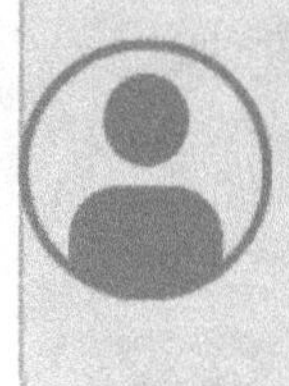

"Fucking hell…"

Austin stared at his inbox notification for a solid minute. He could feel the tequila sweating out of his body and his stomach twisted hard launching him up off the bed. Running to the bathroom, he barely made it as the contents of his stomach emptied out into the toilet. His body heaving with nothing left to give the porcelain god for a sacrifice.

"Austin? Austin?"

"I'm in…" He stuck his head back in the toilet as he heaved nothing but air.

Hearing her footsteps behind him before feeling Calliope's hand on his back, "Tequila is not your amigo."

He heard Jackson chuckling as he joined them. He finally pulled himself up and washed his mouth out once he felt his stomach relax. They all made their way out into the living room of his suite. He handed Calliope his phone with the app open.

"You read it first. I don't think… I don't think I can."

Her eyes softened as they looked down at his screen. Austin watched them widen before snapping up at him.

"Austin Jameson, did you really send this to her?"

"Her? Who her?" Jackson asked with a huff.

He watched as the wheels within his friend's head started grinding the clues together and the light bulb went off when he put it all together.

"Tell me you didn't. Tell me you weren't stupid enough to message a fan on a fanfiction site."

Austin rubbed his fingers over his forehead pinching it together in the center, "I need coffee and waffles."

Runaway
Chapter One – On the Run
@PackNerd71

Present Day

Noelle woke up breathing heavily as the last vision of Andrew faded. She sat up slowly not feeling as nauseous as she usually did. Looking at the clock, she had slept for a couple of hours. She stretched her body before laying back down again. She knew she needed to sleep some more in order to keep heading west.

Taking a few deep breaths, she closed her eyes again. Sleep did not come as easily the second time around. Once she did fall asleep Noelle had the oddest dream and for the first time in over a week, she did not see Andrew's face.

***

Noelle was in a motel room with the blinds open and the sun shining through. She was reading a brown leather-bound journal on the bed. Her clothes looked newer, and she looked more relaxed than ever before. There were no bruises visible, and a genuine smile graced her face.

Glancing up to the bathroom door a tall, muscular man walked out dressed in jeans and a plain black t-shirt. His warm brown hair slicked back from a shower. It was his eyes though that made her heart flutter and breath catch in her throat.

They were a deep emerald that reminded her of the first blades of grass after winter. They were welcoming, comforting and when he looked over to her all she could feel was intense admiration. His lips curled up revealing his perfect teeth and breathtaking smile.

"Hey pretty girl, aren't you tired of reading my dad's journal?" His deep raspy voice sent warm currents throughout her body.

She heard herself giggle, a sound foreign to her, "Never. I find everything you and your family have done fascinating."

The man walked over to the bed leaning down his lips hovering over hers…

***

She woke up staring at the ceiling in her motel room. Alone. A warm, steady current flowing down her veins that she didn't know she could feel. For the first time after the mysterious dream with the handsome man, Noelle felt desire flooding every inch of her.

That dream followed Noelle as she traveled to Corpus Christi, Texas. His emerald eyes and charming smile gave her the strength to keep going and when she saw the ocean off the coast of Texas, she let out her first breath of relief. Checking into a seaside motel, Noelle allowed herself to settle in one place for a while. She could finally start over again, being thousands of miles away from her broken life in Maine. Sitting outside on the beach with a brand-new journal she had purchased at a local thrift shop. She wrote the date in the corner as she began to write about the life, she wanted for herself.

One thing I do know is I would love to find the man from my dream.
Maybe I'm crazy for thinking he could be real but something deep within me says he is
out there somewhere. My only hope is that one day he will find me and take me away.
Making me forget about my life before this date.

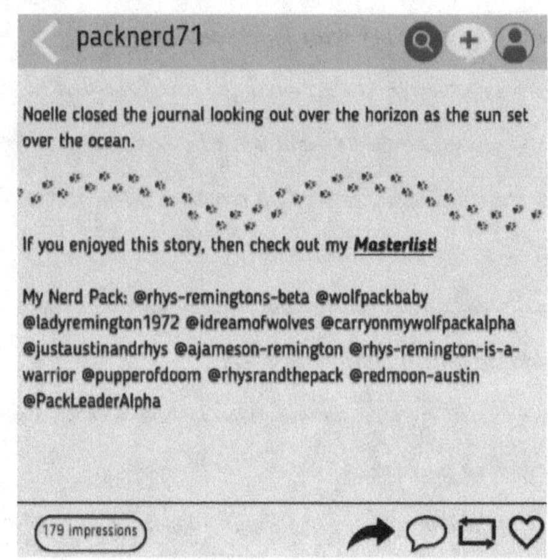
packnerd71

Noelle closed the journal looking out over the horizon as the sun set over the ocean.

If you enjoyed this story, then check out my *Masterlist*!

My Nerd Pack: @rhys-remingtons-beta @wolfpackbaby @ladyremington1972 @idreamofwolves @carryonmywolfpackalpha @justaustinandrhys @ajameson-remington @rhys-remington-is-a-warrior @pupperofdoom @rhysrandthepack @redmoon-austin @PackLeaderAlpha

179 impressions

RAELYN

Rather it was the stress of the new school year or working too much, Raelyn's body decided she needed a break. After a week of fighting to breathe and Maren yelling at her, she finally made an appointment to see her doctor. Her aversion to doctors began when she was a kid. It was always the same thing, causing any illnesses she was diagnosed with.

You have asthma because you're overweight.

Your foot fractured because you're overweight.

You have Major Depressive Disorder because you're overweight.

You have the flu because you're overweight.

She hated doctors, however this time she hated that the doctor was right. Raelyn's weight was now affecting her lungs making her normal seasonally upper respiratory infection much worse. She will never forget sitting in the doctor's office and looking down at herself in disgust. She had always been a big girl, but she had never let herself get above 230 pounds as an adult. That was until her divorce. Now she a few pounds from being over 300 pounds and the heaviest she had ever been.

Over the next couple of weeks, she was poked and prodded at a thousand different medical offices to make sure the rest of her body was functioning. The worst being when she had to do an extensive sleep study the first week of school. Raelyn hated that she would not be there to meet her new students.

After the first couple of days, she understood why her doctor insisted she take it off. For it being a test to observe her sleep, she got very little. She was exhausted from being wired up like a stereo system for multiple nights.

With all the time off and appointments, Raelyn was able to complete her new series. She was proud of the story she had created and spent one entire evening scheduling every chapter to post along with a few extra ones she had written. As she scheduled the last chapter to post, Raelyn realized she had never responded to PackLeaderAlpha's message.

"Crap." She felt a bump on her leg, reaching down to pet her cat, "Cordy, what should we say to him?"

He meowed up at her before jumping up into his window hammock. Raelyn pulled up his message seeing that there was a second message. Before she read it, she remembered not tagging him in her scheduled posts.

"Double crap. Alright Cordy, we have some editing to do and make sure this guy is tagged in everything."

It was nearly an hour later and one break to give Cordy some attention, Raelyn finally had all her posts fixed. The chapter that had posted earlier in the day, she reblogged tagging him with a special message. She stared at her inbox icon suddenly riddled with butterflies fluttering in her stomach. Raelyn pulled up her text thread with her online best friends, Katy, and Zuhra.

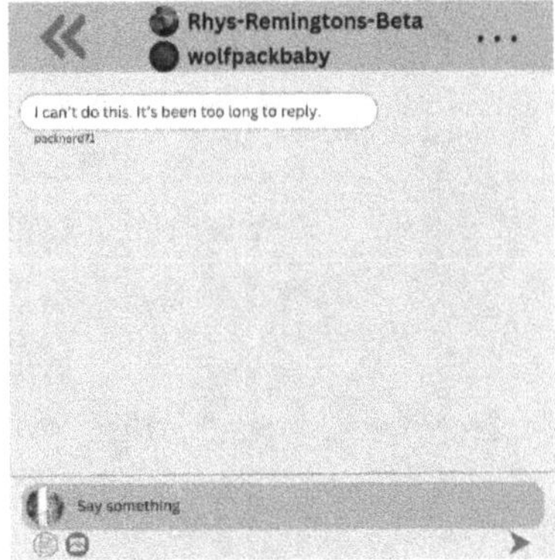

Immediately Katy replied as if she had been waiting for Raelyn to get cold feet.

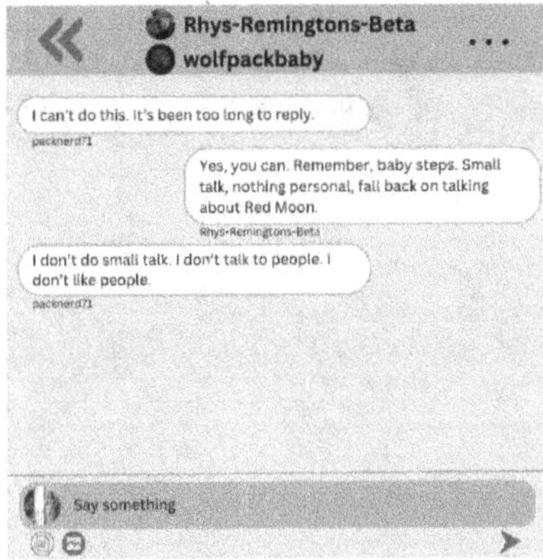

Zuhra chimed in.

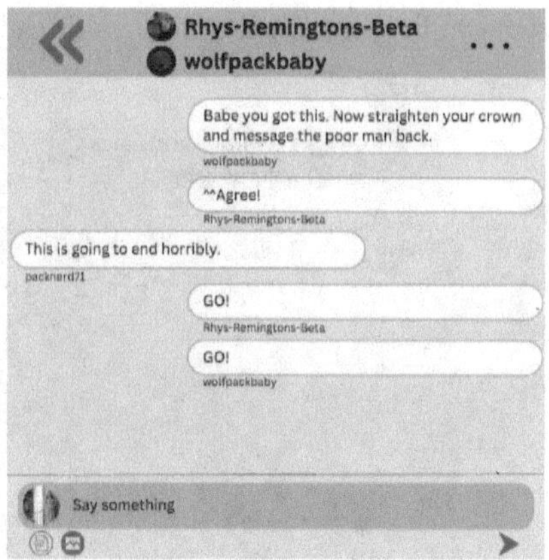

Raelyn chuckled sending the rolling eyes emoji. Taking a deep breath, she clicked on her inbox and opened PackLeaderAlpha's message. Her smile faded and tears sprung immediately in her eyes. She took a screenshot of his message and sent it to her friends.

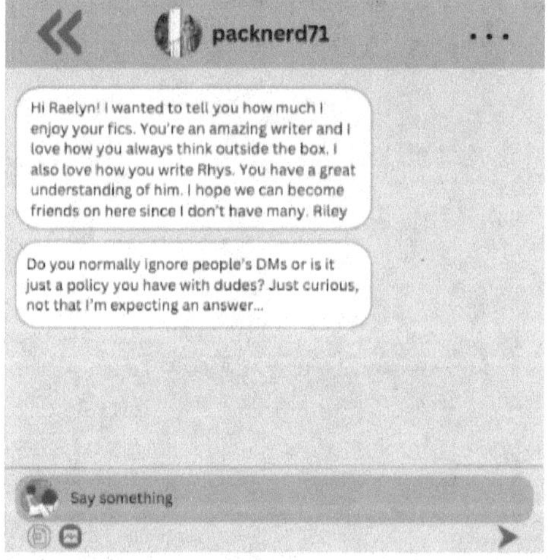

Their replies were identical.

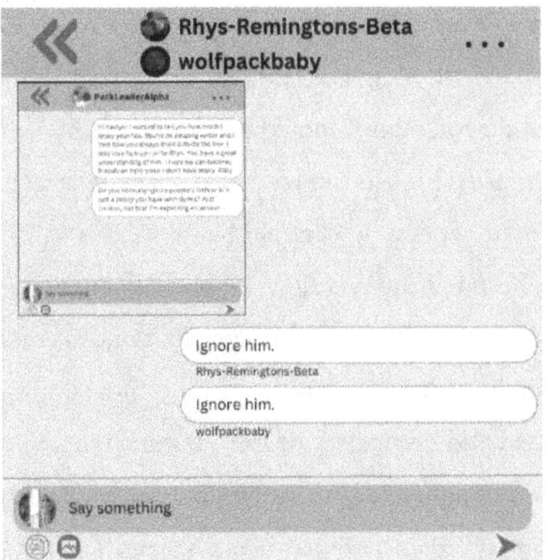

Raelyn's fist clenched in her lap. It was stupid of her to even be phased by one guy she had never spoken to. She hated the fact that she was upset and soon that turned to anger. Her inner voice chiming in with an all too familiar reminder.

Now you remember why you shouldn't trust anyone. They will only disappoint you.

Raelyn said goodnight to Katy and Zuhra with the promise of texting them tomorrow. She stared at his message, her anger stewing in the pit of her stomach. She began typing out a reply then deleted it. She typed out a longer reply with more fuck yous allowing her frustration to choose her words. Her finger hovered on her mouse to hit send. She decided that maybe the best course of action was to ignore him as her friends had suggested.

She closed out of all her browsers and shut her computer down. She headed towards her room but turned walking to the living room instead. Her hands were trembling as his message repeated like a teleprompter in her mind. Flopping down onto her couch, Cordy jumped up settling in on her stomach. His seafoam eyes stared at her.

"What do you think I should do?"

He stretched his legs out his paw brushed against her cheek. Smiling, she closed her eyes and ran her hand over his soft fur. The slight vibration from his purrs and repetitive motion of petting him instantly calmed her and allowed her to see through her clouded emotions.

Raelyn wasn't upset at Riley, not truly. Sure, it was a jerk thing to write, but she had also been a jerk by not answering him in the first place.

As she continued to pet Cordy, she realized that she was frustrated and angry at herself more than anything. Tumblr was the only safe place she felt she could be herself and talk to people. Meeting a whole new group of friends who knew her better than Maren or anyone else in her life.

Rarely were their male fans active in her fandom and she had hoped to get to know him. That seemed impossible now and that was why she was upset.

Opening her eyes, she found Cordy with his closed and content to laying there.

"You're right. We should sleep on this and then reply."

Raelyn carefully picked him up and headed to her room. Putting Cordy in his cat bed by the window, she crawled into her bed and turned on her favorite episode of Red Moon. It wasn't too long after that her eyelids were too heavy to keep open and she placed her glasses on the bedside table. That night, her dreams were filled with her favorite pack leader coming and whisking her away.

The next morning, she woke up to Cordy meowing for his breakfast. Deciding that she needed some orange juice and breakfast before finally replying to Riley. She brought her breakfast to her office sitting in her favorite reading chair by the large bay window. Her phone lit up with a text from Maren.

> Maren Gilmore: What are you doing next Friday night?

> Probably the same thing I do every Friday night, Pinky. Nothing. Writing. Pretending to not exist.

> Maren Gilmore: Not anymore, you're not. You're going to come with me to the first away football game.

Raelyn groaned. Maren was the cheer coach and spent most of her free time in the fall at cheer practice or games. In five years, Raelyn had been able to avoid going to any games as she had done when she was in high school.

> No thanks. I'd rather stay home and rest.

> Maren Gilmore: You don't have to go crazy like the others watching. You can sit down with me and the girls. You might even have a little fun. Please?

She knew there had to be more to Maren inviting her out. She never made a big deal about going to a game, especially one out of town.

Of course, her best friend was scheming, Raelyn rolled her eyes before continuing to read the text.

She sent a link to the school page. Any time Maren had tried to set her up it had always ended in a dumpster fire. However, curiosity got the best of her, and she clicked on the link.

Her jaw nearly dropped seeing a man who looked similar to Austin Jameson on Red Moon. She clicked on his name, Bryce Tucker, and read his school biography. He had been at Bradbury High for six years teaching freshman and junior history classes. The last two years he had been the assistant coach of the varsity football team and head coach for the girls' basketball team.

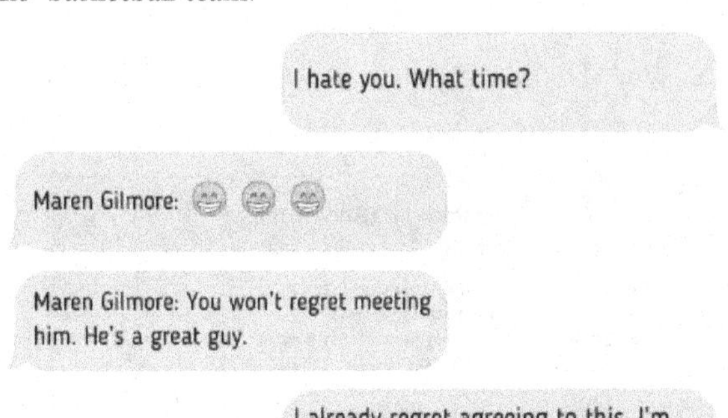

Maren texted her all the information for the football game as Raelyn stared out her window watching her neighbors playing in the front yard. The two kids were riding their bikes while their parents were talking on the porch. The man leaned down kissing his wife wrapping his arms around her. She felt the cold of loneliness creeping over her. She looked at Bryce's picture again.

"This is a good thing."

As she closed out of the website the Tumblr app stared at her from her home screen. Her shoulders slumped forward as if something heavy was resting on them. Opening the app, Raelyn went to Riley's message rereading it and typing her response. She hit send, closing the app and deciding today was a great day to unplug.

Raelyn spent the day catching up on her reading and taking Cordy outside on his harness. She didn't look at her phone until it was nearly dark outside. Making sure, Maren or her mom hadn't tried to text her. Instead, she found only one notification.

This time she didn't hesitate to open his message, the walls around her heart firmly in place to take whatever he threw at her.

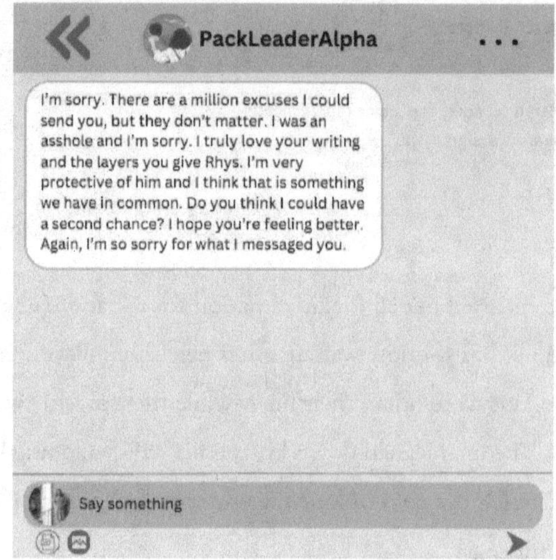

She reread his apology a few times before taking a screenshot and sending it to Katy and Zuhra. Within minutes, Zuhra replied.

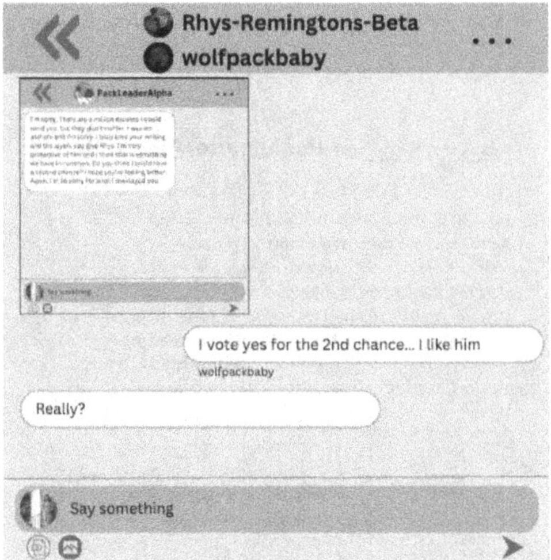

Zuhra sent a GIF of Tibs nodding in his wolf form making her giggle.

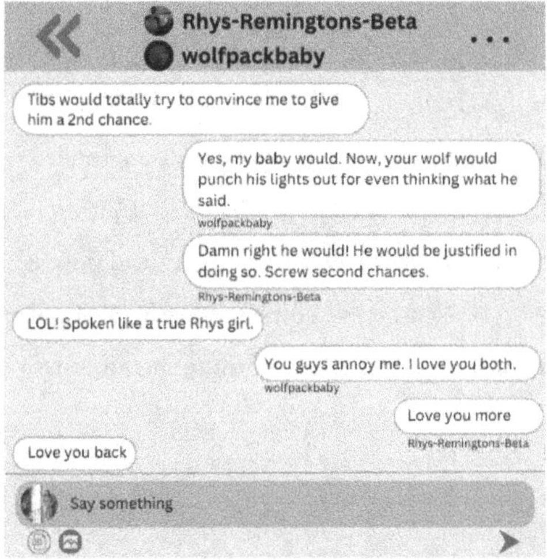

Raelyn smirked imaging Rhys beating up on some random guy that looked in her direction funny. She knew part of the reason why she loved Rhys was because of how protective he was of the pack. She always wanted someone there to protect her.

As Katy and Zuhra continued to chat, Raelyn switched back to PackLeaderAlpha's message.

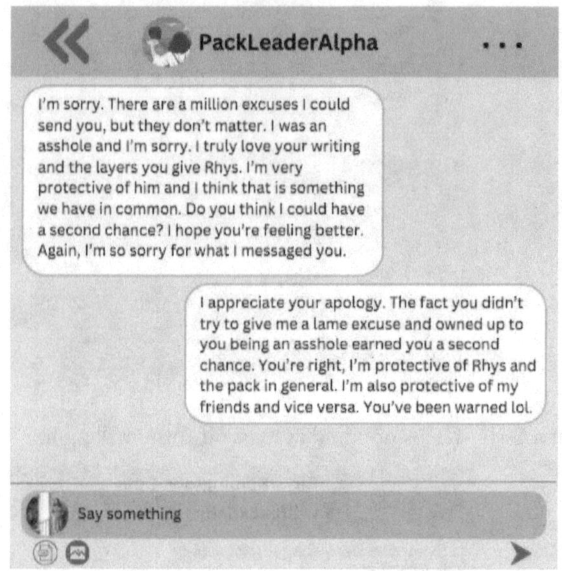

Raelyn set her phone on her desk and pulled up her fanfic folder. Creating a new document, she titled it *Honest Apology*. When she finished typing the summary, a new text thread popped up on her screen.

Raelyn bit the corner of her lip as it pulled upward into a smile. The butterflies had returned fluttering around in her stomach.

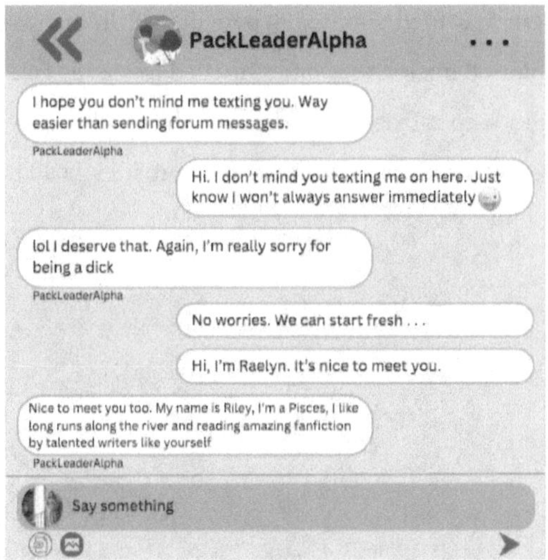

Raelyn rubbed her aching cheeks from the grin on her face. He was a charmer which normally annoyed her, but she found it endearing coming from him. They continued chatting until Raelyn saw what time it was.

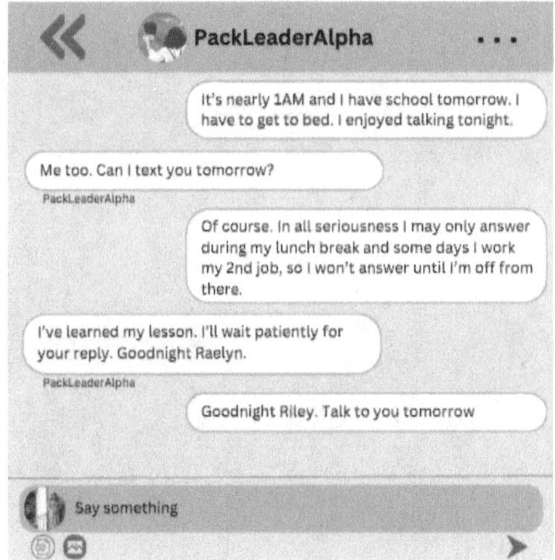

As Raelyn settled into bed that night, her dreams were filled with a mysterious blurred man. Every time she tried to see his face; he would do something to keep it from her. When she did finally catch a glimpse before waking up to her alarm blaring, she swore it looked like Rhys Remington.

7

RUNAWAY
CHAPTER TWO – SAVING ME
@PACKNERD71

Noelle walked to her room, kicking her shoes off then suddenly, a pair of thick arms wrapped around her. The ground beneath her feet disappeared as he lifted her up. Fear and panic filled her body as she let out a blood curdling scream. Thrashing against the person holding her, Noelle brought her elbow into their stomach.

Breaking free from their grasp, she turned around quickly trying to push her way outside. That's when she saw the man's eyes, the same as the darkest night sky.

He chuckled, "You can't get passed me, Noelle. Please keep trying though because I would so enjoy bruising that pretty face of yours."

Noelle backed away slowly from him as he stalked towards her, "H-How do you know my name?"

Her stomach dropped as her worst fear popped into her mind. He had finally found her and now she was going to die.

"My boss. He sent me here to retrieve you."

She felt the wall against her back as he closed in on her. Suddenly the door busted open, and Noelle ducked down into a small ball covering her head from wood flying everywhere. She didn't dare look up as she heard the black-eyed man cry out in pain.

Then she heard the one voice she had only heard in her dreams. Looking up she watched as black smoke came out from the mouth of the man who attacked her.

His lifeless body fell to the ground. Standing in front her was the man who had been giving her the strength to continue living life through her dreams. Looking up, she was met by the all too familiar pair of emerald eyes, soft lips, and strong, stubble covered jawline. That was the last thing she saw before everything went black.

Flashes of green and black were blended together. Calming, soothing green faded into cold, endless black as her body fell back into the abyss. An unimaginable panic flooded her body. The man's words repeatedly ran in her mind.

He sent me here to retrieve you.

Noelle's eyes snapped open as she flung herself upward panting. Everything that had happened hit her as she looked around for the man Andrew had sent for her.

"Whoa, darlin'. Calm down you're safe now." The deep voice sent chills down her body as she looked over to the man in her dreams sitting next to her bed.

"W-Who are you?"

She felt ridiculous asking a question she knew the answer to, or she thought she knew to answer to. His name was etched into her memory and brought a sense of calm to her soul that she hadn't felt in a long time.

The man from the diner was standing in front of her bed, "I'm Tiberius Greyson and this is Rhys Remington. We've been tracking the guy who attacked you for a couple of days now. What's your name? Did he hurt you?" he asked.

"I'm Noelle and no, I'm alright." Noelle said running her hand through her hair.

She could not bring herself to look over at Rhys. Her rapid heartbeat was echoing in her ears, feeling his eyes locked on her.

"Why were his eyes black?"

Rhys chuckled as he stood up from his chair, "Give her the talk, Tibs."

Tiberius took his spot as she swung her legs over the bed, "That man was a demon. From what we can tell he has been making his way down here over the last week from Maine."

Noelle took in a shaky breath as Tiberius continued, "Don't worry he won't be back. We took care of him."

She shook her head getting up, quickly starting to pack her things, "It's Andrew… must have been Andrew. I need to leave. I need to get far away from here." She rambled as she was throwing her things in her bag.

"Slow down, what are talking about?"

Rhys's voice stopped her in her place as if he had control over her body. Looking up she saw both men look at each other curiously then to her. Noelle began to explain what had happened to her in the last month, leaving out the gory details of what Andrew had put her through.

Tiberius crossed his arms over his chest, "Maybe Andrew made a deal to get to her. Which means there could be more coming. We should all head back to the compound, it's the safest place for her to be."

Rhys nodded grabbing her bag, "Agreed."

Noelle knew she should feel a little more frightened since she had no idea who these two guys were. There was something deep within her telling her to go with them. She knew they would protect her, and she belonged with them.

Noelle followed them out of her room and to the silver Chevy Chevelle. Climbing into the backseat, they pulled away from the motel.

AUSTIN

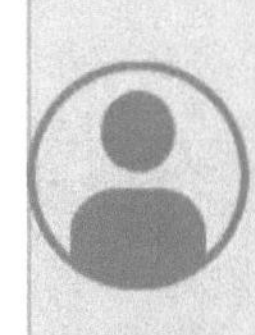

PackLeaderAlpha
What an exciting chapter! How is Noelle dreaming about Rhys? Is she psychic? Or is this fate? We all know how Rhys feels about that. LOL! Can't wait for more!

Austin clicked on *post* and the reblog went up on his dashboard. Chapter two of Raelyn's series had been posted during his lunch. He had been the first to like and reblog. Within minutes of his reblog he was rewarded with a message from her.

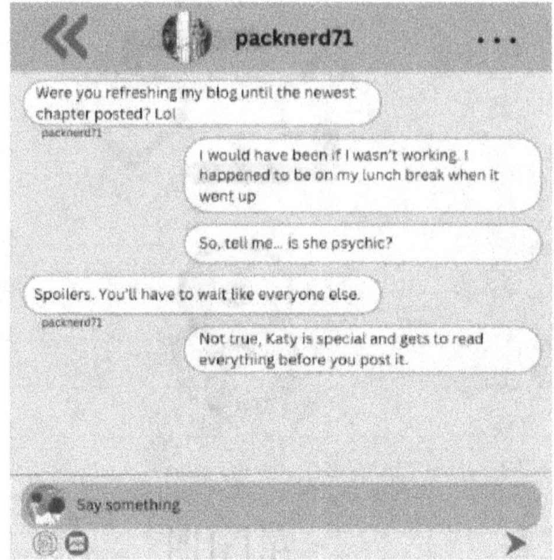

He had recently been added to Raelyn's group chat with her friends Katy and Zuhra. Austin found them hilarious and easy to talk to. If they knew who he truly was they would freak out. For now, he was enjoying getting to know his fans on a personal level.

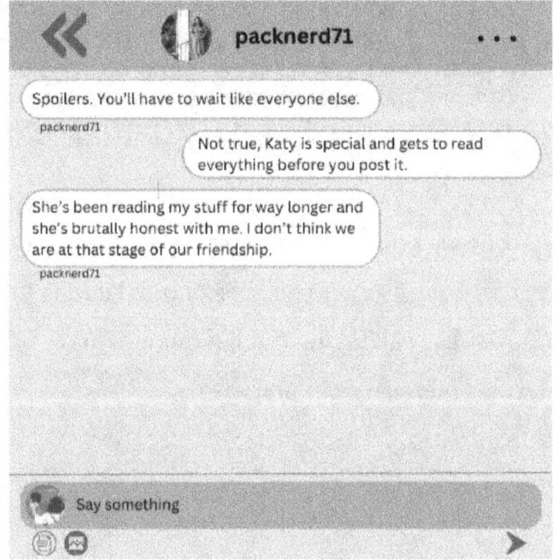

Austin stared at the word friendship. There hadn't been a day in the last few weeks that they hadn't talked to one another. Every day they found something new they had in common or adamantly had opposite opinions on. He found himself wanting to know everything he possibly could about her and often had to hold back from asking her a million questions.

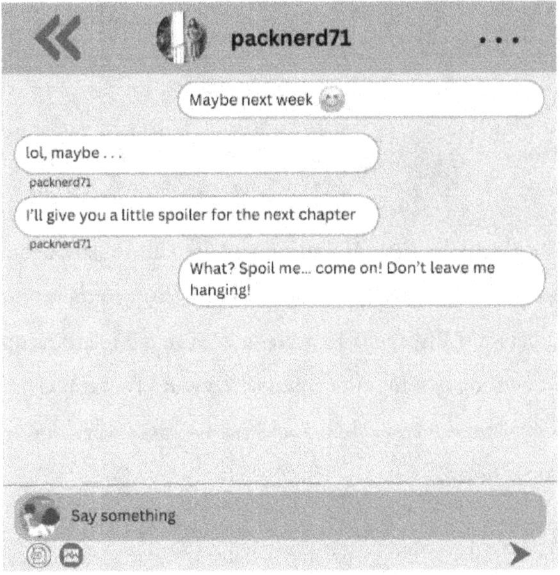

Austin waited impatiently for her to send the text. He sent her a GIF of a cat stretching its paws out with the caption *gimme*.

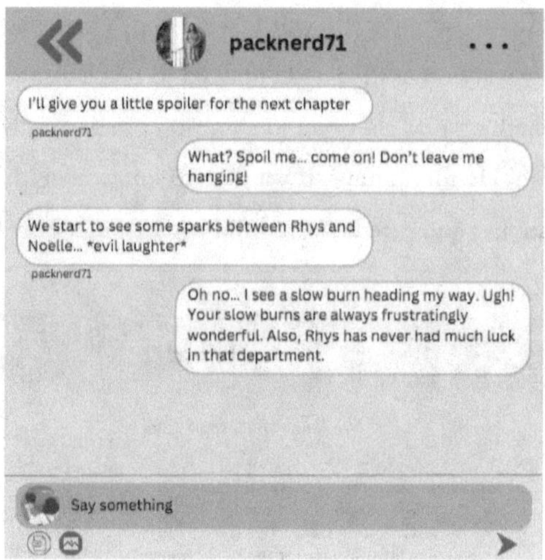

Chuckling, he thought back on all the failed relationships his character had on the show. The producers and show runners always felt fans would hate it if Rhys or Tibs were in committed relationships. Fans proved them wrong in a big way when at the end of season eight they had killed off Tibs love interest. Their social media pages were flooded with messages to fix it.

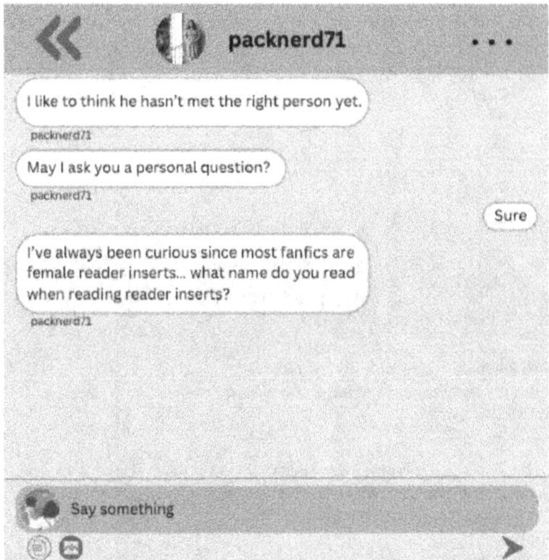

His body had frozen, every muscle tightening at first but then relaxed as he let out the breath he had been holding in his chest. Suddenly, his face became warm as he typed his answer.

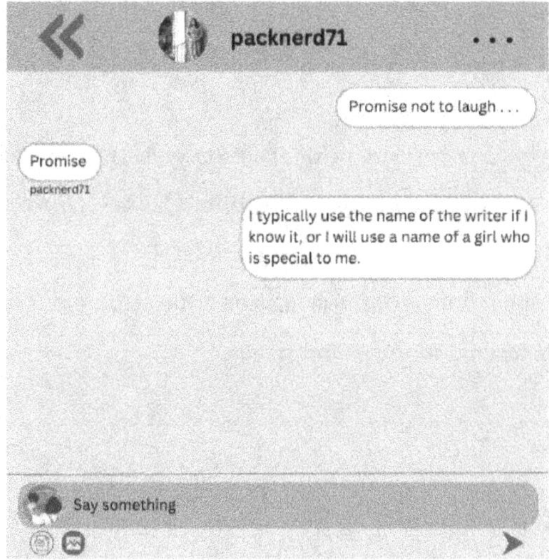

The longer he waited for a response from her the more his stomach churned. He was startled when three knocks came from his trailer door.

"Austin, they're ready for you."

"Thanks Maya, I'll be out in a minute."

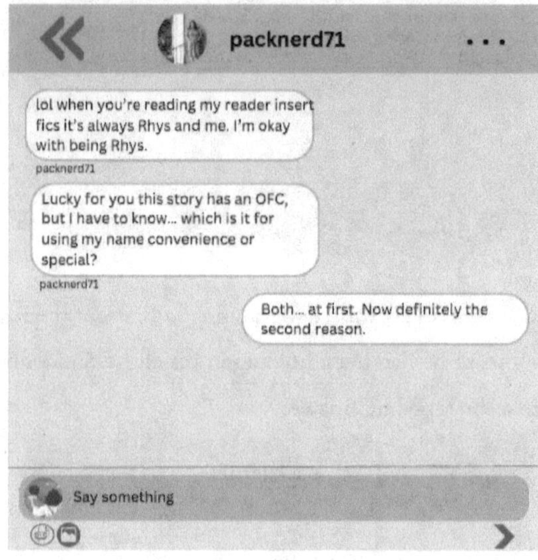

"Austin, get your ass out here now!" Jackson yelled from outside.

Austin chuckled before calling out to his co-star who was banging on his door now, "I'm coming jerk face!"

He opened the door walking down the steps and typed out a message as he headed to the sound stage.

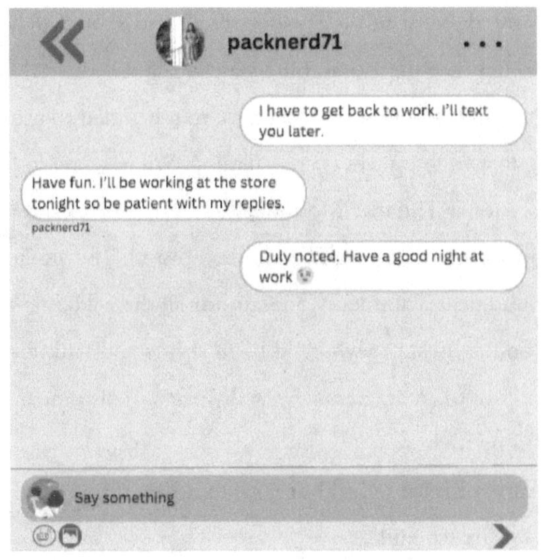

"Please tell me you're not texting the fan?"

His eyes snapped up to Jackson with a warning, "Don't."

Jackson grabbed a hold of his shoulder stopping in front of him, "This will only end one way and it's not good. She will either freak out whenever she finds out who you are then use it to her advantage. Or, if you're very lucky, she will freak out and she will never watch the show again."

"Maybe, we'll be friends and that's that. There's no harm in talking to her, Jax."

"Then why not tell her who you are?" He crossed his arms over his chest.

Austin continued walking, "She would think I'm some weird creep and instantly block me. I plan on telling her, just not yet."

Thankfully, Claire and Eli from make-up came over to touch them up before Jackson could say anything else. Calliope was walking up to them with the director of the episode. He knew immediately from the expression on her face that something was wrong.

"Hey guys, so the sound stage we're scheduled to use isn't ready. We're having to switch up what we're filming. We're going to head out for some night scenes at Thunder Mountain."

Now he knew why Calliope looked pissed. The studio had a small compound near Thunder Mountain for all the wilderness scenes. Most of the time it meant they would be in shorts and tank-tops from shifting in and out of their characters wolf forms. It also meant they were in for a cold, long night.

"I know this isn't ideal but it's either we do this or add an extra day and half to our schedule."

Austin pulled Calliope into his side rubbing her arm, "We'll grab our stuff and be ready for transportation in ten minutes."

The director gave him a thankful glance before heading back to rally the rest of the crew. Suddenly, there was a sharp pain in Austin's side.

"Ow! What the hell?"

Calliope stepped out his grasp, "I would rather add days than work all night in the cold."

He rubbed his side, "So you would rather film all night then fly out for a convention this weekend and come back to filming another night?"

"Oh. I forgot we have a convention in Tampa this weekend." Once more she wrapped her arms around his waist hugging him, "I'm sorry for hitting you."

Austin looked up at Jackson rolling his eyes, "Forgiven. Let's go grab our stuff and get this over with."

As they were walking back to their trailers, Austin noticed Jackson reach out for Calliope's hand. His heart gave an extra hard thump against his chest as Raelyn popped into his mind. He pulled out his phone, a smile spreading across his face seeing a text from her.

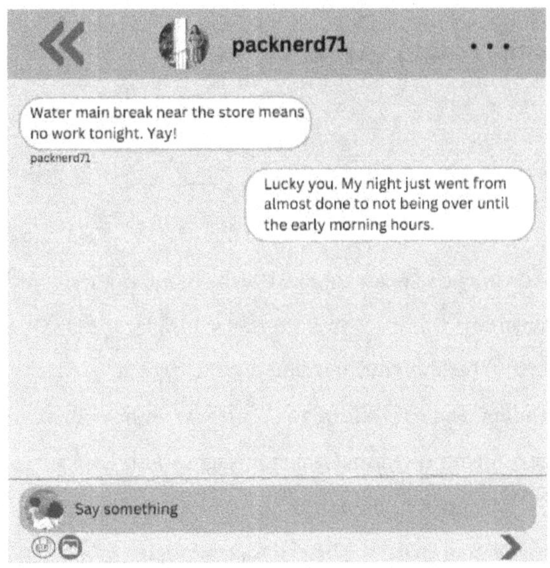

Entering his trailer, he grabbed his backpack and go bag with extra clothes. He made sure he had an extra hoodie in his bag in case Calliope needed it. His phone chimed with another text except this time it was from his daughter.

Austin groaned. Of course, Bernadette's mom picks the weekend he's at a convention to visit their daughter.

"Austin, we're ready to go." Clifford said, popping his head inside his trailer.

He grabbed his stuff heading out the door to see Jackson and Calliope standing next to Clifford's SUV. It was an hour drive to Thunder Mountain and Austin spent that time messaging with Raelyn. Occasionally, he caught Calliope smiling at him while the man she was resting against would shake his head disapprovingly.

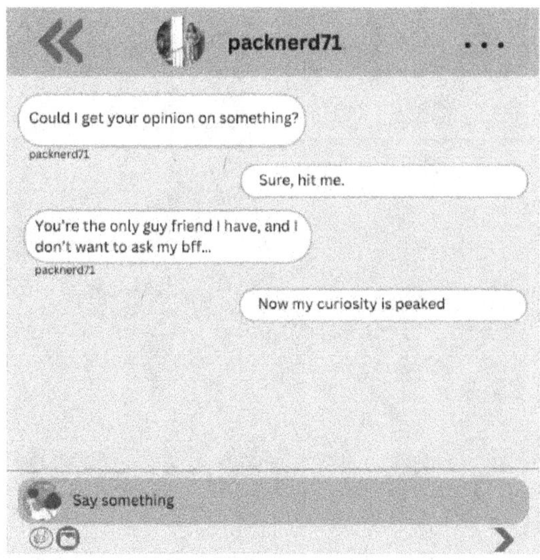

Curiosity was not the word he wanted to use. Dread was pooling in his gut that she was going to ask him for guy advice. For some reason the thought of Raelyn being with someone else made it hard for him to breathe.

When her text popped up a cracking sound echoed in his ears as a sharp pain shot out from the center of his heart. Swallowing the large lump in his throat he began to type.

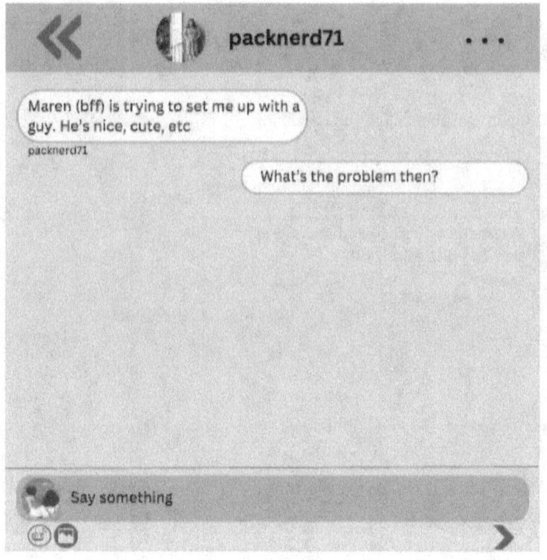

Waiting for her reply was agonizing. Chewing on his blunt nails, each second felt like a year passing. He looked over to Calliope when she bumped her leg into his. She had one eyebrow arched silently asking him what was wrong. He shook his head looking back down to his phone.

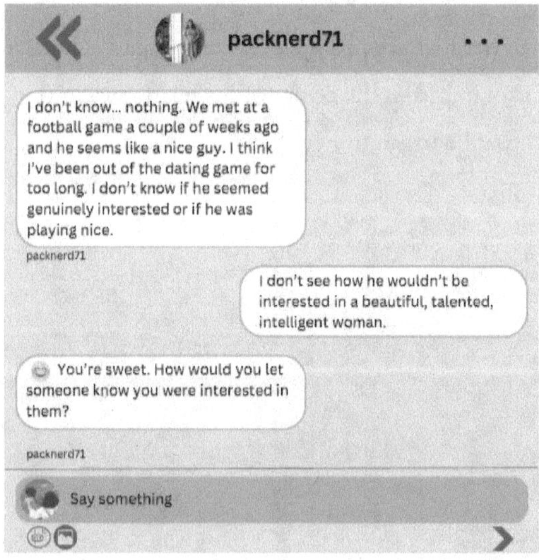

Austin took a moment to think about his response. It had been a long time since he consciously pursued a relationship. He didn't want to come off as over eager, but still be honest with her. Finally, he began typing then hit send. Glancing out the window, Austin saw they were exiting the highway towards the studio compound.

"Hey, you good?" Calliope whispered.

"Yeah, I'm good."

He looked down seeing Raelyn had messaged him again then heard Calliope chuckle.

"Fan or not, I think whatever this is between you and her is good for you."

Austin smiled, leaning in towards her, "Between you and I... I like her."

Calliope slipped her arm through his squeezing it tight, "Oh, I know which is why I want you to keep talking to her."

"You both realize I can still hear you and still think this is a terrible idea."

They laughed at Jackson who had his head resting on his seat with his eyes closed. Austin looked at Raelyn's message and his cheeks grew warm instantly.

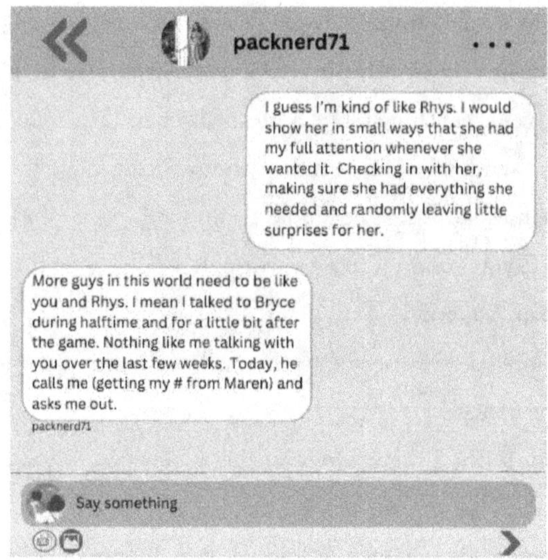

Austin immediately put the name *Bryce* on his list of character names he would never play. Other names including any names beginning with J, Andy, and Michael.

The car stopped, he looked up to see they had arrived, and Austin knew he would have to start getting ready to film. They all piled out of the SUV and made their way to their onsite trailers. Austin quickly changed into his wolf clothes and waited for Maya to come get him when they were ready.

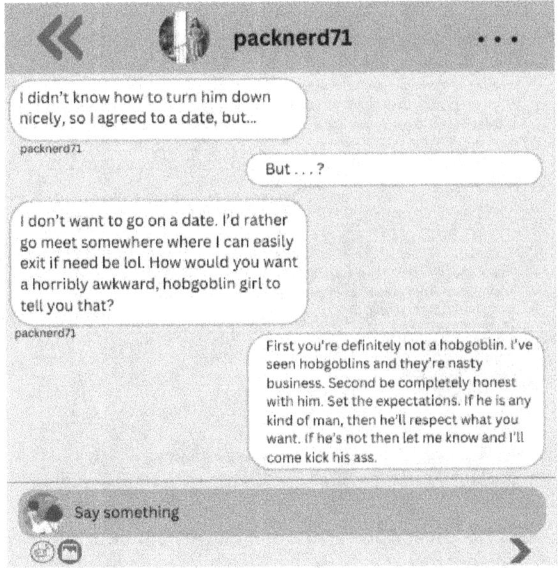

There was a knock before his door opened as Calliope walked in. Her long, dark blond hair was pulled up into a high ponytail and she was layered in hoodies.

"It's going to be a little bit while they get Jax bloodied up."

Austin nodded looking back down at his phone. Calliope curled up next to him on the couch reading the message thread.

"Boy, you really do like her. I'm a hundred percent for this."

"Shut up." He muttered.

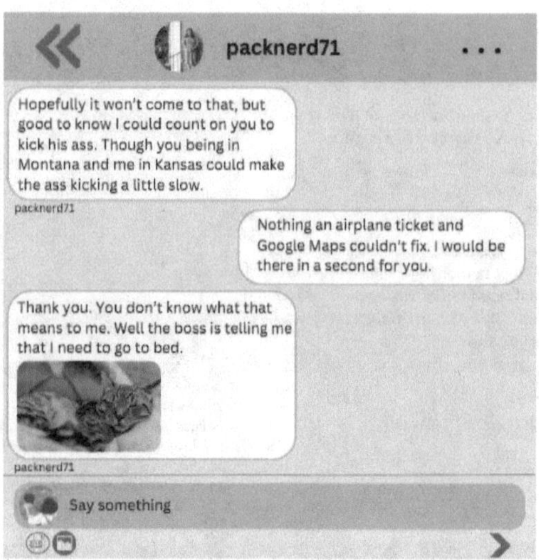

Austin had never been jealous of a cat, but currently he was. The gray and brown, stripped tabby looked extremely comfy sleeping in Raelyn's arms. He also made the mental note that she trusted him enough to send him a picture of herself even if her cat was the central focal point.

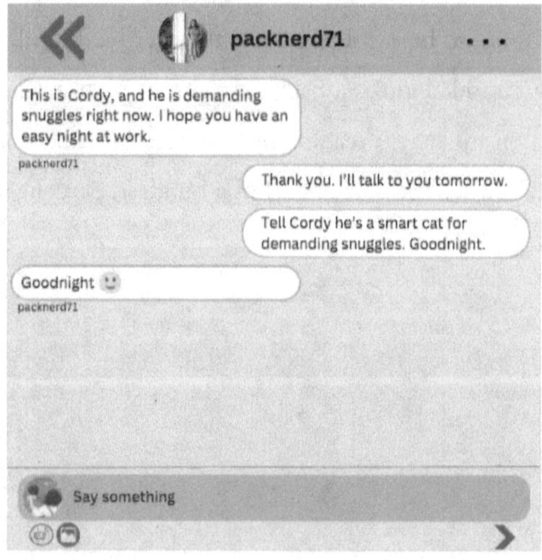

Calliope suddenly threw her arms around his neck hugging him, "I'm so happy for you!"

"What are you talking about? I'm literally just talking to her."

"Yeah, but you want more. The fact that you want more is huge. You deserve to be happy with someone." She gave him a squeeze as the familiar knocks from Maya sounded in his trailer, "We'll be out in a minute."

Austin hugged her back, "Believe it or not I've always wanted to find someone to be happy with."

She smiled softly, "I know. I have a feeling you may have finally found the right one."

They were going into hour ten when the director called a rap on Calliope and Austin. Jackson still had a few solo scenes to film. Austin had to carry Calliope the last few feet to her trailer. Helping her onto the small couch, he covered her with a blanket.

Tonight, had been an emotional rollercoaster for her character as Ash squared off with Tibs. Like in real life, their characters were falling in love and terrified that their Alpha would not allow it. Austin had enjoyed playing the tough guy, jerk towards Jackson. Even though the day had been long, it was one of the best nights of filming he could remember having,

The cast and crew of Red Moon were buzzing with excitement as the countdown to their winter hiatus began. Austin's manager made a visit to set with his convention schedule for the last half of the year. The last convention of the year was set to happen in Kansas City, Missouri. Pulling out his phone he messaged Raelyn.

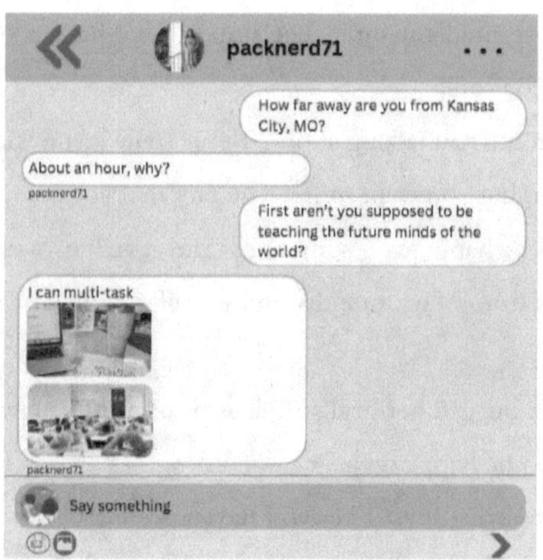

He sent a GIF of Rhys laughing which was both parts awkward and hilarious to him. Before his conscious mind could process what, his fingers were typing, he hit send and the butterflies in his stomach began raging with nervous energy.

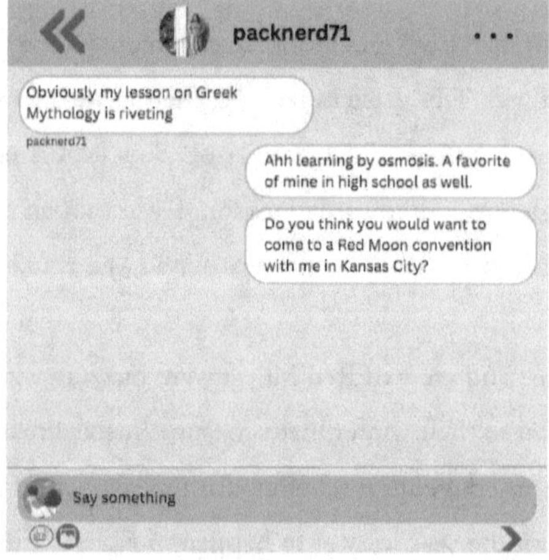

RAELYN

Nearly a week went by since Riley had asked her to the Kansas City convention. Raelyn had spent every second of the last seven days thinking about going with him. She wanted to say yes to him immediately, but something kept her fingers from typing those three letters. She kept staring at his text as her heart and mind were at battle with one another.

She was sitting at her desk well after the end of school trying to focus on grading essays one of the teachers had asked her to help with.

"Are you crazy?"

Her head snapped up as Maren made a beeline to her. Her blood ran cold, fearing that somehow her best friend had found out about Riley's invitation.

"W-What are you talking about?"

Maren slid a chair next to hers, "You turned down Bryce. A perfectly well balanced, normal, good-looking man. You turned him down for a fictional man that you're obsessed with."

She let out a sigh of a relief mixed with annoyance, "I didn't turn him down for a fictional man. I respectfully declined his date because I'm not sure I'm ready to be with anyone. I thought I was being honest by not stringing him along."

"Not ready? Raelyn, it's been years since your divorced. At some point you have to get back in the game or you're going to be a lonely, crazy, cat lady."

"I'm okay with being a crazy cat lady. Cordy loves me and respects my need to be left alone." Raelyn joked, turning back to the papers on her desk.

Maren turned her chair back around, "BFF to BFF, tell me the real reason why you turned him down."

Raelyn wanted nothing more than to tell her the real reason. The only problem was she didn't know what the real reason was.

"I did tell you. If there was any other reason, then I would have told you and Bryce. I'm not hiding anything."

As if the universe wanted to remind her that she was in fact hiding something, her phone chimed with a new message from Riley. Before she could grab her phone, it was being snatched up by Maren.

"Your online friends can wait. We're dealing with real world problems and not fictional problems."

"Mare, I love you. You're my big sis and I would do anything for you." Maren smiled with nod as Raelyn continued, "But if you don't give me my phone then I'm disowning you and never speaking to you again."

Her best friend rolled her eyes handing over the phone. She swiped the message open and instantly her lips pushed upward into a smile.

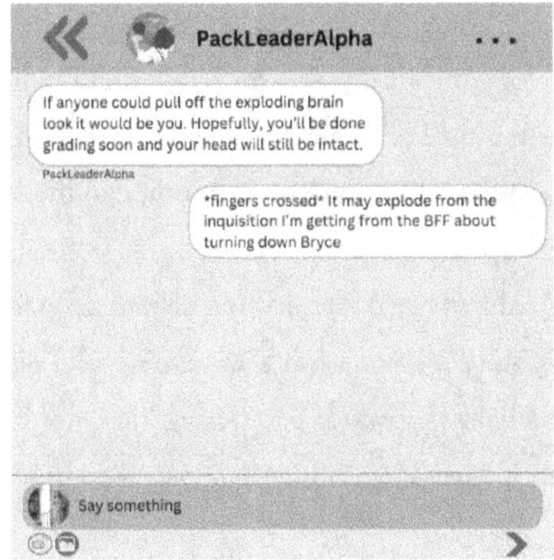

"Who are you texting?"

Maren was trying to look over Raelyn's shoulder to read her screen. She held her phone against her chest to keep her from seeing.

"An online friend."

"You're smiling and blushing…" She could see the wheels working within Maren's head, "Oh. My. God. You're talking to a guy!"

Raelyn set her phone faced down away from her friend, "Yes. He's a guy and he's a fan of Red Moon. He read my newest series and we're now friends. End of story."

Maren shook her head, "I can't believe this. You would rather talk to some random, weird fanboy who you have no idea who the hell he is or even if he's a man in real life."

In all the years they had been friends, Raelyn was usually good about leaving a conversation with Maren before she would snap. Today was not one of those moments and she had had enough of Maren's judgmental comments.

"You know what, I'm tired of you always putting down everything I like. So, what if I like a stupid TV show or write fanfic or obsess over an actor. At least it makes me happy and I'm not the miserable, depressed, shell of a woman I was after my divorce. If you don't like who I am then ditch me like every other godforsaken person in my life has."

Raelyn grabbed her things, leaving behind the piles of papers and walked out of the classroom. Her skin burning with rage as she stormed down the hallway towards the parking lot. Once in the safety of her car, she finally looked at her phone and instantly her body calmed down.

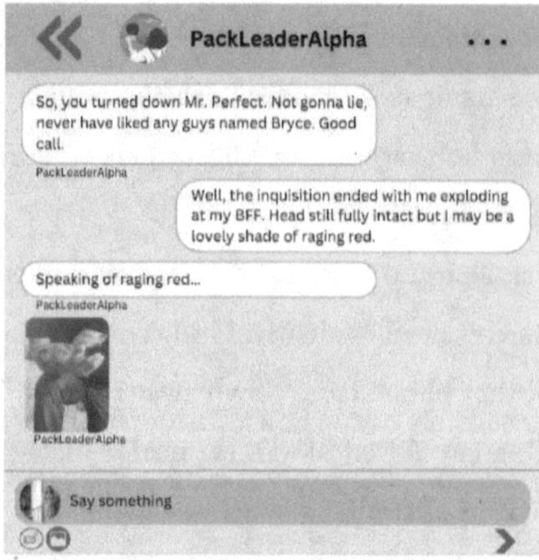

Raelyn watched as a photo popped up of a muscular arm covered in red. He was leaning on his knee while holding his phone. Seemingly relaxed, she still noticed the defined lines of his bicep.

In one of their earliest conversations, they had talked about their jobs. Riley had told her about how he got into Red Moon by working on their set crew. He told her about how he didn't interact with the actors much but a lot of their sets he had built or painted himself.

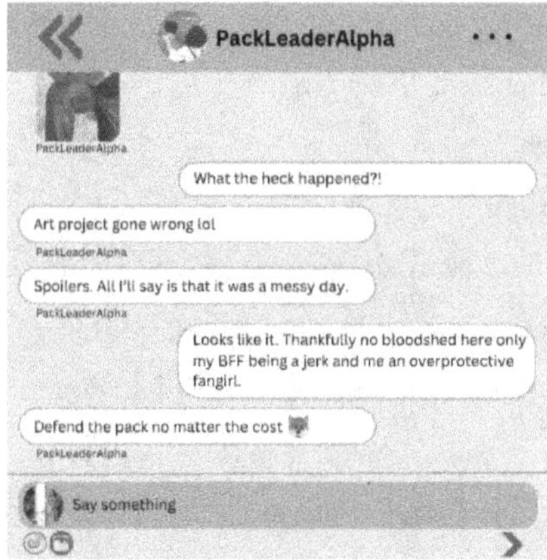

She smiled reading the famous tagline from the show.

Later that night, Raelyn was working in her office when there was a knock on the front door. Looking out her window, she saw Maren's car in the driveway. Raelyn opened the door, her friend held out a bottle of her favorite soda and favorite bag of candy.

"I'm sorry I was a bitch."

She pulled Maren into a hug, "I'm sorry I was equally bitchy back at you."

They walked inside heading to their favorite spots in her living room. Cordy jumped up next to Maren and snuggled up beside her.

"Traitor." Raelyn muttered.

"Awe, Cordy you love and forgive your Auntie Mare." He started purring louder while Maren continued petting him, "What I said back at school was uncalled for, but I want to explain where I'm coming from."

Cordy must have felt the shift between them as he jumped down and headed towards Raelyn. She smiled as he snuggled against the back of her chair placing a paw on her shoulder.

Maren chuckled, "No matter what no one will ever compare to his momma though."

"Damn right."

"I'm grateful every day that you found something to put your passion into. Watching you wither and falling apart was terrifying. I never knew if or when I would get the call that you had done something to yourself."

Watching her friend trying to control her raw emotions was difficult for Raelyn. She always felt like a burden to everyone which is why she figured they all left in the first place. There were only two people in the world she knew would never do that and one of them was sitting in front of her.

"I don't care if you date someone or not. All I care about is you being happy."

Raelyn waited for her to continue before prompting her, "But… there's a but."

Maren smirked, "But, I don't want you to hide behind your fandom and show because you're scared to put yourself out there again. There has to be a balance between your fangirl fantasies and real life."

"I know there has to be a balance between the two. When I meet the person who makes it worthwhile to have that balance then I will. Until then, I really am content with writing about love and not experiencing it."

Riley's name popped into her mind and her heart skipped a beat or two. Raelyn had been trying to ignore the feelings bubbling up from the depths of her heart that she thought were locked away for good. Feelings that once led her astray and broken.

"Okay, but you can't meet anyone by sitting behind your computer." Maren held her hands up defensively, "I don't mean anything against your online friends. I know they mean a lot to you. I'm just saying to be open to meeting someone you have to actually go out where people are."

Her inner voice chimed in.

Anyone will take one look at you and think one thing. Fr-reak.

She ignored her inner voice, "You're right. I do need to try and get out more."

Fr-reak.

Maren smirked, "I was hoping you would say that…"

Now Raelyn immediately regretted not listening to her inner voice.

No saving you now, Fatty-McGee. I'm out.

"Maren…"

"Hear me out. Tomorrow night we go out to our normal hole-in-the-wall bar and have a girls' night. If we get approached, then great. If not, then we'll have fun shooting darts and drinking."

It had been a long time since she had gone out with Maren. Surprisingly, a night out with her BFF sounded like a lot of fun.

"Alright."

Maren's smirk widened into a full grin, "Really? You're not going to back out?"

"Yes, really. I promise to be bright eyed, and bushy tailed all for you."

Raelyn was surprised when her best friend leaped off her seat and tackled her into her chair.

"I'm so excited! We're gonna have a great time!"

Her inner voice echoed in her mind as Maren went back to her spot and turned on the TV.

Yeah, enjoy being the large lump on a bar stool while Maren gets all the attention.

Raelyn had an early morning shift at the grocery store on Saturday. They were typically busy during the day, but with a Kansas University game going on everyone stayed home to watch. She was helping stock when her phone buzzed. Hope billowed in her chest that it was Riley. Her heart only dropped slightly seeing it was a notification from Instagram that Austin Jameson had a new posted.

He, Calliope Melton, and Jackson Powell were all standing in the woods covered in red paint. The three of them smiling and laughing with a short caption that made Raelyn's heart stop.

"Raelyn? Could you come up front to check, please?"

She looked up to see her manager and put her phone in her back pocket. Her mind was wildly jumping to conclusions about the caption Austin had used.

Maybe Riley had said it to him… or maybe they talked more often than he wanted to let on to. Then an unbelievable and crazy thought crossed her mind that made her stomach lurch towards her throat.

What if Riley was really Austin Jameson.

That thought stayed with her while she was getting ready to go out with Maren. Could she possibly be talking to her favorite actor?

You've lost your damn mind…

Her inner voice sneered trying to push the thought from her mind. Raelyn looked at the picture he had sent her and compared it to the photo Austin posted. There was no way to tell if they were different or the same. The only thing for sure was they were both covered in red paint.

She jumped slightly when a message from Riley popped up on her screen. Suddenly her body was buzzing with nerves and her hands trembled slightly.

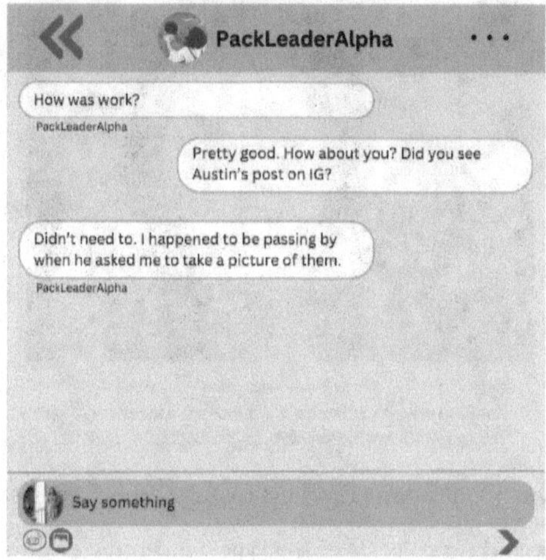

The breath that was burning in her lungs blew past her lips and her body relaxed. Her cheeks burned from the ridiculous thought that Riley could be Austin.

Yeah, keep dreaming that Austin Jameson will even acknowledge your existence. Loser.

Raelyn shook her inner voice to the back of her mind as she typed her reply.

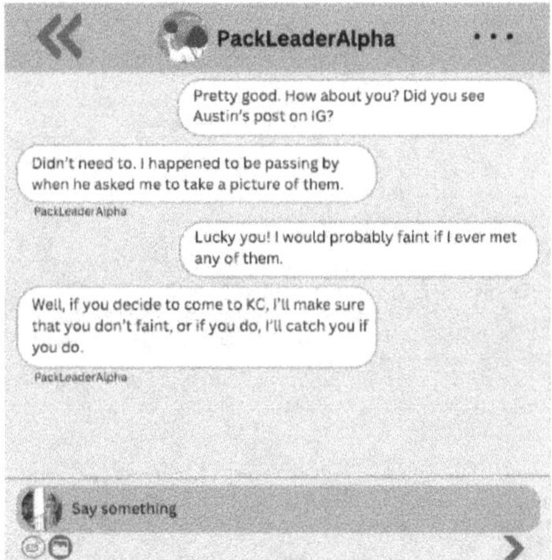

For a moment, she had forgotten about his invitation to go to the Red Moon convention. The familiar pull to go tugged hard on her heart.

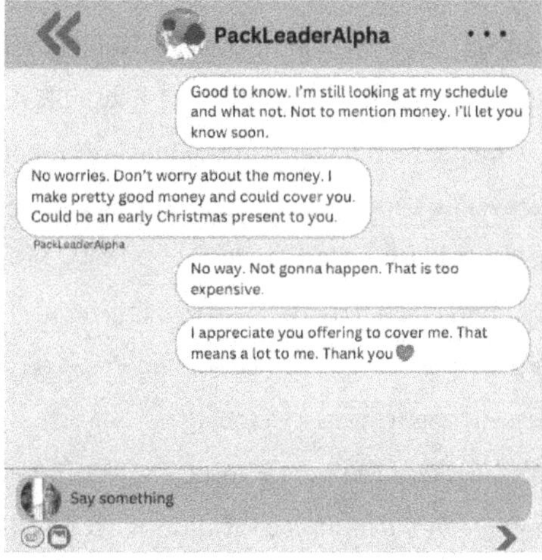

An ember of an old familiar feeling sparked deep within her. An ember that the more she kept talking to Riley began to spread igniting more feelings that had been long lost to her.

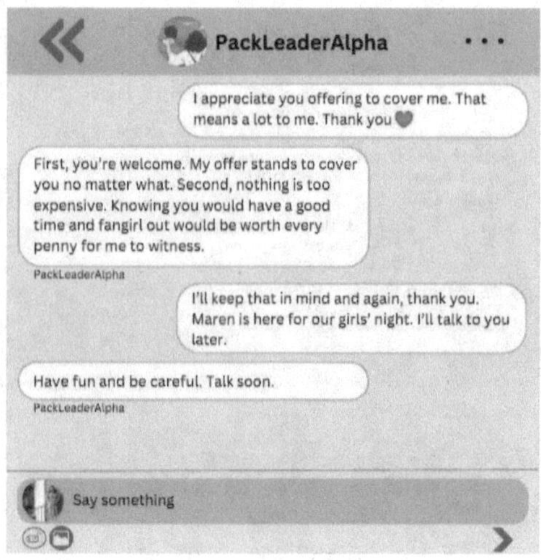

Another tug of her heart had her fingers typing an answer to him until she heard Maren honking her horn for a second time. Quickly she erased the text and grabbed her purse.

She took one more look in the mirror. Her hair was down and straightened. She attempted to put make-up on that looked more natural than glam. She wore her favorite buffalo plaid tied off to the side and a black tank underneath it with a pair of dark jeans. She deemed herself presentable and headed out to Maren's car.

"Really? You could have dressed up a little more."

Raelyn rolled her eyes, "You know I don't *girl* very well. This is as good as it gets and you're lucky I did this."

Maren's laughter filled her car as they took off down her street. The Rec Room was only a ten-minute drive from her house and was already packed. A lot of the people were regulars with KU students mixing in. Raelyn was able to find a dart board for them while Maren had gone to get the first round of drinks. After several minutes of waiting, she went in search of her friend only to find her surrounded by men of all ages.

Her best friend was in her element as she soaked up all the attention they were giving her. She couldn't blame any of them. Maren was gorgeous and with a great, big, loud personality. She was everything Raelyn had once been before her ex-husband and desperately wanted to be again.

After a few games of darts and interruptions from guys buying Maren drinks, Raelyn was left on her own again when a familiar voice came from behind her.

"I never expected to see you here." Bryce walked up to the high-top table leaning against it, "So, you do like to have fun."

"Yes, I do… sometimes. Tonight, was supposed to be girls' night, but as you can see…" She pointed to Maren downing a shot with her arm hooked through some college guy's arm.

Bryce chuckled and Raelyn noticed the adorable laugh lines flanking his eyes. Maybe it was the three or four Jack and Diets she had, but Raelyn also noticed how handsome Bryce truly was. He had a backwards cap on with a black t-shirt showing off his well-kept body and jeans that hugged in all the right areas.

"Here," Bryce slipped his arm over her shoulders holding his phone out for a selfie, "Smile."

She leaned in, resting her temple against the side of his clean-shaven cheek. He showed her the picture and was surprised how good they looked together.

"That way you don't have to stare, you can have a picture of me to look at." He chuckled as her face burned.

"You can tell I'm out of practice with the whole checking guys out subtly."

He pulled her tight into his side leaning in, "Feel free to check me out any time. Subtle or not."

Her breath caught in her throat, "Uh… o-okay."

Bryce laughed then pulled her off her stool, "Now come on, Maren told me you're a hell of a dart player. Let's see if you can kick my ass."

"Challenge accepted." Raelyn down the rest of her drink grabbing her darts.

It was the early morning hours when she arrived back home. Raelyn indeed kicked Bryce's ass in darts and more importantly had more fun than she had in a long time. Pulling out her phone, she dropped down onto her bed seeing several notifications from Riley.

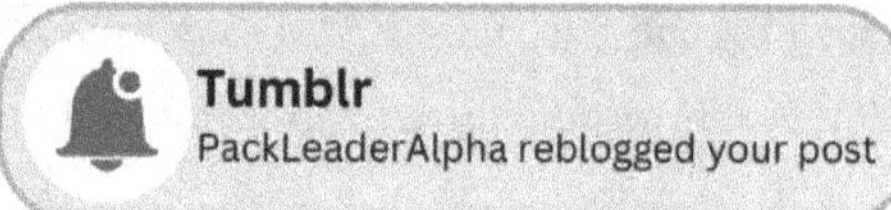

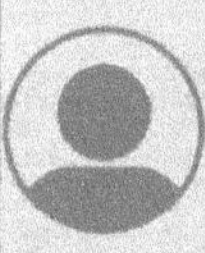

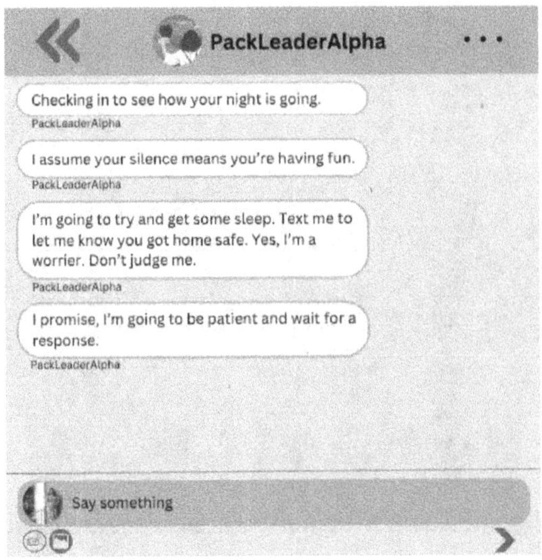

Raelyn felt tears slipping down her cheeks as that same ember burned brighter with hope fueling it to spread throughout her chest. An ice-cold realization snuffed out the warmth that was blanketing her.

Rather it was Bryce or Riley or any other guy who would want to be with her. She was too damaged to burden anyone with her issues. She was too fucked up in the head and no one deserved to have to deal with her bullshit. More tears flowed freely down her face as she messaged Riley.

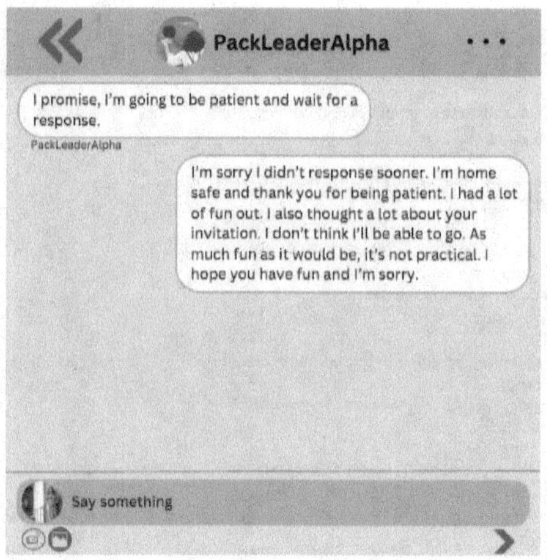

Raelyn turned off her phone, crawling beneath her blanket and allowed her self-pity and doubt to drag her under into unconsciousness.

Runaway
Chapter Three – New Beginnings
@PackNerd71

Summary: At the Red Moon compound, Noelle, Rhys, and Tiberius try to piece everything together between the demon and Andrew.

Characters: Rhys Remington, Tiberius 'Tibs' Greyson, Noelle Clark (OFC)

Warnings: Angst / Fluff

Rating: M - Mature

Word Count: 2408

Rhys turned towards Tiberius, "Sounds like he was fixated on her from the get-go. Maybe targeting her from the start." Tiberius nodded in agreement.

"Why? I'm nothing special." A cold coil tightened around Noelle's chest thinking of Andrew targeting her before she even knew him.

Rhys leaned back keeping his hand over hers, "I don't know, I think you're pretty special."

Her eyes snapped up at him, feeling her cheeks burning. He flashed a charming smile and winked at her, making the heat from her cheeks spread down her neck. He chuckled at her reaction before letting go of her hand. Noelle resisted the urge to inch her hand forward to hold his again.

"Noelle, do you mind if we look into your background. We might be able to find out why Andrew was so focused on having a child with you." Tiberius asked, bringing her attention back to what they had been talking about.

She nodded, "That's fine. Can I write it all down for you tomorrow morning? I think I'd like to head to bed."

The night was cool, and the moon was almost full. Off in the distance, she could hear howling. Picking up her pace, Noelle headed towards her home. She was getting ready for bed when there was a knock on her door. Opening it, Rhys's concerned eyes were staring down at her.

"Hey. I… uh, just wanted to say goodnight and make sure you're okay." He looked down at his feet bashfully.

A small smile spread across her lips, "Oh, okay. Do you want to come in?"

Rhys nodded as she stepped aside for him to walk in. They both stood there awkwardly for a moment. Noelle could feel the tether between them pulling her towards him. As if he could feel it as well, he

reached out pulling her into his arms. Her body was stiff, not knowing
how to react, and then Rhys's soothing voice filled her ears.

"Noelle, no matter what, Tiberius and I will protect you. You're
safe here."

Letting out a shaky breath, she wrapped her arms around his
waist. His arms tightened around her, pressing her ear against his chest.
The steady beat of his heart became the baseline to calming her mind and
body.

RAELYN

Raelyn's mind had been in a dark place after declining Riley's invitation. She was allowing the darkness to consume her to reinforce the walls of protection around her heart. Meanwhile Bryce had called her a few times leaving a couple of voicemails.

Hey Raelyn, checking in to see how you're doing. I had a lot of fun the other night and was hoping we could hang out again. No expectations or anything, just a couple drinks and maybe you can kick my ass in pool this time. Call me back.

Hey, I was hoping to hear from you. I'm going to be up at the Rec Room after school today. I'll buy the drinks and you can school me in darts again. I really hope I'll see you there.

He finally stopped calling after a week and a part of Raelyn was relieved when he did. Riley, on the other hand, was a different story. They continued to chat, but now it felt superficial. They would talk about their day but never in detail and discuss the latest episode of Red Moon.

This season of Red Moon was another layer of darkness consuming her. The current show runner was taking Rhys's character down a dangerous path that she felt he would never take. Lying to Tibs and Ash, making secret deals with a rival pack and then there was a new love interest that Raelyn hated. She was fine with Rhys having a love interest, but not this one.

"Miss B?"

Raelyn looked up from her spot in the commons seeing one of her seniors standing there. He was new to Collins High and struggling to catch up to keep his grades and stay on the football team.

"Hey Vin, what's going on?"

He sat across from her, and she could see in his dark eyes that he was upset. His fist clenched on the table and his body was a solid wall of tension. Her heart broke watching as he searched for the words to say.

"I knew coming here was going to be hard, but man… everyone here seems to hate me."

"Why do you think that?" She had a pretty good idea of why but knew he needed to say it to confront his feelings.

Vin let out a long sigh, "People look at me funny. They avoid me in the halls or talk about me behind my back. Even my teammates stay clear of me."

"I don't think it's because they hate you. I think they're intimidated by you." Raelyn smiled softly, "May I be honest with you?"

He nodded and Raelyn was taking a big risk by saying what she was about to say. She knew he had a lot of discipline marks for fighting with peers and staff. He was known at his other school for having a short temper, especially when he thought he was being look down on. She kept her voice as light and calm as possible to ease the nervousness rolling over her.

"I was intimidated by you. I'm nearly old enough to be your mom and you stand almost a foot taller than me. You're a strong man and that sometimes can intimidate people. I also think you're incredibly smart and that also intimidates people."

He chuckled, "I'm not that smart."

Raelyn knew differently. When speaking about any of his core subjects, Vin was able to recite facts and terms easily. However, ask him to write a paper or read and he would struggle. He had recently been diagnosed with Dyslexia which is why Raelyn was working with him during study hall periods.

"You are Vin. You're smart, you're a great player and teammate for your team. You're a good-looking guy."

His head perked up and she chuckled, "I've heard a few of the senior and junior girls talking about you. I think you need to take a chance and put yourself out there. Try to make a couple of close friends and you'll find your place here at CHS."

Vin's fists relaxed on the table, and she saw the hints of a smile on his face.

"Thanks Miss B." He stood up walking past her table.

Suddenly two large arms wrapped around her, squeezing her tight. Vin's deep laughter filled the commons as he startled her and then he jogged off towards the gym. Raelyn sat there laughing to herself and her heart feeling full for the first time that week. She immediately thought of Riley wanting to share with him what happened.

She had been putting up boundaries for herself with him. Carefully navigating them as if they were land mines. Right now, she didn't care and wanted to share her happiness with someone.

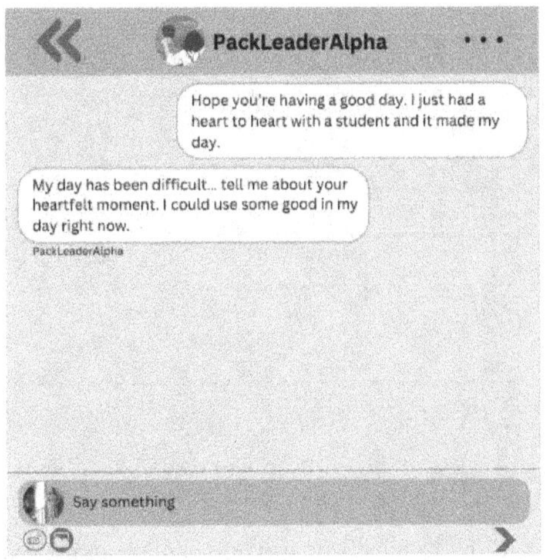

Raelyn bit her lip as her mind and heart fought for what to do next. In the end, her heart won. She typed out her text hitting send then there was a long pause before his reply appeared on the screen.

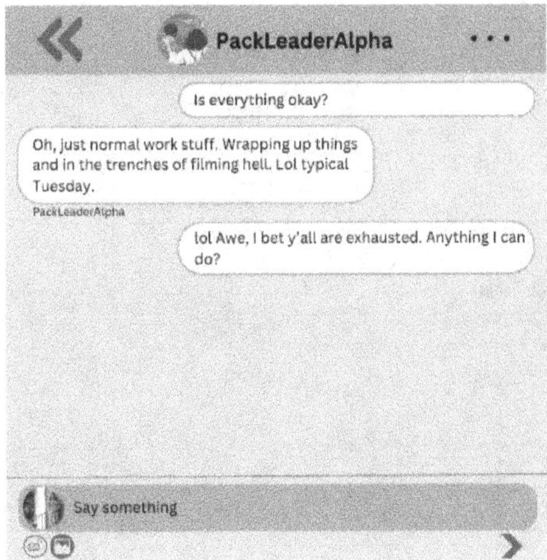

She hit send before thinking about what she had typed. She could already feel the guilt seeping into her chest waiting for the guilt trip coming her way from him.

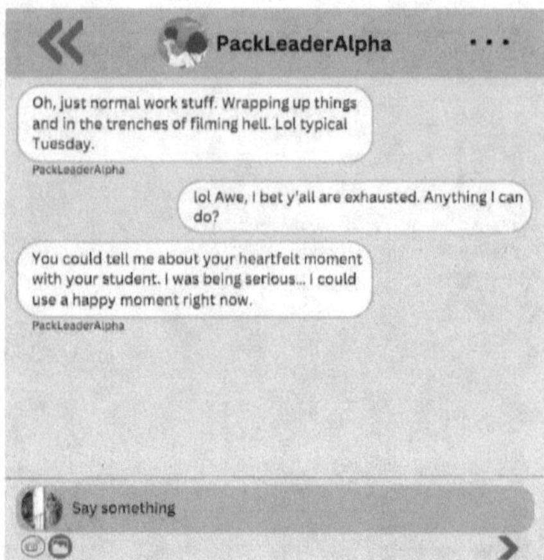

Raelyn told him all about Vin and their conversation. As she was telling him, something stirred within her. A sense of comfort that she hadn't felt since the early days with her ex, Jacob. It felt nice to have someone to share her day and little moments of joy with.

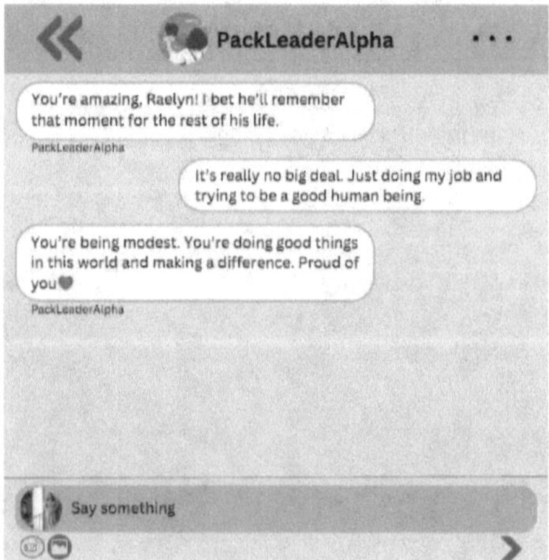

Raelyn felt her cheeks heating up and let out a shaky breath rereading his text a few times.

Proud of you

She had no idea three words could have such an impact on her, but she found it hard to hold back the tears filling her eyes. Maren, her mom, Katy, and Zuhra always told her how proud they were of her. This was different. Why was this different?

You're falling in love with him, dumbass.

"Raelyn, you alright?" Maren's voice pierced through the hard truth being declared by her inner voice.

"Huh? Yeah, I'm fine."

Maren sat across from her narrowing her eyes. Before her best friend could say anything, Raelyn stopped her before one of her famous inquisitions began.

"I'm fine. Truly."

"No, you're not. You haven't been for the better part of two weeks. Now, I respect it if you don't want to get into it at school. You can't bottle it up."

Raelyn sighed, "Come over tonight and I'll make dinner. I'll tell you everything."

"Shredded chicken tacos?"

She laughed, "Yes, if that's what you want. You bring the whiskey."

"Oh boy… wait." Maren glanced down at Raelyn's phone then back up, "Does this have to do with…"

"Tonight, Maren, tonight. Now I have to get to Lacey's English IV class."

Raelyn was able to leave without another word. She pulled out her phone before going into the classroom.

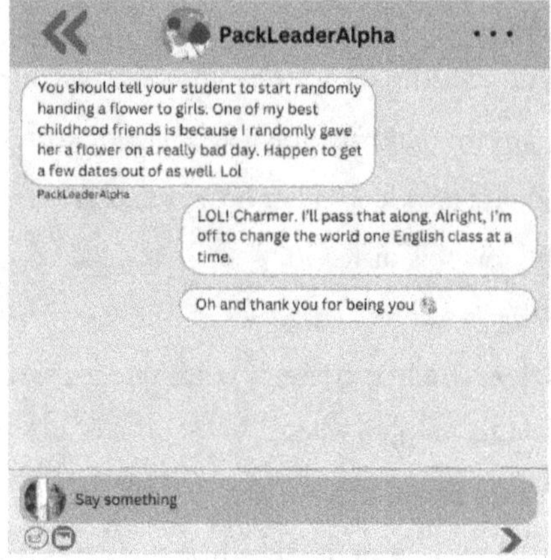

The rest of her day was a blur and before Raelyn knew it the last bell was ringing. She headed off to the grocery store to pick up what she needed for dinner. She found the manager in a panic as the only other cashier had called in with the flu.

Taking pity on her manager, she jumped on the register and started checking customers out. When she had a free moment, she texted Maren.

Around 7:30 pm, Raelyn clocked out and headed home with her own groceries. Walking in, she could hear multiple voices and panic spread down her body.

"Finally! You're home. I thought you might want a couple more friendly faces to greet you."

On her TV was Katy and Zuhra on a video call. Zuhra was still wrapped in her blankets and tired looking being it was nearly four in the morning for her.

"What is going on here? Zuhra, shouldn't you be sleeping?"

On queue her friend yawned, "Yes, but I was informed that it was important I was here. I will do anything for you my beautiful Queen."

Raelyn's heart thumped in her chest trying to let out the joy overflowing from it. Maren hooked her arm with Raelyn's and walked her over to her favorite chair.

"We're here for you, no matter if we understand it or not." She pointed to herself as they all laughed, "We want you to know that you are supported and loved."

She hugged her friend, "I'm definitely feeling that right now. Thank you."

Maren and Raelyn ate their dinner along with Katy while Zuhra sipped on some coffee trying to wake her brain cells. When Maren poured the first round of whiskey for them, she got down to the real reason why they were all here.

"Now, tell us what the hell has been going on with you."

Raelyn downed her first drink before telling them everything. From everything that happened with Bryce, to talking to Riley every day and his invitation to going to a convention. She even came clean about developing feelings for him.

"I like him. I don't want to like him. I don't want my heart to get broken again. I can't go through that again. It's like my heart can't help it and I know how ridiculous it sounds. I've never met him. I've never even seen a picture of him, but I feel like I've known him my whole life."

Taking a chance, Raelyn glanced up from her empty glass. Maren was sitting there, stone face while Katy and Zuhra were smiling knowingly.

"Well, I can tell you that Riley definitely has feelings for you. On more than one occasion he messaged us asking what he can do to make things better or how he could make your day better. He genuinely cares about you."

Zuhra nodded in agreement, "Yeah, he definitely cares a lot about you. I do find it odd that he's never sent a picture to you. Just a random picture of his arm covered in red paint."

"What?" Maren's eyes snapped up to hers.

"Riley works on the Red Moon crew in Montana. He's a part of set design or something. They hire locals to help them. He took the picture of Austin, Calliope and Jackson being covered in red paint. He had sent it to me because I sent him a photo of Cordy hiding my ugly mug."

There was an exchange of looks between her friends.

"What?" she asked refilling her glass.

"Not to sound like a crazy fangirl," Maren turned towards her computer, "no offense, but is there a possibility that Riley is one of the actors?"

"I told you I wasn't crazy, Zuhra."

Zuhra chuckled, "You're still crazy, but this time your crazy is valid."

Raelyn felt all the blood from her body pool at the bottom of her feet. Hearing her suspicion out loud made her feel less crazy and more panicky.

"Raelyn?" Maren's hand squeezed her shoulder, "Is it possible?"

She shrugged, "I guess anything is possible. I... I really don't think so."

"There's only one way to find out for sure." Zuhra took a sip from her mug, "Take him up on the sweet offer to go to the convention."

"No way. I can't afford to go, and I have two work schedules to ask off from. Not to mention the stress of meeting my favorite actors, from my favorite show and the guy I'm falling for. T-That's too much."

"Unless Riley is one of the actors. My guess would be Austin since it's all over the interwebs that Cali and Jax are officially a thing." Katy mentioned.

Now Raelyn's stomach plummeted to her feet, "No way..." she muttered putting her head in her hands.

Maren lifted her chin, "Hey, you're probably right and that he's just a regular guy. Now I have a question for you."

"What?"

"Does he make you happy?"

She couldn't stop the smile spreading across her face, "Yeah, he does."

Maren gave a short nod, "That's all that matters. I think you should reconsider his offer and I'll even go for the moral support of it all. Who knows maybe going will make me want to watch the show."

Raelyn busted out laughing, "Now that would be a small miracle."

"I agree with Maren. I think you should go to the convention. If anything, to meet our sex god Mr. Austin Jameson." Zuhra chimed in, "And on that note I'm going to get a couple more hours of sleep."

They all waved goodbye to Zuhra then Katy spoke up, "I agree with the rest of them. Personally, I'm hoping Riley turns out to be Austin and you get to live out every fangirl's fantasy."

"I think I'm going to vomit." Raelyn groaned.

AUSTIN

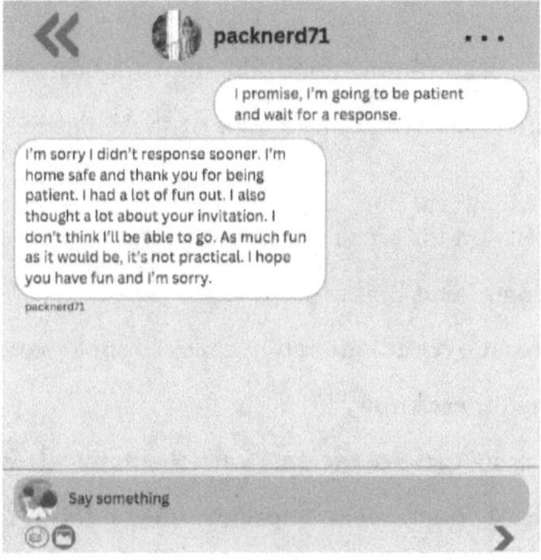

Austin had been thankful for the convention that weekend and taking his mind off the stinging disappointment running throughout his body. He focused on being there for their fans and trying to have fun with his extended Red Moon family. It was only when he went back to the hotel at night that it was hardest to keep the sadness from consuming him.

Tonight, a visit from his manager was the distraction keeping his mind from spiraling. She knocked on his hotel door a little after ten o'clock.

"What's up Rachel?"

She walked in slightly in a huff, "Before we head back to Montana, the execs want a meeting with the three of you. We're flying out of Florida first thing Monday morning and heading to Los Angeles."

"Will this affect our filming schedule at all?"

"It will push you back a day," He groaned as she continued, "They're insisting, Austin."

Her eyes never met his and he knew she was holding back, "What is it?"

"There's been rumors about the network being sold in the next three to five years. That would mean a lot of shake ups in the current lineup of shows."

Austin sat on the small couch at the end of the bed, "Do you think they're going to end Red Moon?"

She looked over at him and her silence spoke volumes.

"Do the others know?"

"Their managers are meeting with them now. It would be a good idea for the three of you to meet before the meeting with them. See where you all stand with the show ending and how you all want your lives to look after Red Moon."

Rachel gently squeezed his shoulder, "I'll be at the bar for a little while if you care to join or need me."

"Thanks Rach, I'll be fine."

He walked her to the door and locked it after she left. He hadn't been prepared to think about the ending of Red Moon. For the last ten years, that's all his life had been. It was the only life Bernadette knew for him and it was a good one. Thinking of his daughter, he grabbed his phone texting her.

> You awake? Think you could call your ole dad for a moment.

Within a minute, her beautiful face filled the screen, and he smiled instantly seeing her sitting in her favorite spot at his parents' home.

"Everything okay daddy?"

He nodded, "It is now. I just need to see and hear from you. Tell me about your day."

As he listened to her talk, he thought about how much of her life he had missed. His career had provided a comfortable life for them but took away a lot of time. The only reason why Austin had sole, physical and legal custody was the support system he had put in place when Bernadette was born. There was no way Britney could fight him on it and because of her own shady past she had limited visitation.

"Dad, are you sure everything is, okay?"

Her concerned voice caught his attention, "Yeah baby, I'm fine. I can't wait to see you in a week."

"Me too. I better get to bed, or Pop will be upset if I'm late for our morning run. Love you daddy."

"Love you more, Birdie. Goodnight."

She waved then ended the video chat. His heart felt almost whole, but there was still a small piece missing. Glancing down at his phone, he pulled up the Tumblr app and went to Raelyn's message thread. His fingers hovered over the screen.

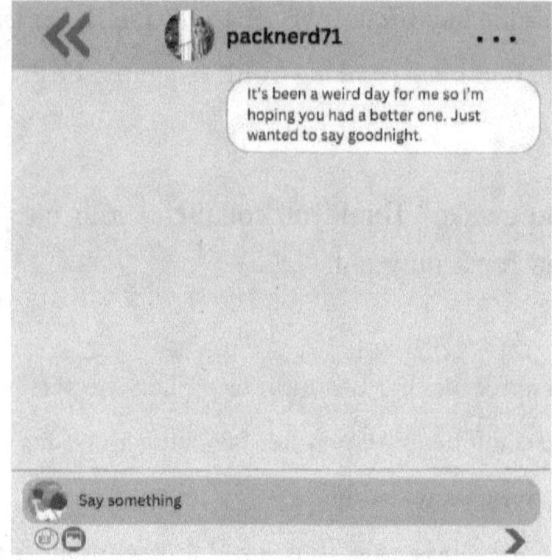

After a half hour there was no response and Austin felt the weight on his shoulders push down a little harder. Deciding to see if Rachel was still downstairs, he made his way to the bar. He found her talking with Calliope at a table while Jackson was getting some drinks.

"Well, I guess none of us could sleep." Calliope tapped the seat beside her.

They all made idled chit-chat about the convention and a few fun stories about the most interesting photo ops they had so far. There was a question burning at the end of Austin's tongue that he wanted Rachel's opinion on. A question that had been running through his mind for weeks now. With the third scotch in him, he finally was brave enough to ask.

"Rach, can I ask you a hypothetically question?"

"Sure." She looked over to Calliope and Jackson who were both staring at him curiously.

"How would you handle one of your clients falling in love with a fan?"

All three of them had immediate reactions. Jackson groaned then downed the rest of his drink. Calliope's eyes went wide as she excitedly clapped her hands. Finally, Rachel stared at him dumbfounded and slightly paled.

"What did you do, Austin?"

He scoffed, "Why is it you immediately think I've done something?"

"You have a 13-year-old daughter with a fan so I will ask again. What did you do?"

Austin signaled to the bartender for another round, "Nothing... really."

Rachel ran her hands down her face, "Oh god..."

"He's been lurking on fansites under the name Riley and has been talking to a fan on there." Jackson said as Calliope smacked him on the chest, "What? That is what's happening."

"Is that true?" Her eyes snapped to his as he nodded, "Seriously Austin?!"

"Look it's no secret I get on the fansites or talk to fans on socials. This time, I happened to read some fanfiction and reached out to the author. We've become... friends."

"Friends? That's all?" Rachel asked, downing her drink, and ordering another immediately.

"Yes... for now." He mumbled the last two words as he took a drink.

They all leaned in towards him as Calliope asked, "What was that? Did you just say..."

Austin sighed, "For now."

Calliope got up and hugged him. He was thankful at least one of the three could be happy for him as Jackson and Rachel looked disapprovingly at him.

"Look, I'll be straight with you. I like Raelyn a lot. I invited her to a convention close to where she lives with the intention of telling her the truth about everything. By the way, she declined my invitation. I didn't set out to fall for her, but it happened. Now, I'm not sure where we stand."

Calliope rubbed his back, "I'm sorry she's not coming out to meet you. Maybe, she'll change her mind."

"Let's hope not." Rachel muttered earning a nasty look from his friend, "I'm sorry but relationships between celebrities and fans never work out. Fans think they can handle being with a celebrity but after a few months of not seeing one another and schedule changes they break up."

Austin could hear his heart slowly cracking, "I don't know. I don't think Raelyn would be like that. She knows what it's like to go through a terribly heartbreak."

Rachel reached over grasping his hand, "Tell me the god's honest truth. Are you in love with her?"

Austin's answer was out of his mouth before his brain could even register what he was saying. It was the same answer he had given himself when he asked the same question.

"Yes."

"Fucking hell… I need to process this. I'll see you all in the morning." Rachel walked off towards the elevators leaving the three friends sitting together.

His friends both stared at him as if a second head had appeared on his shoulders.

"Alright. Come on with it. Give it to me." Austin waved his hand for his friends to unleash their thoughts about everything, "Come on! Get it over with it and tell me how dumb and stupid I'm being."

"Do you really love her? Never meeting her? Never speaking to her?" Jackson asked.

"I've talked to her nearly every day for months now. At first, I only wanted to be friends and build a unique friendship with a fan who really gets our characters."

Austin paused, looking down at his phone. His heart longed to talk to her. To meet her, hug her, to be with her.

"When we started to get to know each other I found that the part of my day I looked forward to the most was hearing about her day. Hearing about what student she helped get a better grade. How she volunteered for another committee that she has absolutely no time to be a part of. I wanted to know how her shift at her second job went and how Mr. Bernard's new recipe came out. I found someone I wanted to share my day with and hear everything about theirs."

He noticed Jackson look down at Calliope smiling, "I get that."

"I don't know where the line vanished between friend and love or fan and actor. All I know is when she told me she didn't want to come my heart broke. I don't know what to do or say now."

His shoulders sagged from the weight of everything he had been holding inside of him. He placed his head in hands and held back the tears threatening to fall.

"We'll figure something out. No matter what, we've got your back."

Austin was surprised to hear that come out of Jackson's mouth, "You don't think I'm a dumbass?"

"Oh no, I still think you're a dumbass, but not for following your heart. I'll never think your dumb for that." Jackson slapped his back.

Calliope wrapped her short arms around both of them, "I love you guys so much."

As the end of the week approached, exhaustion was hitting Austin harder than ever. The meeting with the executives had gone fine. They could all tell that some big changes were on the horizon and had him, Calliope and Jackson seriously thinking about their lives after Red Moon. Thankfully with their winter hiatus coming up, they all would have plenty of time to think about it.

He had a few conversations with Raelyn but things between them had seemed to shift since he invited her to a convention. Many times, he found himself typing out messages to her and deleting them. He didn't want to come off as clingy or needy, especially since they were simply friends.

The longest conversation they had was about her helping a new student. The pride that had filled his chest hearing her go above and beyond for her kids. He knew then it was official. He was falling in love with her.

As that realization settled in his mind, he still tried to give her space. He also never brought up the convention again. It was only a few weeks away and he would send up a nightly plead to any higher being listening that she would change her mind.

Before he knew it, Austin was flying home to New Orleans. His home welcoming was filled with hugs and tears. His parents and Bernadette had a big home cooked dinner waiting at their house.

It felt good to be home with his family. As he listened to Bernadette talk about school and a new writing club she joined, Austin's heart thumped painfully against his chest. The missing piece grew as he glanced down at his phone.

"Everything okay, daddy?"

Austin smiled, resting his arm on the back of her chair, "Absolutely. Everything is perfect now that I'm home."

Bernadette had gone to bed around nine o'clock since she still had a couple weeks of school before winter break. He stood in her doorway for a long time simply watching her sleep like he did when she was little. She had grown so much in the last few months, turning into a young woman seemingly overnight.

"Hey." He turned to see his mom standing there, "She's not going anywhere. I'm sure you're exhausted."

He nodded, following her back downstairs to where his room was. His parents had a small home on the same property for Bernadette to remain in their house. He was grateful for his parents being willing to help them while he pursued his career. One thing he didn't want for his daughter was the constant travel he made to different events.

"Are you sure everything is, okay? You seem a little off." His mom walked towards the kitchen pouring them each a glass of juice.

"I met someone, and I don't know where things stand between us."

He watched as his mom perked up, "Does she know about your life and Birdie?"

Austin shook his head, "That's a small part of the problem. Her name is Raelyn and I met her on a fansite…"

For the next twenty minutes or so, Austin told her all about Raelyn. How she made him feel and ended with inviting her to a convention. When he finished, she got up taking his half drank juice and getting the hidden bottle of scotch out.

"I think we need something a little strong." They both chuckled, "So, you love her."

It wasn't a question, but he answered anyway, "Yes. I know it sounds crazy since I'd never met or spoken to her in person."

His mom's smile never failed to comfort him immediately, "Not as crazy as you would think. Your great, great, grandpappy met his wife through a pen pal service during the war. They wrote letters every day to one another and fell in love. It was nearly two years before they met each other."

His great, great grandfather, Austin Everett Jameson was his namesake. He had never met him but could remember his grandmother telling stories about him all the time.

"I never knew that… wow."

"One way or another, you need to be honest with her." She poured a little more scotch in his cup before putting it away.

He took a sip of it allowing the smoothness to calm the raging butterflies in his stomach.

"What if she tells me to take a hike? I don't think…" He bit his lip hard to keep the flood of emotions from falling down his face.

His mom placed her hand on top of his, "Then we'll be here for you. Love is about taking risks and being daring. If it wasn't then it wouldn't be worth fighting for. So, answer me this... Is Raelyn worth fighting for?"

Again, his answer was immediate, "Absolutely. A thousand percent."

"Then give it all you have." The table vibrated as his phone lit up.

His lips pulled into a grin seeing a notification from her. He looked up to see his mom smiling as well.

"I will say this, if she makes you smile like that then I like her already." She hugged him before heading out towards the walkway connecting their homes, "Goodnight and love you."

"Goodnight momma. Love you too and thank you."

He watched her walk down the path connecting their homes until he saw his dad waiting for her. Austin grabbed his phone and headed toward his bedroom. Falling backwards onto the mattress, the exhaustion from non-stop filming and traveling hit him like a Mack truck. Before he allowed sleep to take him, he opened Raelyn's message.

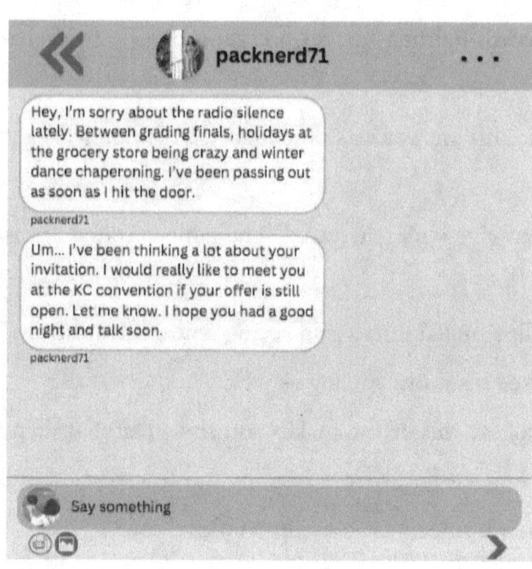

packnerd71

Hey, I'm sorry about the radio silence lately. Between grading finals, holidays at the grocery store being crazy and winter dance chaperoning. I've been passing out as soon as I hit the door.

packnerd71

Um... I've been thinking a lot about your invitation. I would really like to meet you at the KC convention if your offer is still open. Let me know. I hope you had a good night and talk soon.

packnerd71

Say something

Runaway
CHAPTER FOUR – FALLING HARD
@PACKNERD71

"Tiberius, will you stop acting like a high school girl and get to the point?" She said looking over her book to him.

He chuckled, "Alright. Do you have feelings for Rhys?"

She closed her book sighing, "Are you asking as my friend or as Rhys's seemingly second in command snooping for information. Which, by the way, is there some kind of hierarchy I should be aware of? Feeling like I'm missing the punch line of a joke with y'all."

Tiberius gave her a pointed look answering her question silently. She bit her lip nervously debating in her head if she should tell him or not. Noelle could tell by Tiberius's expression that he could piece together her internal argument. He stood up from the table reshelving his book.

"For what it's worth Noelle, I think you two could be good for one another. Don't tell him I said that." He stopped beside her chair, his jaw clenching as he spoke, "As for your other question. Only Rhys can tell you. In our little world, he is top dog."

Noelle snapped her eyes up to Tiberius, a small smirk on his lips as he walked out of the library. She spent the rest of the night sitting in her favorite spot since coming to Red Moon. It was the one place she would always go to keep calm if she was having a rough night.

She propped her pillow against the car door and stretched out over the backseat of the Chevelle with her blanket. The car smelled of old leather and pine since Rhys had recently driven her through the woods. She could not explain why she felt so comfortable and safe within the car, but it never failed that she would drift into a peaceful sleep within it.

She was dreaming of running through the woods as howling echoed all around her. Nothing was chasing her, but she kept running until coming to the edge of Red Moon. Turning slowly, she found a large golden-brown wolf jogging up beside her. She expected to be afraid of a wolf bigger than she was. His muzzle slipped beneath her hand, and she threaded her fingers through its thick fur. Lifting its large head, Noelle's eyes were met with crimson ones filled with love and warmth.

"R-Rhys…" She muttered, slowly opening her eyes as she felt her body being picked up, "W-What's going on?"

"Shhh, I'm just taking you back to your home. Go back to sleep, Noelle."

She looked up to see Rhys carrying her and she wrapped her arms around his neck snuggling into him. The familiar leather and pine smell filled her nose as she quickly drifted back to sleep feeling the safest, she ever had cradled against him.

She woke up the next morning stretching and swinging her legs over the edge of her bed. Her feet bumped into something solid that was on the ground and she instantly brought her feet up onto her bed. Noelle looked over the edge and found Rhys sleeping in a sleeping bag.

14

Fourteen

AUSTIN

Austin was floating on cloud nine the next few days after Raelyn accepted his convention invite. As he sat in his home office, he prepared himself for the phone call to his manager he needed to make. He knew Rachel would give him a lot of push back on Raelyn coming to the convention and him taking care of all the cost. He pressed her name on his phone listening to the rings.

"Not that I don't love hearing from you Austin, but I'm on a beach, on vacation like you're supposed to be."

He chuckled, "I need your help with something and you're not going to like it."

"I'm hanging up."

"Hey! Come on, please." He begged, knowing she wouldn't say no to him.

There was a long sigh on the other end of the phone, "I have a feeling this is about your fan and coming to a convention to meet you."

"And this is why you're the best and I hired you as my manager."

"Yeah, yeah. Okay, so you want to hook her up with some con tickets or a VIP ticket."

Austin sat a little straighter, bracing himself for the lip lashing he was about to get.

"I want her to be able to do whatever she wants at the convention. If she wants eighty-five photo ops with Cali, then so be it. If she wants front row seats and first in line for autos, then she gets it. I also want her stay at the same hotel as me and all meals paid for. I don't want her to spend a penny unless she wants to."

There was a long pause. He checked his phone to make sure their connection was still good. Finally, Rachel unleashed her whirlwind rant onto him.

"Have you lost your *DAMN* mind?! Austin the whole way conventions work is for people to pay for the goods and services received. That is how you make money and in return how I make money. If you give it to one fan, then other fans will start to expect that. We can-*NOT* have that happen."

Austin held his phone from his ear patiently waiting for her to stop ranting, "I never said it wouldn't be paid for. It will come out of my personal account, and I'll have my financial manager make sure it is all paid for in advance."

"Is there any possible way of me being able to talk you out of this?"

"Not even in the slightest. I will find out from Raelyn what she wants to do and email you a list." She groaned and he continued, "Rachel, thank you for doing this. It means a lot to me."

"You're lucky I'm nice and have a soft spot for you. Send me the email asap, so I can get things rolling."

He ended the call and he saw a new notification from Raelyn.

Immediately, he brought up the newest chapter for Runaway and read it. If he didn't already love Raelyn's writing enough, her new series was mirroring his own experience of falling for someone. He liked the chapter and hit reblog.

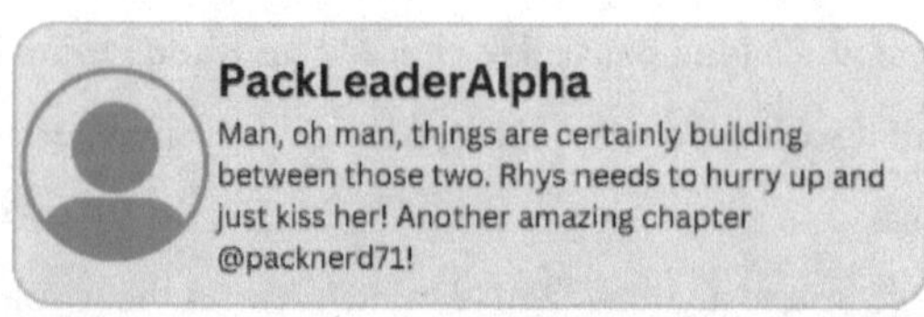

Austin hit post then pulled up his message thread with Raelyn. Ever since she had decided to come to the convention their conversations had returned to normal. Talking everyday about anything and everything they could.

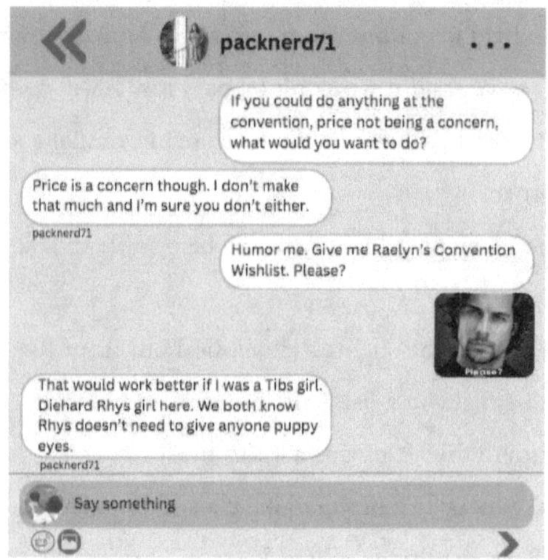

One of the many reasons why Austin loved playing Rhys. He had confidence and swagger unlike himself. Over the years, a little of Rhys had rubbed off on Austin and vice versus as they were going to see in this newest season.

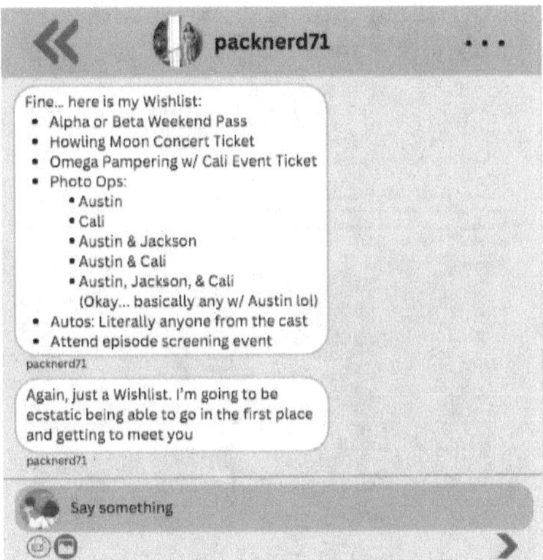

Austin smiled, as he typed up an email on his laptop to Rachel. He listed everything Raelyn wanted, only changing that she have a front row seat and the Red Moon Pack VIP pass. That way she could come back to the green room any time she wanted.

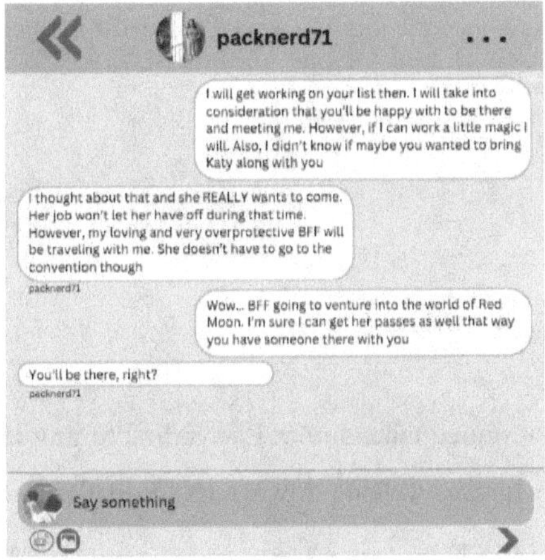

He cringed as another block of guilt was added onto his shoulders. He hated lying to her and kept reminding himself it was only for a little bit longer.

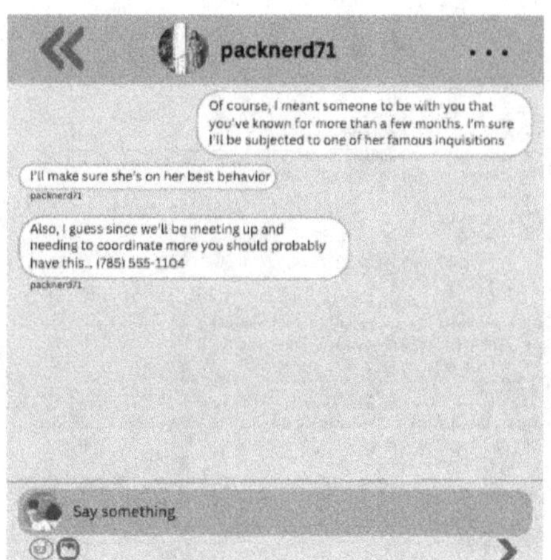

He stared at the number. He always figured they would text through the app, but he knew a lot of times it wasn't reliable at conventions. Austin saved her number in his phone and pulled up a new text message thread.

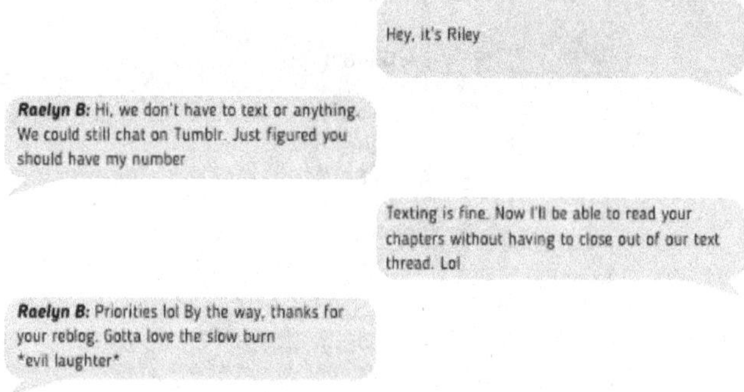

They continued talking until Raelyn had to go to the grocery store to work. As he was walking downstairs, Bernadette came walking through the front door.

"Hey baby, how was school?"

She looked up from her phone, her forehead furrow, "Dad, is it true?"

A sickening pool began to form in the pit of his stomach, "Is what true?"

"You and Cali are dating?"

She held up an article from an online publication known for celebrity gossip. There was a picture of him and Cali from the convention in Florida. They were standing off to the side in front of the hotel waiting for their car. Their arms wrapped around one another, and Austin was resting his head against the top of hers. To the world, it looked like a happy couple. For those who knew him and Calliope, they saw two best friends and nothing more.

He skimmed through the article and shook his head, "Oh please…"

Seen together, Austin Jameson and Calliope Melton, waiting for their ride to take them to the airport after a convention in Orlando, Florida. Jackson Powell was seen earlier heading out before his co-stars. Jameson and Melton have always been reported as close friends, but now it seems they have crossed the line to lovers.

Long time Red Moon fans have always shipped the two actors creating a whole sect of fans shipping their characters that are siblings. Even though, Melton has been sited to be dating Powell like their characters in the series, it seems maybe Powell left early due to a broken heart from his co-star stealing his she-wolf.

"These tabloid articles are getting worse and worse." He muttered handing the phone back to Bernadette, "Sweetheart, Cali and I are friends. She's one of my best friends and we're close. That's all."

"Good because I love Aunt Cali and wouldn't want to lose her."

Austin watched as she headed upstairs and made a mental note to talk to Rachel about the article online.

"Just what I need… a rumored romance with a co-star when I'm trying to impress a fan to like me." He mumbled, heading towards the kitchen.

By the end of the week, Rachel had called to let him know everything was set up for Raelyn. Everything she wanted had been set aside for her to be picked up the night of registration.

"Rachel, I can't thank you enough."

"You could by calling all of this off and not getting involved with a fan." Rachel said in all seriousness in her voice.

Austin chuckled, "Not even gonna happen, but still thank you."

There was a long pause before Rachel spoke, "Can I ask you something personal not as a manager but as a friend?"

"Absolutely."

"Why have you never considered getting back with Britney? Wouldn't it be nice to have your family whole?"

Her question caught him off guard, "Um, I guess I've never thought about it. Things between Britney and I were not real. She had this fantasy dream of being married to a celebrity who had an A-list career. Not someone who was a simple TV series actor. Plus, she was certifiable… so there's that. Why?"

"No reason. The small publicist in me always loves to see a redemption story." She laughed softly, "Alright, enjoy the rest of your hiatus and I'll see you in Kansas."

He ended the call with an uneasy feeling in his stomach. Deciding to push it aside, he went upstairs to talk with Bernadette. She was at her desk with one earbud in and head down in a textbook.

"Do you have a moment for your ole dad?"

She turned around with a smile spread across her face, "Of course. All my homework is done already. This is a little extra so I'm ahead."

Austin sat on her bed, "You never cease to amaze me. I have a question for you, and it may seem a little strange."

She arched one of her eyebrows, "O-Okay…"

"Would you ever want your mom and I to get back together?"

"Permission to speak freely?"

He knew that was her way of asking if she could curse and he chuckled, "Granted."

"Why in the hell would you ever want to do that? I love mom and always will but from far, far, *far* away."

His chuckle turned into a full laugh, "Okay, that's good to know. Just wanted to make sure we're on the same page."

"Does this have to do with the article I showed you?"

Austin shook his head, "No, not at all."

Bernadette rolled her chair closer to him, "Then what?"

For a moment he debated rather to tell her about Raelyn. Austin had always been careful about keeping his daughter out of the lives of women he had seen. He always knew deep down that none of them would be around long, and he didn't want her getting attached. However, with Raelyn, it was different. She was different and how he felt about her was different.

"I have been talking to someone for a few months now. We're meeting at the convention I'm going to in Kansas City."

"She's special, isn't she?" Bernadette asked.

"Yes, she is. I didn't want you holding onto a dream that one day your mom and I would get back together because I'm hoping there's a future with this special woman."

"You and mom together sounds like a freaking nightmare that I want no part of." She leaned forward placing her hand on his, "Just please be careful and don't get hurt. I don't want to see you hurt or have to ask Cali to help me kick some poor woman's butt."

Austin pulled Bernadette from her chair to sit beside him and hugged her, "Kiddo you don't have to worry about kicking anyone's butt. I promise to be careful with my heart."

She pulled away kissing his cheek, "Thank you. Now, I need to finish my science flash cards so I can start studying."

"Alright smarty-pants. Love ya Birdie."

"Love ya more, daddy."

Going into the week before the convention, Austin began to doubt his decision on meeting Raelyn. It was getting harder and harder to keep his secret from her. He was terrified that he would lose her once she did find out who he was. One night, he found himself calling Calliope after a few whiskeys.

"I don't think I can go through with meeting Raelyn. What if she hates me for lying to her? What if she is some crazy fan like Britney was? What if— "

Calliope cut him off, "Whoa Austin, slow down. Take a deep breath."

He inhaled counting to ten and then released the breath counting to ten again. He repeated the motions as Calliope continued talking.

"First, you might as well get it through your head that she's going to be kind of pissed you've been lying to her. Hopefully, she will be able to see that everything between you two has been honest except for your identity. Secondly, I truly believe if you thought she was anything like Britney you would have ditched her a long time ago."

Austin chuckled, "That is true."

"So, what's with the cold feet suddenly?"

"I don't know. Rachel asked me a week ago if I had ever considered getting back with Britney. That made me think to ask Birdie if she had any secret hopes of her parents getting back together."

Calliope scoffed, "Which she doesn't because we've had many conversations about it."

"Well, that's news to me. Anyway, I also told her a little about Raelyn…"

"Really? You've never told her about anyone who've dated."

He looked down at the photo of him and Bernadette a fan had taken at a convention. He was doing his solo panel and she kept walking out on stage to be next to him. Finally, he picked her up and held her while continuing to answer fan questions. By the end of the panel, Bernadette had fallen asleep, and a lovely fan had taken a picture of him holding her.

"I know. I've never wanted her to get attached to anyone, but with Raelyn…"

"It's different. I won't lie, you've been different since talking with her. A good different, but still different." There was a moment a silence before she continued, "I know Rachel would kill me for saying this to you…"

"What?"

He heard her let out a breath, "I'm happy you fought to meet Raelyn. Just because she's a fan doesn't mean you can't make a real connection with her. You've always been guarded and isolate yourself from getting too close. I know that was for Birdie's benefit."

"Yes, because she's my number one priority."

"I know, but you can't be the best dad for her when you don't allow yourself to flourish. You have to take care of yourself first and in return it will take care of her. That means allowing yourself to be loved and to love someone else. It's the only way Birdie will learn how to love others."

Austin was speechless. He had never thought about his love life that way. He always figured the less Bernadette knew the better. She had great role models with her grandparents being married for fifty plus years and his own parents being happily married since their early twenties.

He knew Calliope was right and a small spark of pride burned in his chest for her, "When did you get so smart?" He chuckled.

She scoffed softly, "When I fell in love. Now, stop with the cold feet and negative thoughts. Focus on the positive and pray she forgives you for lying to her for so long."

"Thanks Cali, I love ya."

"Love ya too Austin."

After making the rounds to check the doors and Bernadette, he was crawling into bed when his phone buzzed with a text.

> **Raelyn B:** Just wanted to say goodnight 🖤

> Goodnight Raelyn, can't wait to see you in a week 🖤

RAELYN

There was only a week until the Red Moon convention and Raelyn was a wreck. Thankfully, she was on winter break from school and only had to work one job for the week. Raelyn spent her free time either texting with Riley or working on a new writing project she had recently thought of. She had spent the afternoon at a coffee shop writing while waiting for Maren to go shopping for convention clothes.

Raelyn looked up seeing a disheveled Maren walking in and waved her down. She couldn't help the wide smile on her face as she locked her phone and shut down her computer.

"I love my parents, truly, but they're a great big pain in my ass sometimes."

Raelyn slid over a large cup of Maren's favorite coffee, "This will make it all better."

Maren took a sip closing her eyes and humming, "Raelyn Burton, you are a goddess and my savior."

"Bless you child." They both started laughing, gathering their things, and heading across the street to the mall.

Raelyn hated shopping for clothes but had absolutely nothing nice to wear. All her clothes were either jeans and t-shirts for school or uniforms for the grocery store. Other than that, she was always in leggings and hoodie or leggings and a flannel. She knew only one person would be able to help her find clothes.

"Now Maren, don't go completely wild. I want to be comfortable and look nice."

Her best friend had already dragged her into the first clothing store and was going through a rack of clothes. She loved Maren, but sometimes she forgot that Raelyn was a size twenty-four and not a twelve like her.

"What about this?" She held up a cute flannel crop-top hoodie.

Yeah, put that on and see your rolls unravel.

She shuddered from her inner voice, "It's cute but not quite what I was looking for."

Raelyn found a cute blouse that was a dark teal color with a plaid pattern at the bottom. She looked for the largest size and grabbed it. She turned around to see Maren holding several items in her arms and she immediately regretted bringing her clothes shopping.

After the first few shirts she tried on not fitting at all, Raelyn stepped out without bothering to try on the rest. Maren was still in her dressing room trying on clothes while she returned all her items.

"Nothing?" Maren asked.

Raelyn shook her head and headed towards the registers so Maren could pay for her stuff. Three stores later, Raelyn was beyond frustrated and over shopping. Pulling out her phone, she tried to smile seeing a text from Riley.

"You, okay?"

Before she could answer Maren or reply to Riley her phone started to vibrate. The picture of her and Bryce flashed beneath his number.

"Hello?"

"Hey Raelyn, I was beginning to wonder if you would ever answer my calls."

Maren mouthed to her, "Who is it?"

"I'm sorry Bryce, I got really busy at the end of the semester and I'm going to be taking a trip to Kansas City next week. What's going on?"

Her friend sat back sipping on her smoothie with a wide grin on her face. Raelyn rolled her eyes.

"I was hoping to grab a drink or maybe dinner with you. Are you free any time before you leave for KC?"

"Like… on a date?" she asked, making her stomach twist.

"Yeah. Maybe on Saturday?"

Raelyn's chest tightened making it hard to breathe. She had felt guilty for blowing him off a few weeks ago, but the thought of going on a date with him made her feel uncomfortable.

"Raelyn?"

"Yeah, I'm still here. Um, sure I can meet up with you on Saturday. Just text me where and when."

He chuckled, "Now it wouldn't be a date if I didn't pick you up. Text me your address and I'll see you on Saturday at seven o'clock."

The rope around her chest tightened more as every warning bell and whistle went off.

"Okay. See you then."

She ended the call sucking in a harsh breath. The panic was spreading throughout her body making it impossible for her to move. Every muscle was freezing in place.

"Raelyn, try to take a breath. Come on, take in a breath and I'll count to ten."

She listened to Maren's soft voice and did as she said. Taking in a breath listening to her count and then let it out slowly. She did it once more counting for herself.

"You, alright?"

Raelyn nodded, "Better, thank you."

Maren squeezed her hand, "Not to make you panic again, but if you're falling for Riley then why go out with Bryce?"

"I have no clue why I agreed to go out on a date." Raelyn bent over resting her head on her arm, "I guess I feel guilty for brushing him off before."

"Alright, I get that. However, that's not a good reason to go out with someone. So, here's what we're going to do. You go out with Bryce, and I will be available in case you need an emergency out. You text me and I will come get you."

Raelyn pulled her friend into an awkward hug over the table, "Thank you."

Once she collected herself enough to focus on walking, they went to one last store with plus sizes. Raelyn was able to find a few outfits for the convention and a new blouse for her date with Bryce.

As Saturday inched closer and closer, Raelyn began to panic more about her date. It had been nearly five years since she had been with anyone and longer since she had been on a real date. Maren had offered to help her get ready on Saturday, but Raelyn decided she didn't want to put too much effort into it.

"I'm going to be honest with him, Mare. I'm going to tell him that he's a great guy but there is someone else in my life right now."

Maren was sitting on her bed as she got ready, "Remember to text me if you need me. I'll be here with Cordy watching cat videos all night." On cue, Cordy jumped up and snuggled in on her lap.

Raelyn had decided to wear a pair of black skinny jeans with her new burgundy blouse and black flats. Her hair was loosely pulled back off her face and she decided no make-up was needed. At seven o'clock on the dot there was a knock on the front door.

Maren hugged her quickly, "Good luck and remember text me if needed."

"Got it and thank you."

She opened the front door and could already tell this was a horrible idea. Bryce was in a school hoodie with a backward cap and jeans.

"Looks like I'm a little over dressed." She joked.

"Not at all. You look great!" He held out his hand for hers and they were off.

Bryce drove them to the Rec Room making Raelyn's stomach twist tighter. He even picked the same table they had sat drinking and playing darts at. He ordered two whiskey and cokes for them, grabbing a dart board.

"Figured we could hang out here for a while and then maybe head back to my place."

Red flags went flying in her mind. Even her inner voice was sounding the alarms.

Oh hell no. Nope, No way, No how. Not even if we were desperate to get laid because we're not.

"Well, I'm good with hanging here for a while then going home. I have to be up early tomorrow." She looked down at her glass and pushed it aside.

Smart girl!

She felt her phone buzz in her pocket. Pulling it out, the guilt rushed over her like a tidal wave.

> **Riley:** Haven't heard from you all day. Just saying hi.

"Who's Riley?"

She looked up, seeing Bryce looking down at her screen. No better time than the presence to get this date over with.

"He's the friend I'm going to meet up with in Kansas City."

"Friend?"

She could see him working through a little internal dialog, "Yeah. We meet online a few months ago and we're meeting for the first time at a convention for our favorite show."

"Oh. Sounds kind of nerdy." He chuckled, "Wasn't expecting that from you."

Raelyn gawked at him for a moment, "You didn't? Most everybody who sees me immediately thinks 'nerd'. The glasses and graphic tees are a dead giveaway."

Bryce wrapped his arm around her leaning in close to her ear, "I was more focused on other parts of you."

"Oh." She shivered feeling her stomach twist into a knot, "Let me tell Riley I'm busy and then we can play around of darts."

Bryce nodded, going to set up the board. Raelyn pulled up Maren's text thread and sent a bunch of red flag emojis.

Please come get me. We're at the Rec Room

Maren: Leaving now

Raelyn left a twenty-dollar bill on the table and walked over to Bryce by the dart board.

"Hey, I think I'm going to go ahead and go home now. I just don't think I'm ready to date anyone quite yet. I left a twenty on the table for my drink and I hope you have a good night."

She didn't give him a chance to respond, turning and immediately headed towards the doors. Stepping out into the cool night, she walked down to the corner and watched for Maren's car.

"Raelyn! Wait!" Bryce called out, "What happened? One moment everything is good and the next you're leaving."

"I'm sorry Bryce. I should have never led you on and gone out with you tonight. I'm…" Riley popped into her mind, "I'm not ready for anything serious."

He chuckled, "It's just darts and drinks. Maybe a little something more later…"

"Exactly. I'm not ready for that and I'm sure you could find someone who is more suited for you."

"What's that supposed to mean?" His eyes hardened as he looked down at her.

Raelyn took a step back, "I only meant that you're great looking, athletic guy and I'm a nerd. I'm sure there is a beautiful woman who would love to be by your side."

His head tilted slightly, "Sounds like you think you're too good for me."

"Not at all. Quite the opposite."

"You know what, whatever. I only went out with you since Maren turned me down and I figured you two would be a lot alike. I was wrong. You're like all the other chubby losers who want nothing good in their lives."

She watched as he headed back inside as Maren pulled up along the curb. When Raelyn was safely inside the car, she could no longer hold back the tears.

"What happened?" Maren asked, taking off down the road.

Raelyn shook her head, "Nothing. Just nothing."

It took a few days before Raelyn told anyone about what Bryce had said to her. When she did, Riley did not take it lightly.

Raelyn laughed as she stared down into her empty suitcase. Her body was buzzing with nervous energy as she began to pack for her trip to Kansas City.

Raelyn scoffed, mumbling to herself, "Good luck to them making me look good."

Okay, good to know. I think I have everything. Maren and I are driving out around 2pm and will get to Kansas City around 3ish. When are you coming in?

Riley: I'll be there Friday afternoon. I have a few things I need to do before I can meet up. I was thinking maybe we could meet for a late-night dinner after the concert

I don't know, my track record for bad dates is not in my favor

Riley: I promise it will be nothing like that douchebag's date. We don't even have to call it a date. Just two people meeting for dinner

Okay, it's a date

happy dance

Raelyn started laughing seeing a GIF from Riley of Rhys smiling and doing a little dance. Her heartbeat sped up thinking to herself how she went from no one asking her out to having two guys ask her out.

As nervous as she was to go to her first Red Moon convention and meeting her favorite actors. It was nothing compared to the nerves fluttering in her stomach thinking about meeting Riley finally. She only hoped that the bad feelings trying to creep over her were for nothing. Either way, in twenty-four hours she would be in Kansas City on a whirlwind adventure.

RUNAWAY
CHAPTER FIVE – THE MONSTER
@PACKNERD71

Over the next few days, Noelle spent most of her time going for walks around the perimeter trying to figure out the dynamics between Tiberius, Hunter, Ash, and Rhys. There's was something more than friendship or respect between them. Something that allowed him to control them and what they said.

She feared maybe her heroes were turning out to be some weird cult and now she had traded one terrible situation for another. Noelle decided to do what she did best, which was read and study everything she possibly could about cults, mind-control, and anything that would explain what was going on.

One night in the library, she was going through the last pile of books when Brynn surprised her with a large tome.

"You want to know what's going on?"

Noelle nodded, too stunned to say anything to her.

"Read through this." For the first time ever, she saw Brynn smile, "Sometimes it's good to be a rule breaker."

Noelle looked down at the ancient, worn book with a crimson cover and gold etching reading, The History of the Red Moon Lycanthropes

"Lycanthropes…" She had heard that before in a Folklore and Legend class in college, "Werewolves."

Over the next few days, she ordered a few books online. She had them sent to Rhys's mailbox in the nearby town once she had exhausted all the books in the Red Moon Library on lycanthrope.

It took her hours to work up the courage to walk to the car Rhys had fixed up for her at the garage. She turned the key in the ignition and sat gripping the steering wheel tightly. Taking a few deep breaths, she gently pressed her foot on the accelerator driving up to the gate sensor that opened the main gate to the compound.

"Alright Noelle, you can do this. Just drive to the post office. Everything will be fine." She said to herself as she pulled out onto the main road heading towards town.

A couple hours later, after getting lost, she had her large order of books in the trunk. She was about to get in the car when suddenly everything went black, and she let out a blood curdling scream.

She was thrown harshly into the back of a vehicle. Her hands bound behind her back along with her feet. Tears were slipping down her cheeks as she silently cried out to Rhys.

"There's no use in trying to call out to anyone, your wolves can't hear you in here."

The dark voice made her body tremble in fear. A voice she was all too familiar with and had been running from all this time. The hood was pulled from her head, blinking a few times only to be met by the cold stare of her husband, Andrew.

RAELYN

Raelyn was giggling in her seat beside Maren. They were cruising down highway 70 towards Kansas City when her phone chimed with a reblog from Riley.

"Something he said?" Her best friend asked.

"Yeah, he read the latest chapter of my series. A lot happened in it and he's not too happy."

Maren chuckled, "I guess one day I'll have to find your blog and read it."

Raelyn joined in with her laughing, "Any time you want too. There's about a million words of Red Moon fanfiction on there."

"Really? Where do you find the time?"

"I make the time because writing is important to me. However, the flip side is I typically look like an extra from a zombie show. My exhausted writer looks keep all the boys out of my yard."

They both started giggling as Maren turned up the volume of their favorite band. Raelyn could not remember the last time they had taken a road trip together. It must have been before she was married and that was far too long for them to go without a trip. They sang along to Maren's playlist, tossing snacks at each other and playing dumb road trip games.

Before she knew it, Raelyn watched as the hotel and convention center came into view. The butterflies in her stomach were waking up and shaking out their wings. When they checked in at the front desk, Raelyn was stunned to hear they had a suite on one of the top floors.

"Are you sure?"

"Yes ma'am. Miss Raelyn Burton and Miss Maren Gilmore. We'll get someone to assist you with your bags and show you to your suite."

When she turned around a young man was loading their bags up onto a cart. They headed to room 1404 and the man rolled the cart inside their huge suite. Maren tipped him as she closed the door behind him.

"Wow, Raelyn… this place is amazing."

She was looking around the suite. In the living quarters was a large couch and TV with a beautiful glass coffee table in the center. On top of the table was a small bouquet of tulips with an envelope. Looking at Maren, she could feel her cheeks heating up.

"Riley?" She pointed to the flowers.

Raelyn nodded, grabbing the envelope, and smelling the flowers. They were a beautiful shade of red representing their favorite show.

Dear Raelyn and Maren,

I hope you love your room. Everything is set up to be billed and y'all will have nothing to worry about. Feel free to call room service, use the spa or whatever else you may need. I know this weekend will be overwhelming. I want to help make it a great and fun weekend any way I can.

Enclosed in the envelope are you convention tickets and passes. You don't need to go to registration since I've already had that taken care of. I hope Maren won't mind that I got her the same things as I got you minus the photo ops and autographs. If she wants these then let me know and I will have my connection get them for her.

Enjoy your first night and I will see you after the concert tomorrow. I can't wait to finally meet you... and Maren too. However, I won't lie... I'm a little terrified to meet her. Hopefully, I'll be in her good graces by the end of this weekend. Enjoy!

♡ Riley

"Damn right he should be terrified of me. I will say, he's already in my good graces with this room and everything. Wow."

Raelyn was speechless as she reread his letter, focusing on one line:

I know this weekend will be overwhelming. I want to help make it a great and fun weekend any way I can.

She hadn't said anything about it being overwhelming for her to be in a large crowd of people. How she was riddled with worry about spending so much of her savings to have a good weekend. How she had been having random panic attacks about meeting her favorite actors. How her stomach was in constant knots knowing she was going to be meeting him. He just knew and for that she fell a little more head over heels for him.

"When's your date with him again?"

Maren's voice snapped her back to the surreal reality she was in, "Tomorrow night after the concert."

Maren grabbed her purse and keys, "I think we need to up your game a little for tomorrow night's outfit. Come on, let's find a mall and at least find you a dress. Did you bring make-up? Nevermind, we'll stop and get some of that to."

Raelyn was slightly dazed as Maren tugged on her arm. All she could do was look around the room at everything Riley had done for them in amazement. No one had ever done anything like this for her, especially someone who had never met her.

"What is it?"

There was one nagging thought her inner voice was sing-songing loudly.

"What if... what if Riley really is Austin Jameson? What if he sees me and goes running for the hills or laughing to his co-stars about the fat fangirl who fell hook, line, and sinker? What if— "

"Raelyn Burton, stop it right now." Maren took a hold of her shoulders, "I know I had my doubts about Riley in the beginning, but he's proving time and time again that he truly cares for you. You know if I was getting any runaway vibes, I would drag you out of here in a nanosecond."

Raelyn forced a small smile on her face, "Yeah... yeah you're right."

"Now, I'm thinking we head straight to your favorite clothing store and find something comfortable yet sexy for you to wear on your date." She nodded, following Maren out of their suite and back to the elevators.

There were fans already lining up for registration for the convention. A lot of them were in flannels and Red Moon shirts and it was surreal to see so many likeminded people around. As they walked outside there was a replica of Rhys Remington's 1971 Chevy Chevelle parked outside for fans to take pictures with.

"Once we're back and settled in for the night, you're going to have to introduce me to your show. I don't want to sound like an idiot if anyone comes up and talks to me."

Finally, she could put a genuine smile on her face, "I would love to do that. Honestly, it will help with my nervous to watch my comfort show."

Within a couple of hours and a few detours to a local grocery store for some whiskey and wine. Raelyn and Maren settled into their suite with a delicious meal from room service. Raelyn had her laptop connected to the TV and queued up the pilot episode of Red Moon.

"Now, before we begin, I think I must warn you that you are going to fall hard for one of the main characters." Raelyn said, settling in next to Maren.

"Oh really?"

"Yes, I do believe you will fall for Mr. Tiberius Greyson who is the Beta beneath Rhys and his best friend."

Maren rolled her eyes as she took a sip from her wine glass, "And why, pray tell, do you think I'll fall for him? Is he handsome, charming and devil may care kind of a guy?"

Raelyn laughed softly, "No, I mean yes, he is but he's more like the men you typical date. Goofy and short tempered."

"Not funny. Now hit play so I can see this Tiberius Greyson. The name is a mouthful though." She laughed.

"Everyone calls him Tibs for short. I happen to like his full name." Raelyn chuckled, hitting play.

They made it through three episodes before Maren was head over heels for Tiberius and looking up everything on Jackson Powell. Raelyn didn't have the heart to tell her that Jackson and Calliope were now a couple since their characters started dating on the show.

It wasn't long after they both fell asleep. Raelyn's dreams were filled with scenarios of what she would say to Riley when she met him but then he would morph into Austin Jameson.

Friday at the convention turned out to be a relaxing day. There were a lot of panels from guest stars and Calliope's solo panel. Raelyn and Maren were off to the center left side of the stage in the second row. The moment Calliope came onto the stage, Raelyn went from a reserved woman to cheering fangirl.

"Hello everyone! Wow, it's so lovely to see so many of you here on a Friday afternoon."

Calliope took her spot center stage and started taking questions from the fans who had lined up.

"Don't you want to ask a question?" Maren whispered.

"No. I would rather sit here, listen and take pictures."

Raelyn had made only one major purchase before coming to the convention and that was buying a new camera. She always loved and appreciated the fans who would spend their own time and money to take amazing pictures at conventions. They had inspired her to take a few classes over the summer in photography to learn how to take true photographs and not just pictures.

They were halfway through Calliope's panel when a newer fan asked a fandom taboo question, making Raelyn cringe.

"Hi, I'm Becky from Kansas City, Kansas. I'm newer to the Red Moon fandom."

Calliope had taken to walking the length of the stage towards each fan asking the question, "Lovely to meet you, Becky. Welcome to our fun little pack family!"

"I recently read that you and Austin were dating," The crowd began to grumble and groan as the poor girl continued, "I was wondering if that was true?"

Calliope chuckled, "It's okay everyone, she's allowed to ask the question. I don't necessarily have to answer it."

She walked back towards her seat as Maren leaned in towards Raelyn whispering, "I agree, that's an awfully personal question."

Raelyn nodded in agreement, "It's an unspoken rule to not ask about their personal lives or shipping questions." She looked up when Calliope began to answer.

"However, since that so-called article came out Austin, Jackson and I have had a few conversations about how to answer questions about it. Austin and I are best friends. That's all. Much like Rhys and Ash, we are like siblings and that comes from me growing up around him on the show."

Calliope paused for a moment a small smile appearing on her face as she continued to answer the fan's question.

"Now, I will say this. I am in a relationship with someone and it's wonderful. We're both very happy with how things are going. Also,

Austin has someone new in his life who is very special to him. That's all I'll say about that. Thank you for your question and again, welcome to our wolf pack."

Many in the crowd began to howl, making Calliope laugh as she took the next fan question.

"I don't know what you got me into, but I'm scared now." Maren chuckled.

Raelyn nodded absentmindedly as she replayed Calliope's answer in her mind.

Also, Austin has someone new in his life right that is very special to him.

Her inner voice sing-songing once more the sneaking suspicion Raelyn had been trying to push out of her mind.

Riley is Austin. Austin is Riley. You're walking right into a heaping pile of disappointment and heartache.

She swallowed the large lump in her throat trying to distract herself by taking pictures for the rest of her panel.

After Calliope's panel, they started the autograph lines. Many of the guest stars had lines and offered selfies at their tables. Calliope had the longest line since she was one of the main cast members of the show. Maren had opted out of getting any autographs for that night; however, she did wait in the lines with Raelyn.

Raelyn was excited to finally have her special Red Moon themed autograph board signed. She had spent the whole week before the convention working on it instead of writing.

On a circle wooden cut out, she painted a fading red moon with all the wolves from Red Moon on it. Each actor who played a wolf on the show happily signed next to their wolf and some even took a picture of her board.

Calliope was her last autograph, and Raelyn was nearly bouncing in her spot. With each step forward, the butterflies in her stomach flutter harder.

"You're not going to pass out, are you? I wasn't prepared for you to pass out over a girl."

Raelyn shook her head, "I've had a girl crush on Calliope and her character Ash since her first season on Red Moon. She's gorgeous, talented, funny, and super smart."

They stepped up to the table as she was finishing up with the fan before her. She handed her board to Calliope's handler who took a picture of it before securing the sticky note with Raelyn's name on it.

Calliope took the board, her eyes widening as she looked it over, "This is amazing! How long did it take for you to do this?"

"N-Not too long. Only a few days in order to let the layers of paint to dry." Raelyn's voice trembled at first, "It's so nice to meet you, Calliope. I've loved Ash since day one and love the growth she's gone through on the show. I also love how she doesn't take any shit from Rhys."

Calliope laughed then her eyes snapped up to Raelyn's as she read the post it note.

"Raelyn? That's such a beautiful name. Not one you hear very often." She took out her metallic red sharpie and signed by her character's wolf form, "Do you mind if I take a selfie with you and your board. I love it so much and would love to post it on my socials."

"Absolutely! Of course." The butterflies were now in a fluttering mosh pit as Calliope walked around her table with her phone.

She took a couple of selfies having a hard time getting the board in the picture and making them both laugh. Maren offered to take the picture for them.

"Thank you so much! Hey, write down your socials so I can tag you in my post." Calliope gave her a hug before returning to her table, "It was great meeting you."

"Thank you, it was amazing meeting you as well." Raelyn wrote down her information, handing it to the handler.

Her cheeks were aching from smiling so much. Maren was laughing softly as they walked out of the main ballroom.

"Wow, I've never seen you this happy and giddy before. Now, I'm even more grateful for this show and for Riley giving me this opportunity to see this."

Raelyn pulled her best friend into a hug, "That makes two of us. Now, we have a couple of hours before the concert and I'm sure you're going to use every minute of that torturing me into being a girly girl."

Sure enough, Maren had spent nearly the entire time working on Raelyn's hair and make-up. About halfway through her best friend's torture session there was a knock on the door. Maren went to answer it, threatening Raelyn if she were to move.

"It's for you." Maren was grinning as she handed her another familiar envelope, "Go on, read it."

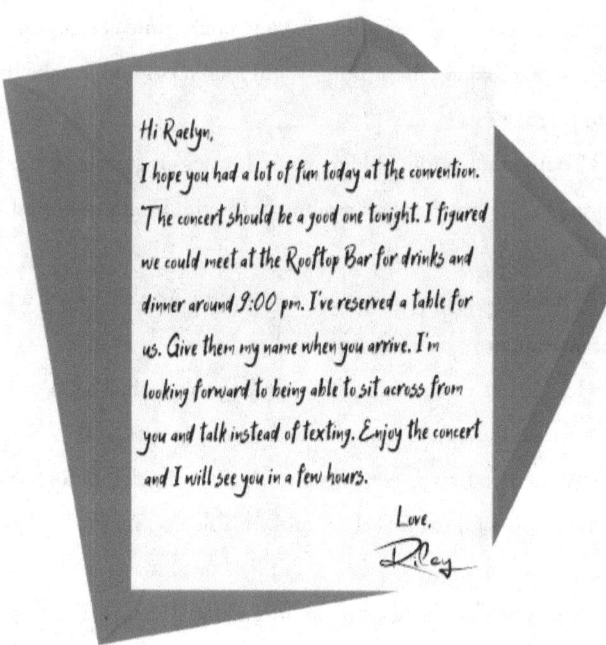

She stared at *Love, Riley* for a long time.

"If you don't end up liking him, please make sure to pass him along my way." Maren joked as Raelyn smacked her arm.

"No way. Find your own guy. I think I'm keeping this one."

She watched as Maren's jaw dropped, "Well I can't believe my ears. Finally, someone swept Raelyn Burton off her feet. About damn time. Personally, I can't wait to shake this man's hand and give him a hug."

"Alright, alright. Will you finish with me so I can get ready."

Raelyn went into the large bathroom to put her dress on. They had found a simple dark teal, A-line sundress, and a crop denim jacket. She put on her black All-Star Mary Janes then looked in the mirror. She was pleasantly surprised that she loved the way she looked. The dress fit her perfectly in all the right areas and hid the not-so-great ones. The denim jacket and Mary Janes were the perfect match to dress it down a little.

Maren had done exactly as she asked with simple make-up and wavy curls for her hair. She walked out into the suite and gave a twirl to Maren who was whistling her approve.

"If he doesn't fall head over heels for you then I think you should steal Calliope away from Jackson so I can have him." They both laughed and headed back down to the ballroom for the concert.

One reoccurring Red Moon guest star had an indie rock band who performed at all the conventions. A lot of the cast members and guest stars would come to sing covers of their favorite songs and if fans were lucky, Austin would come out to sing as well.

Raelyn and Maren were both having a great time singing along to all the songs. Raelyn was able to take some amazing photos of the band and celebrities as they performed. Halfway through the show, the stage went dark, and Raelyn could see someone walking out from behind the curtain.

"Oh my god…" She started smacking Maren's arm excitedly.

"What? What!"

"Austin is singing. Holy crap… Austin Jameson. Is. Singing!"

The stage lights came back on, and the crowd went wild seeing Austin standing on stage, including Raelyn. She caught out of the corner of her eye, Maren laughing as she fangirled then she took Raelyn's camera.

"I'll take the pictures. You enjoy your man up on stage."

She turned her attention back to the stage as Austin began to talk.

"Hey everybody, I thought I might come up here and sing a little for you."

Once again, the crowd went wild as the first few notes of the song began to play. Suddenly, Raelyn froze in her spot. A conversation she had with Riley popped into her head immediately.

***

@PackLeaderAlpha: *Favorite band or song currently?*

@packnerd71: *That's a hard one to answer… ugh*

@PackLeaderAlpha: *Oh, come on. I need some new music on my playlist. Give me one.*

@packnerd71: *…*thinking*…*

@PackLeaderAlpha: **waits patiently like a good friend**

@packnerd71: *There is one band and particularly one song that has been on repeat for me…*

@PackLeaderAlpha: **still waiting patiently**

***

Austin began singing the first verse of that particular song and any doubts she had about who Riley was went out the door. Now her stomach was knotted with sheer panic and the urge to run nearly had her feet moving towards the door.

"You okay?" Maren asked, tapping her shoulder.

She turned to her slowly shaking her head but turning back towards the stage. She watched as Austin took the mic off the stand and moved across the stage. His bright emerald eyes scanning the first few rows until landing on her. He went into the chorus, his eyes never leaving hers.

The urge to run was now pulling against the invisible tether tying her to the man on stage. Raelyn was mouthing the lyrics right along with him. Smiling, he winked at her then moved towards the other end of the stage.

Suddenly she felt like everything was closing in around her. She didn't want to leave, but it was getting impossible for her to take a breath. She grabbed Maren's arm and pulled her towards the end of their row.

"You're worrying me." She asked, "Raelyn, what's wrong?"

Once the cool night air hit her burning face, she finally felt like she could breathe again. Taking a few quick, harsh breaths, Raelyn finally felt like she could speak.

"Riley… has to be… Austin. No other way to… explain it."

"What? Why are you saying that?" Maren directed her to a bench off to the side and pulled out her water bottle for her.

She took a few gulps and let out a long breath, "The song Austin was performing. I told Riley about that song a month ago. He asked me what my favorite band or song was currently. I had told him to listen to that song because at the time it reminded me of us. There's no way, Austin could have known that unless he was Riley."

Maren rubbed her back, "Okay, but there's another explanation…"

Raelyn eyes snapped to Maren's, "Really? How would you explain it?"

"Maybe Riley is closer to Austin and the others than he led on. Maybe he was protecting himself to make sure that fans wouldn't use him to get to Austin or Jackson or Calliope. Maybe Riley told Austin about the song after liking it after you suggested it to him."

The knots in Raelyn's muscles and stomach relaxed as the logic of her friend settled her nerves.

"For once, I'm grateful for your ridiculous logic and reasoning."

Maren laughed, "Do you want to go back in?"

Raelyn shook her head as she glanced down at her phone, "No, it's nearly time for me to head up to meet Riley. I think I need to freshen up beforehand. Mind helping me?"

Maren smiled and pulled her into a hug, "Not at all."

Raelyn left Maren at the elevators, getting into a car by herself and heading to the rooftop. It was a couple of minutes before nine o'clock when the doors opened revealing a small lobby with glass doors leading inside. The hostess greeted her warmly and Raelyn gave Riley's name to her.

"Right this way."

She followed her through rows of tables. A few times she had to pick her jaw off the ground seeing a lot of the guest stars chatting and laughing with one another. She swore at one table she had seen Calliope and Jackson together having a drink together.

Raelyn was led into a private dining area where one person was sitting at a table near the large windows with a view of the skyline. The man was dressed in a light teal suede jacket and his long, golden-brown hair was perfectly set off to one side. She took a deep breath as the hostess left and the man stood turning towards her. He held a single, red tulip like the ones she had received the day before.

I told you! I told you! Now your stinking of heartache and regret.

Her inner voice was right. Katy and Maren were right. She had been right all along.

"Hi Raelyn." Austin flashed his famous, charming smile taking a step towards her.

Raelyn stopped short as Austin's beautiful smile faded slightly. She took a step back followed quickly by another one. His perfect lips parting being the last thing she saw before turning away and walking towards the elevators. Her heart was sinking as one thing ran in through her mind.

It was all a lie.

AUSTIN

"Raelyn! Wait, please!" Austin called out watching her bolt towards the elevators.

He rushed after her through the rooftop bar catching the attention of everyone they passed including his two best friends. He caught her elbow before she could press the down button on the elevator.

"Please, hear me out." He begged, his heart cracking as he saw the tears shining in her beautiful eyes.

"I can't believe I was such a fool. All the signs were there and yet I still allowed myself to play your game. Is that what this was? A game?"

The tears were now slipping down her cheeks, each one adding another crack in his aching heart. He led her away from the elevators afraid she would run before hearing his side.

"None of this was a game. Everything was real. My blog is really mine, but to keep it from getting out to the public I use my middle name on there. The picture of me and Cali is a real picture we took together when I made the blog. Everything I've ever said to you was all me just under another name."

She took a step away from him wiping the tears from her face. That's when he got his first real look of the woman who had turned his world upside down. She was gorgeous. Breathtakingly beautiful and he was having a hard time taking his eyes away from her to focus on keeping her in his life.

"You look beautiful tonight."

Raelyn scoffed, "Oh yeah… I'm sure. Compared to the models, actresses and lord knows countless women that throw themselves at you every day."

"They're not the ones I'm standing in front of trying to convince to come back to the table and have dinner with me. Please, come back to the table and I will answer any questions you want. Nothing is off limits. I'm just asking for you to give me a chance."

She looked him over and his heart raced watching her eyes travel over his body. Her bottom lip disappeared beneath her teeth, and it was taking every fiber of his being not to kiss her. He threw up a silent prayer to whoever would listen that she would come back with him.

Without a word, she walked past him and back into the bar. Austin released the breath that was burning in his lungs. As he followed her back to the table, he caught Jackson and Calliope both headed his way. He shook his head at them, letting them know he was fine. With a nod from Jackson, they went back to their own table and Austin hurried back to Raelyn.

As they sat down, the waiter came up for their drink order.

"Jack and diet tall and a glass of water please." Raelyn ordered not looking up from her hands on the table.

"Scotch on the rocks and a glass of water as well."

The waiter left and a heavy silence fell between him and Raelyn. She was fidgeting with her napkin on the table and her eyes would never lift to his.

"I meant what I said earlier. You look beautiful tonight."

"Thank you." She softly said glancing in his direction, "You look nice as well."

He chuckled, "Thanks. I guess nice is good, right?"

The corner of her lips curled upwards, "I didn't think Austin Jameson had bad looking days."

He laughed, bringing a full smile on her face that took his breath away. Now his single mission in life was to make sure that smile never left.

"Oh, trust me, there are plenty of bad looking days for me. I'm sure Cali would be more than willing to show you."

Raelyn's eyes snapped up to his and her smile faded, "She knew who I was today, didn't she?"

"Yeah. She's the one who encouraged me to keep talking with you. As she says she's fully on Team Auslyn."

"Aus-lyn? Oh god…" Raelyn shook her head as the waiter brought their drinks.

"Were you ready to order?"

He looked at Raelyn who was taking a long drink from her glass.

"I think we'll need another minute. Could you bring out an order of your famous chips and dip?"

The waiter nodded, leaving them alone once more. The awkward silence returned as they sipped their drinks.

"I know you have a lot of questions. I'm willing to answer any of them." He watched as she ran her fingers over her glass and tried shaking the inappropriate images from his mind.

She leaned back in her chair, "I don't know where to begin. What was the end game here?"

"I didn't have one. I like to read fanfiction. I know a lot of actors stay far away from it, but I love seeing our characters through the eyes of our fans. To be honest, ninety percent of what fans write is amazing. There is some weird stuff out there that I skim over. I truly enjoy reading your stories."

The waiter returned with their appetizer and Austin continued once he left the table.

"I came across your new series and loved how it sounded. When I clicked on your blog and saw your picture," He paused when her eyes locked with his, "I thought you were the most beautiful girl I'd ever seen."

If he was going to lose her tonight, then he might as well put it all out there honestly. He wanted her to know everything from their first interaction to now.

"I find that hard to believe." She muttered, taking another long drink.

"It's true. Once I started reading everything you've posted on your blog, I knew for a fact you were the most brilliant woman on this Earth. You get Rhys on a level that I don't think I even get him. It was eye opening to read him from your point of view. I love that you can see all his layers and then some."

Once again, that beautiful smile appeared, "Well a lot of that has to do with everything you put into him. You're an amazing actor."

"Here I thought everyone loved me for my good looks and charm."

"That helps too." Raelyn leaned forward on her elbows resting her chin on her hand, "Be honest with me. Where did you see this going? I'm having a hard time believing that a man of your stature would ever give a woman like me a second look."

"Why do you think that?"

Austin had been more baffled that she hadn't been snatched up by a guy already. He knew a little about her divorce and how she focused on herself after it. He figured men would be throwing themselves at her like that douchebag, Bryce.

"Do you really have to ask? Look at you," she waved her hand up down towards him, "gorgeous, charming, talented, famous. You have millions of fans who adore you."

He leaned in towards her, "And? Why couldn't someone like me fall for an equally gorgeous and talented and strong woman?"

"You're prince charming and I'm a hobgoblin."

"Is that you're only hang up with this? If it is, I can tell you right now what has been running through my mind since sitting across from you. I'm pretty sure no one has ever had thoughts about a hobgoblin that I'm having."

He smiled seeing her face flush, "N-No, that's not the only thing. Though it's a big one. How would this even work between us? No one would ever believe me that I was dating you. I'm sure your management team wouldn't want you telling anyone about me."

"First, no one other than myself and the person I'm involved with has a say in our relationship. My management team has nothing to do with my personal life. Second, anyone who wouldn't believe you can come to me, and I'll set them straight. Third, our relationship is between us."

He wiggled his finger between them watching as she shifted in her seat and her cheeks darkening to a deeper shade of red.

"Now one way you could shut people up if they don't believe you're with me is to show them this."

He stood from his chair and pulled it over next to hers. Slipping his arm around her shoulders, Austin pulled her close to him. He was hit with an alluring mixture of wildflowers and berries. He pulled out his phone and held it up to take a selfie of them.

"Really?" She chuckled.

"Yes, really. Now smile like you actually like me." Austin looked at his phone seeing that Raelyn was looking up at him with a beautiful smile and snapped the picture, "One more."

When he saw she was looking at the camera, he turned towards her and pressed his lips against her cheek. He took the picture as he heard a small gasp come from her. She turned towards him as his mind and heart screamed for him to kiss her.

"Austin…" Her gray-blue eyes went down to his lips, and he leaned in closer to her.

"Excuse me, would you like another round of drinks?"

Raelyn immediately backed away from him as Austin glared up at the waiter, "We're fine. Thank you."

"I think… maybe I should get back to my room."

He nodded, pulling her chair out for her, and following her to the elevator. They were the only ones inside the car traveling slowly down to the fourteenth floor. They stood beside one another, the electric current building between them.

Glancing over, Austin found Raelyn's eyes traveling the length of his body again. When they reached his lips, he felt a zap jump starting his body. He turned towards her before losing his nerve, placing his hands on either side of her face.

The moment his lips met hers, he knew they were the only lips he ever wanted to kiss for the rest of his life. They were soft with a hint of whiskey on them still. He felt her hands gripping his jacket and soon he was pushing her back against the car wall. His hands drifting down her arms slipping over her hips.

"Au-Austin, we have… we have to stop." She placed her hands on his chest pushing him gently.

He forced his feet to step away from her as his body demanded more of her, her body, her lips.

"I'm sorry. I should have asked if I could kiss you. That would have been more gentleman like."

The elevator dinged signaling they had reached her floor. As they walked out of the car, Raelyn grabbed hold of his hand lacing their fingers together.

"I didn't say I wasn't enjoying the moment." She looked up at him with that breathtaking smile melting Austin's heart.

When they reached her room, he pulled her into his arms. She fit perfectly against him as if she were always meant to be there. He tucked a strand of her hair behind her ear watching as her eyes closed leaning into his touch.

"May I kiss you again? I'm dying to kiss you again."

Her eyes fluttered opened as she nodded, "I would like that."

He leaned in pressing his lips to hers and he felt her trembling hand hesitantly brush against his cheek. He smiled against her lips and let out a soft moan as her fingers threaded through his hair. He didn't want this moment to end. He didn't want to let her go. He didn't want to lose her.

Austin pulled away from her watching as her lips chased after his and chuckled. Her eyes slowly opened, shining with tears. He didn't need to ask what she was thinking because he already knew it. They were both feeling the same thing.

"This isn't goodbye. I'm not going anywhere. However, I will give you the space you need to think this out. Dating me is no picnic. My schedule is crazy, and I travel a lot. I also have a daughter and a baby momma that could be classified as crazy. I've got a lot of baggage, but I'm hoping that you might give me a chance regardless of all that."

He kissed her once more and let go of her, "Sleep well. I'll see you tomorrow for all the convention fun."

"Goodnight Austin." She turned towards the door to swipe her keycard.

Austin spun her around for one last kiss. His body demanding to feel hers one last time. His heart sealing its fate that he was hopelessly in love with the woman in his arms. Pulling away from her was excruciating.

"Goodnight Raelyn."

When he let her go this time, he turned away walking down the hallway before he could change his mind and beg her to come back to his room. Beg her to let him show her how he felt for her. When he walked off the elevator onto the floor above Raelyn's, Austin found his two best friends waiting for him outside his room.

"So? How'd it go?" Calliope asked practically bouncing off this ground.

The longing to run back to Raelyn hit him at that moment. Not knowing if he had lost her or if she would be willing to give him a chance. His heart beating at half pace knowing he left part of it in that final kiss with her.

He could feel the tears pushing against the dam he had built. He looked at them and shrugged. Immediately, Calliope pulled him into a hug, and he allowed the tears to fall down his cheeks.

Runaway
Chapter Six – Save Her
@Packnerd71

Rhys pressed his foot down on the accelerator a little more, hitting eighty on the speedometer. His eyes were glued to the road ahead of him. Something was unsettling being away from Noelle. Tiberius sat beside him, slightly annoyed to be missing out on a pack hunt and reminding him repeatedly Noelle had not called or anything.

"Rhys, there is no need to race back. I'm sure Noelle or Brynn would have called if something was wrong." On cue, Tiberius' phone started to ring.

Rhys gave him a pointed look as he answered the phone.

"Slow down Brynn, what?" Tiberius looked over at him, "We're thirty minutes out."

"What happened?"

"Noelle is missing. Her car was found outside Papa Boris's Pizzeria with everything still inside of it. Brynn is there now talking with people." Tiberius lowered his head as Rhys's anger flowed out of him.

Rhys pressed the accelerator further into the floorboard. When they arrived at the pizzeria, Brynn was waiting for them outside.

"What do you got?"

"She was taken by two men in a van outside the pizzeria. Several people tried to help but apparently, they were pinned to the ground as she was put into the van."

Tiberius sighed, "Demons."

"It had to be Andrew which means we need to find her fast before he kills her." Rhys walked back over to his car, "Tibs, track her scent and see how far that gets you. Brynn, you'll head back with me and track the van."

An hour had passed, and Rhys started to pace. He knew they shouldn't have left, but the pack was getting restless sitting around the compound. Rhys had been surprised the other wolves hadn't caught onto Noelle's scent yet. The more she was around the wolves, the more her omega scent was coming out. He knew the time was coming to tell her everything. If not for her own sake, but because he knew soon her scent would allure other Alphas like she was to him.

There was a knock on his door, and he flung it open to see Brynn on the other side. Her eyes were on her feet and the guilt rolled off her. For the first time, he found her submitting to his Alpha instead of pushing against him.

"Did you find her?"

"No, the van had no plates or markings. Several traffic cams are down for maintenance. Tibs has not reported back yet." Brynn answered as he returned to pacing along the side of his couch. "Rhys, may I ask you a personal question?"

He nodded as she asked the question, he had been asking himself for weeks, "Noelle, she's your omega, right? Your true omega."

"I don't know..." However, deep down he knew she was his omega, and he wasn't ready to take on that responsibility of being someone's true mate.

RAELYN

Raelyn walked inside the suite, leaning against the door as she shut it. Her mind was racing with thoughts of everything that had happened. Her lips were still tingling from his kiss and her body was buzzing with renewed energy to run after him. The need to be with him was foreign to her after so many years of denying herself any kind of desire.

Don't forget why you denied yourself those feelings. Let's go through our list again, shall we!

Her inner voice was opening the file cabinet of her mind labeled, *Reasons to Never Fall in Love Again.*

Broken heart, depression, being alone, losing a family you were a part of for many years, betrayal, eating your feelings away, emptiness, self-loathing… oh wait, that's supposed to be in the Everyday File.

Raelyn took in a shaky breath as she felt her phone vibrate within her small clutch. Pulling her phone out, she saw it was a message from Riley.

The text was short and was followed by the selfies Austin had snapped of them.

Maren walked in from the bedroom of their suite. At first, she wasn't looking at Raelyn as she leaned against the door.

"How did the…" Looking up, concern filled her eyes, "Are you alright? What did he do? Do I need to kick some ass?"

That's when the tears began to flow freely down her face.

Her best friend immediately pulled her into a hug, "Raelyn, tell me what happened?"

They walked over to the couch, and she showed Maren the pictures he sent her.

"Oh my god... we were right. Riley really is Austin."

Raelyn nodded, "Yep. Apparently, he really does have feelings for me. I… I don't know what to do."

Maren kept staring down at the picture on her phone, "What do you mean? He likes you; you like him. What don't you know?"

"Guys like Austin do not like girls like me." She saw a familiar disapproving look on Maren's face as she continued, "This is not my own insecurity saying this. I'm serious. Austin is a famous actor who has women throwing themselves at him all the time. Why in the world would he ever settle for a woman from small town in Kansas who can barely get by? I may write fanfiction, but I don't live in it."

Maren handed her phone back, "Did you tell him that?"

"Basically, yes."

"And? What was his response?"

Raelyn smiled remembering what he had said, "He told me they were not the ones he was standing in front of trying to convince to have dinner with him."

"Tell me the truth. What is really keeping you from being with him?"

The answer to that was simple and the toughest to say out loud. She swallowed the large lump of emotions lodging in her throat.

"I'm scared I won't be enough for him, and he'll leave me like Jacob did. Except, this time I don't think I would survive my heart being broken." She leaned her head on Maren's shoulder as more tears fell.

"Babe, you are more than enough for any man. You're beautiful inside and out, you're talented and smart. Most of all, you love with all your heart, body, and soul."

Raelyn lifted her head as Maren continued, "I can tell you without a doubt in my mind, you are the only woman strong enough to be with a man like Austin and everything that comes with him. I can see that you truly love him."

"I think that's what scares me most. I really do love him."

They both started laughing and turned into a fit of giggles.

"Come on, let's get in our pjs, order room service dessert, watch your man on TV and relax."

Which is exactly what they did until falling asleep in the early morning hours.

The convention would be buzzing with excitement as it was the first day Austin and Jackson would have solo panels, photo ops and autographs. As they were getting ready, there was a knock on their suite door. Raelyn's stomach twisted thinking, hoping it would Austin on the other side.

"Raelyn, it's for you." Maren walked into the living area with a small stuff wolf holding a red tulip with a small note.

"The man has some charm. Whew!"

"You have no idea…" Raelyn murmured setting the little wolf next to her vase of tulips.

They went down to the convention, taking a walk around the vendor's room. Raelyn ended up picking up a few little trinkets and a Rhys

Remington hoodie. As soon as Maren saw it, she started laughing uncontrollably.

"Please, please, for the love of all that is good in this world. Please wear that in front of Austin and let me know his reaction."

Raelyn looked down at her hoodie that had Rhys looking stoic and authoritative. Then across the front it said Rhys Remington is my Alpha.

"Does this mean, you're going to…"

Raelyn shushed her, "I don't know. I want to pursue whatever it is between him and I."

"But?"

"But I don't see it working out in the end as much as I want it to. I think someone more suited for him will come along."

Maren rolled her eyes as they walked into the main ballroom, "If those selfies say anything, it's that he only has eyes for you. Just saying."

They sat in their seats chatting with the fans sitting around them. Raelyn felt her phone vibrate and saw a text from Riley.

"Guess I need to change that." She muttered then decided to keep it so no one would know who he truly was in her phone, "Holy crap."

She looked up scanning the stage area before seeing Austin peeking around the stage curtain.

"What?" Maren asked, as Raelyn showed her the text and pointed out where Austin was.

Maren practically pushed her up out of her seat, "Come on, I want to meet this man."

"Oh god help me."

They walked to the edge of stage where a burly man stood in front of the curtain. He smiled as soon as he saw them approaching.

"You must be Raelyn. Nice to finally meet you, I'm Clifford. Come on back."

They walked through the curtain to see the backstage area. A lot of the guest stars were milling around along with Calliope. When she saw Raelyn, she made a bee line straight to her.

"Hi, I'm so sorry I couldn't say anything to you yesterday. I'm so happy to officially meet you, Raelyn."

She chuckled as Calliope hugged her, "It's okay. It's nice to meet you again."

"Cali, let her breathe."

They turned to see Austin and Jackson walking towards them. Maren let out a soft whistle and elbowed Raelyn gently in her side.

"Damn they're better looking in person than on TV."

"Shut it, Mare."

Austin walked up with his hand extended to Maren, "You must be the BFF. I'm Austin, it's nice to meet you."

"It's nice to meet you as well."

Raelyn watched Austin flinch as Maren squeezed his hand.

"If you break her heart, I'm gonna break that pretty face of yours."

"Maren!" Raelyn covered her burning face with her hand.

Jackson started laughing, "I like her! She's got spunk."

Raelyn went to apologize when Austin spoke, "If I break her heart then I deserve to have my face broken. I accept those terms."

He looked over to her with a smirk then let go of Maren's hand. Raelyn didn't know what to do as they stood there across from each other. There was something pulling her towards him. To feel his arm around her and his body pressed against hers. However, her feet were rooted to the floor, and she stood unmoving.

"Hey Maren, would you like a little tour of our backstage area?" Calliope asked, looking from Austin to Raelyn.

Maren looked at her asking silently if she was okay. Raelyn nodded and Maren followed Calliope and Jackson.

The air shifted between herself and Austin as they both stood awkwardly. Austin chuckled running his hand over the back of his neck.

"I was hoping this wouldn't be awkward, but it is. I don't know what to do." He admitted.

"That makes two of us. I really don't know what's allowed and what's not."

Austin closed the distance between them. His hands slipped around her waist locking at the small of her back. Her heart was pounding in her ears, but all the tension that had built up in her released once she was in his arms.

"You feel that too, don't you?"

"What?" she asked, letting out the breath she had been holding.

He held her a little tighter, "That you were meant to be here. I felt it last night. You fit perfectly right here and makes everything feel right."

She couldn't form words to say. All she could do was look up into his stunning eyes and nodded.

"I really want to kiss you, but I feel like I'm pressing my luck if I do. The ball is in your court as to what happens. I don't want to push too hard, but I also don't want you to think I don't want this. I'm having a hard time finding a balance."

Raelyn reached up and brushed his hair back behind his ear, "I think you're doing a great job and I appreciate you being patient. This is all overwhelming. I'm trying to separate the fangirl feelings from the real woman feelings."

"I mean, if you want to fangirl over me, please do. However, I think I would prefer the real woman feelings." He leaned in close enough she could feel his lips brush against hers, "I also know you can't have one without the other."

He placed a quick kiss on her lips making them spark and tingle instantly. She smiled against his lips as they mirrored hers. They pulled away from each other when someone behind them cleared their throat.

"Sorry Austin, but it's time for your panel." Clifford said.

"Duty calls. Clifford will make sure you and Maren get back to your seats. See you later." He kissed her quickly again and took off towards the stairs leading up to the main stage.

Maren suddenly appeared at her side, hooking her arm with Raelyn. Clifford let them out from the curtain when everyone was distracted by the hosts introducing Austin onto stage. He came walking out as the crowd roared with praise for him. Raelyn sat in her seat in complete awe of him. She was reeling from his kiss, and he was calmly sitting up on stage playing it up for the crowd.

"How is everyone this beautiful Saturday morning?"

He scanned over the fans until his eyes landed on her. She took out her camera and started snapping pictures of him. She caught a great one of him laughing when he saw what she was doing.

"Now, before we get to questions. I know there was a question in Cali's panel yesterday that I want to address."

Raelyn's stomach dropped as her hands began to tremble holding her camera.

"I know there are a lot of rumors about Cali and I being together. As she said yesterday, we are best friends. I couldn't imagine life without her, but she's like the annoying little sister I never knew I wanted. Plus, she has a great person in her life that is perfect for her."

Fans all around them were whispering to one another. Raelyn glanced off to the side to see Maren was listening as well to the fans around them.

"Do you think he'll mention the special someone that Calliope mentioned?"

"I wonder why no one will come out and say that Cali and Jax are sleeping together. We all know it."

"That means Austin is still single and I have a chance. Whoo-hoo."

Maren started giggling when they heard the fan behind them say that.

"Now, I will tell you that I have someone special in my life as well. It's all sort of new and exciting. I care about this person a lot and I'm hoping that everyone will be kind and respect that us actors have lives outside of our little Red Moon bubble.”

“He cares about you.” Maren whispered.

“Shut. Up.” Raelyn whispered back through gritted teeth.

Austin clapped his hand down on his thigh, “Now, let’s get to your burning questions.”

Throughout his panel, Raelyn would catch Austin looking down at her. She distracted herself by taking as many pictures as she could of him. Her favorite moment was when a little boy asked if he could give him some Scooby snacks. She caught the moment where he picked the boy up and they did their best werewolf growl.

“He’s good with kids.” Maren bumped her shoulder into Raelyn, “Another check in the pro column.”

“I hate you so much right now.” Raelyn laughed.

At the end of his panel, he waved goodbye to the crowd. Then Austin looked down right at Raelyn as she snapped a picture of him blowing her a kiss. All the fans around her were screaming out for him thinking it was for them. Part of her loved knowing it was truly for her only. It suddenly made her heart race with excitement.

The girls ended up staying for a few more panels until Raelyn had her first round of photo ops. She had decided to buy a Jackson and Calliope op for her and Maren. They waited in line like everyone else and when they saw them in line all of them started laughing.

“My BFF here, has a major thing for Tiberius and I have a girl crush on Ash. So, we were hoping that we could each get a squishy hug pose.” Raelyn explained feeling her cheeks burning.

“Absolutely! Get on in here beauties.” Jackson held his arms out for Maren who instantly fell into place.

Calliope hugged Raelyn then whispered, "I'm gonna give Austin hell for his girl having a crush on me. This will be entertaining."

"Oh boy…" Raelyn chuckled nervously.

They had a little time to kill before Raelyn had a solo op with Austin. Maren decided she was going to go up to their room and take a short nap.

"Have good dreams about Tibs." Raelyn called out.

"Oh, I will, trust me."

Raelyn went to a nearby lobby table to sit and look through some of the pictures she had taken. Each picture of Austin she scanned through made her smile wider. You could see the love he had for all his fans and how much they meant to him. He always listened intently to their questions or stories. His full attention was always on whoever was speaking to him.

She couldn't help but assume that he was like that with the women he dated. Giving them his full attention whenever he was with them. Her mind wandered to how attentive he would as a lover and she found herself shifting in her seat as desire pooled in the pit of her stomach.

"Raelyn?"

She looked up to see Clifford, "Hi."

"I saw you sitting here by yourself and wanted to make sure you were okay."

"Did Austin send you?" she asked, smiling.

He looked in every direction but at her, "Nope. Not at all. Respecting your space and all."

They both laughed, "I'm fine. I'm going to be getting in his photo op line soon. I kind of want to be the last one though. I'm scared if fans see us then the rumors will start like wildfire."

"That's a good idea. I'm going to be in the op room. I can signal to you when to come up."

"That would be great. I appreciate that, Clifford."

He nodded, walking back towards the op room.

Raelyn was amazed by the line of fans for Austin's op. Most of them women. Most of them gorgeous and model-like. Most of them way more interesting and exciting than her.

As she watched woman after woman go in and out of the op room. A heavy realization settled deep with her chest. A realization that had her grabbing a notebook from her bag and writing her raw feelings down.

Clifford walked out and gave a low whistle towards her just as she was finishing writing. She picked up her bag heading towards the op room. It was playing music and she found Austin bouncing along to the beat before the next fan walked up to him.

Clifford offered to hold her things as she walked up to the person collecting tickets. She watched as the fan, who was obviously familiar with Austin and had many ops with him asked for a dipping pose. He pulled her into his arms and with ease dipped her backwards. They stared into each other's eyes and the picture was taken looking like the cover of a romance novel.

Instantly Raelyn's stomach churned with envy and sadness. She would never be able to do that with him. He belonged with someone who looked like that fan and not someone like her.

You're doing the right thing. You must protect us. The only way is to be alone forever.

Her inner voice was right, and Raelyn hated that.

"Hi darlin'!" Austin's voice drugged her out of her daze, and she forced a smile on her face for him.

"What pose would you like?" The photographer asked.

Raelyn shrugged, "Whatever pose is Austin's favorite."

Immediately, Austin wrapped his arms around her shoulder pulling her flesh against his body. She wrapped her arms around his lean waist and tried to commit to memory the feeling of his firm, tone body against hers. She couldn't remember if she smiled or looked at the camera. Before she knew it the photographer called it perfect and was getting ready for the next round of ops.

"Hey Jay, hold up. I think we need a redo. I want to go with my other favorite pose."

The photographer laughed, "Sure thing Austin."

Austin pulled her into the same hugging position, but this time when Jay snapped the picture, she was positive she smiled this time. As the click of the camera echoed in her ears, Raelyn felt Austin's lips press against her cheek. Everyone in the room looked a little stunned at first until Jay broke the tension with his laughter.

"Perfect!"

As Raelyn stepped away, Austin caught her elbow pulling her towards the back of the room. She could see Clifford distracting the others in the room before Austin led her through a back door into a hallway.

"This is how we go to and from different rooms. Only convention and hotel staff are allowed back here."

Raelyn looked around the service hallway, "Where are we going? Clifford has my stuff."

Austin stopped, looking around, before slipping his hand behind her head and pulling her lips to his. Each kiss was more powerful than the last, striking her heart hard. Feeling his teeth graze against her bottom lip before pulling away from her. Raelyn was thankful she was holding onto his arms since her knees wanted to give out.

"I would apologize, but I'm not sorry for ditching my handler to kiss you. I needed that."

She giggled, "At least you're honest… now."

He flashed her his famous smile, "Now that I am sorry for. Come on, I'll show you back to where Clifford will have your things. I'm sure my handler is freaking out."

Austin kissed her again, "I just can't get enough. I love kissing you."

He showed her out a side door where Clifford was waiting with Maren. Austin waved at her before running down the hall towards the main ballroom.

"How mad is his handler?" She asked.

"On a scale of one to ten…" Clifford paused, "About a twelve. He's running about thirty minutes behind for autos."

The guilt flowing over her must have shown on her face as Clifford patted her shoulder.

"Don't worry, he's always late. Austin always makes sure the fans get a great experience and often will run late to make sure an op or meet and greet is done right."

"Sounds like a great man to me." Maren chimed in as Clifford excused himself.

"Yeah, he is a great man." Raelyn could feel the weight of her notebook doubling in her bag, "Come on. You can stand in Austin's ridiculous auto line with me."

Once again, Raelyn made sure she was the last fan for the evening to get his autograph. She walked up with her small poster for him to sign. When his handler slid it over for him to sign, he looked up with a proud smile.

"Hello beautiful, I love this aesthetic." He wrote a little message on it and signed it, "I just got the notification for the newest chapter. Can't wait to read it."

"Thank you. By far my favorite series I've written. I also hope you don't mind me giving you this letter to read later. I just want to say thank you for all the time and energy you put into Rhys. His character makes a big difference in the world and particularly in my world. Thank you for being amazing."

Austin brought his hand up over his heart, "The pleasure is all mine. I'm glad I could make a difference. Thank you for all your support and love. It's what fuels us to keep going."

As she walked away the heaviness on her heart was nearly too much to take. The tears were already streaming down her face and Maren was pulling her off to the side.

"What's wrong?"

"I just made the hardest decision in my life, and I don't think my heart can take it." She let out a quiet sob feeling her heart crack in half.

AUSTIN

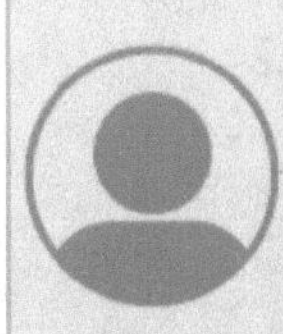

PackLeaderAlpha

I was scared Rhys wasn't going to make it in time, but I should have never doubted him. I really wish he could have taken a chunk out of Andrew. I hope he'll be able to help Noelle through this. Can't wait to see how their relationship changes after this. Loving this series @packnerd71

Austin was riding on cloud nine that night at the cast dinner. The only thing that would have made the night perfect was Raelyn being there by his side. He watched Calliope and Jackson as they danced together in the middle of the bar that was rented out for all of them. They were always holding hands or stealing kisses from one another. He couldn't help to be a little jealous of them when the woman who had stolen his heart couldn't be by his side.

That's when he remembered Raelyn's letter. He pulled it out from his back pocket, his nose filled with flowers and berries bringing a smile to his lips. Seeing his name written in her beautiful handwriting made him never want it to be written in another script ever again.

Austin,

This weekend has been amazing and it's not even half over. I feel like I'm living in a fangirl dream and I'm going to wake up in reality again. A reality where you're still a famous actor who doesn't know I exist and I'm a content, but lonely woman who works two jobs. No matter how much I want to stay in our little dream bubble, I know reality is going to pop that bubble sooner or later.

You're an amazing man. I'm not saying that as a fan. I've never had a man do what you've done for me. Going out of your way to make sure I'm well taken care of even when you were simply just 'Riley'. I love the way you make me feel. I feel like I can do anything, be anything. In the same breath, it scares me how you make me feel. That I'm right where I'm meant to be, by your side, in your arms.

Austin stopped reading, the heaviness on his heart causing his chest to ache. He walked past Calliope and Jackson to the balcony suddenly needing air. He didn't want to finish Raelyn's letter. He knew where it was going and in a desperate attempt to keep it at bay, he refused to read it.

"Hey man, you alright?"

Jackson stepped up, handing him a drink. He downed it in one swallow letting the burn of the whiskey flow down his throat. He handed the letter to Jackson who began reading it out loud.

"My heart, my body wants to be with you. Needs to be with you and that scares me. Nothing scares me more than losing you. A man like you surrounded by beautiful and talented people, it's inevitable that I will not be enough. I will never be enough. Deep down, I know you need a woman who can contend with the millions of women who will be fighting for your attention.

As much as I have loved living in this little fanfiction fantasy, I know I can't stay here. I can't be by your side. I can't hold you back. I can't be with you. I will always be a fan of yours and will support everything you do from afar.

I love you. I love you enough to let you go. Keep inspiring people through your characters. Keep loving your fans. Keep being you, Austin. Goodbye.

Love, Raelyn"

"Oh man." Jackson gripped his shoulder pulling him into a one arm hug.

Austin tightened his jaw trying his damnest to hold back the tears. His heart ripped into pieces with each word of her letter. He thought he could handle walking back inside until Calliope found them. The moment he saw her everything he was holding inside his chest came out from his lips. Burying his head into her neck as she held him allowing him to get all his agony out.

The next morning, Austin didn't want to get out of bed. He hit snooze on his phone twice and ignored Jackson's phone call. He knew he had obligations to uphold, but he couldn't gather the strength to put on his professional mask for the day. There was a loud knock on his door as he pulled his covers over his head. He heard the click of the lock and footsteps approaching.

"Come on Austin, you have to get up." Calliope pulled open his shades letting the sun's rays shine through, "You have exactly a half hour to get your ass in gear and downstairs."

"Can't you and Jackson handle the morning panel?" He pulled the covers tighter around his head to block out the brightness.

Calliope pulled the blankets from the bed, "We could, but we're not going too. We already have Ben and Tricia stalling. Now get up, in the shower and dressed."

"Sometimes, I don't like you." Austin glared at her.

"I know, but you're always grateful for me."

Now that was the truth. He was grateful to have so many people who loved and cared about him in his life. He didn't want to let them down or the fans. Austin swung his legs over the side of the bed rubbing his eyes with the back of his hands.

"I also happen to know that Raelyn and Maren will be down at the panel. As we speak, Maren is doing the very same thing I am with you to Raelyn."

He popped his head up to see Calliope smirking, "You spoke to her?"

"Raelyn? No. I ran into Maren in the lobby this morning. We had a lovely conversation during an elevator ride up to our floor. We are both firmly Team Auslyn and hate seeing you both miserable."

Knowing he would see Raelyn downstairs gave him the little boost to get going. He grabbed his clothes for the day and headed towards the bathroom.

"I'll be down in twenty. Thank Tricia and Ben for holding down the fort."

"That's my boy." Calliope called out as Austin heard the door close.

True this his word, he was down in the main ballroom within twenty minutes with his hair slicked back from his shower. He could hear the audience laughing at a story Ben was telling about his character, Hunter, chasing after Tricia's character, Brynn. Austin remembered watching them film and Ben tripping ass over tea kettle down a hill.

Austin took a chance, peeking his head out around the curtain. His eyes immediately went to Raelyn's seat only to see it was empty. His heart dropped slightly as he turned back towards his friends waiting for him by the stairs.

"You ready?" Jackson asked.

Austin shook his head, "Nope, but let's do this."

Ben announced the three of them out onto the stage. Their morning panel was for the fans with special weekend passes. Usually, it was only the first fifteen rows of fans, and they would randomly pick fans for questions. Before going out on stage, Austin had told the convention runner that they would go a little longer since they were late.

"Good morning, KC!" Jackson called out as they walked out waving to everyone.

Austin put on his best smile as fans cheered and waved at them. He tried to keep his eyes from going to Raelyn's seat, but his willpower was non-existent. He took a shaky breath seeing her sitting beside Maren.

Her beautiful hair tied up into a messy bun and black rimmed glasses resting in front of puffy eyes. She was wearing her Rhys Remington hoodie from yesterday and looking anywhere but up on stage.

"Thank you for be patient with us as sleeping beauty took his time getting ready."

Jackson playfully pushed him, and Austin chuckled, "Hey I don't just wake up looking like this. I'm old and need all the beauty sleep I can get."

"Let's take some questions before we lose any more time." Calliope called on a fan on the opposite side of where Raelyn was.

It was almost like the fans could sense he needed an easy panel. Their questions were simple with easy answers. He and Jackson were still laughing about the time they were tied together and had to work out Rhys and Tibs' issues when Calliope picked another fan.

"Hi, I'm Maren and I'm brand new to the Red Moon family."

Austin's heart nearly stopped as he heard Maren's voice. Turning, he could see Raelyn shifting in her seat uncomfortably. For a moment, everything around them paused as Raelyn's eyes locked with his. Her pillowy bottom lip disappeared beneath her teeth, and she looked towards her friend standing with a mic.

"Welcome Maren, what's your question?" Jackson had stood from his chair and walked towards her side of the stage.

Maren looked directly at Austin with a smirk that made his stomach clench nervously.

"I was wondering if you ever read any Red Moon fanfiction and if so, what your thoughts were on it?"

Suddenly he felt like a spotlight was placed on him. Jackson and Calliope were chuckling while Austin slowly wished the stage would swallow him whole.

"Personally, I've never read any fanfiction of Red Moon. I imagine reading fanfiction would be like reading my script and I don't

198

want to make a decision for my character that would be based off reading a story online. I've heard we have some talented writers in our pack family."

Jackson looked at Calliope who was grinning, "I love reading fanfiction. Jackson's right, we have some talented writers and artists in our little pack family. I love anything fluffy since we tend to have a lot of drama and angst on the show. Austin?"

All eyes were on him, and he glanced down at Raelyn whose eyes were glued to the floor and faint rosy color on her cheeks.

"I'm with Calliope, I love reading fanfiction. I even have a blog on a fansite where I reblog and share the fanfics I like. I'm reading through one series right now that is amazing. The author is talented and truly gets Rhys."

Austin didn't look away from Raelyn as she looked up at him, "I'm lucky enough that the author and I have talked online and became friends. I love being able to connect with fans on the same level and not as someone famous. Just a normal dude."

"I don't know about normal…" Jackson joked making everyone laugh, including Raelyn.

Austin smiled seeing her cheek color deepen and Maren bumped shoulders with her. Their panel ended and the three of them headed off stage. Seeing Raelyn ignited something within him that had Austin heading off to the green room. They had a little time before any ops were to start and Austin wanted to get his thoughts down before he lost his nerve.

Making his way to the op room, Austin grabbed Clifford and asked him for a favor. At first, Clifford was a little hesitant to go with it, but in the end, Austin knew he would have his back. Photo ops were one sure fire way to keep his mind off the slow ache radiating in his chest as fan after fan came in to pose with him. Thankfully he also had duo ops with Jackson and Calliope ending with their trio ops.

It didn't go unnoticed by him that Raelyn hadn't come through the line even though she had tickets. Part of him was thankful she didn't, making it easier to focus on his job, but with each passing fan the longing to see her deepened the ache in his chest. Jackson and Calliope checked in with him regularly as the day went on, giving him enough space to be but always close enough if he needed them.

Their afternoon panel was the main event of the convention. The three of them took their seats as fans lined up on either side of the stage. Austin glanced down at Raelyn's seat only to see Maren sitting there. She gave him a small wave then pointed towards the line on stage left. His eyes followed until he saw Raelyn standing with the other fans to ask a question.

Again, he didn't know if the fans could sense he needed easy questions, but their panel was filled with funny stories and easy answers. He looked up at the clock letting them know how much time was left for the panel. Austin tried to calculate if Raelyn would get to ask her question or not. He didn't know which he preferred more.

"We have time for one more question." Calliope looked towards the left side of the stage with a wide smile spreading across her face.

His heart began to race as Raelyn's voice flowed over him from the speakers. Her somber, even tone spread warmth over his body that made him feel like he was wrapped in a fuzzy blanket. His body was instantly at ease listening to her speak.

"Hi, I'm Raelyn and I've been a long time Red Moon fan."

Jackson slipped his arm around Austin's shoulders, "Lovely to meet you Raelyn."

"My question is what is one thing you would like for your character on the show to achieve before the show ends?"

There was a low rumble at the mention of the show ending. It was clear from their fans that they wished the show would go on forever.

Calliope laughed, "That implies the show would end. I don't see that happening any time soon. Personally, I would like to see a new generation of Red Moon wolves. Other than our newcomers, the twins… which can we give it up for Shae and Kye."

Everyone started clapping for the newest guest stars on Red Moon. Real life twins who were playing young werewolves, Paisley, and Ronan. The young actors were still getting used to the convention circuit and the Red Moon fandom.

"Other than the twins, my character is one of the younger wolves. I think I would like to see some of the pack have families. Maybe then we old timers could have a break while having a spin off series."

Jackson squeezed his shoulder, "I agree. I think for Tibs I want to see more of his domestic side. I think settling down with Ash exploring their relationship more and how it affects his friendship with Rhys. I would like for the three of them to truly be a family."

"Awe, you break my sister's heart I'm gonna break your face." Austin chuckled, clearly hearing Maren yell out in agreement.

"Damn right!"

"For Rhys… I don't know."

He looked right at Raelyn who was shifting nervously from one foot to the other. He thought about Raelyn's series and how she was writing Rhys.

"I would like for Rhys to settle down and find love. We know him and Brynn had a thing and how hurt he was after it. I would love for him to find someone who would love him for the grumpy old wolf he is and still keep him on his toes. I would also love to play Rhys as a father. I think he would make a great dad."

Raelyn stepped up to the mic, "I think Rhys already shows how good of dad he would be. One of the many layers I love about him."

Ben came out with the rest of the cast to end the panels for the day. Austin's eyes were glued on Raelyn as she made her way back to her seat. Everyone in the audience was standing and applauding. They all waved and blew kisses out to their fans before exiting the stage. Austin, Jackson and Calliope were the last ones to walk off as he did, Austin noticed Raelyn and Maren were already gone.

Following everyone to the autograph tables, his handler was already there setting everything up for him. Clifford stopped by next to him before his autos began.

"She's in line."

Austin's heart leaped in his chest, "Thank you."

About an hour later and countless signatures, he found a familiar name coming across the table attached to a beautiful piece of Red Moon art. Looking up, he found Raelyn standing in front of him.

"Hi Raelyn."

Her chest swelled as she took in a breath, "Nice to see you again."

Once again, her bottom lip disappeared beneath her teeth and Austin suddenly was having a problem remaining in his seat. He looked down at her autograph board seeing his was the last signature she needed. His alpha wolf dead center in the red moon.

"This is a lovely board. You're a great artist."

He glanced up after signing his name to see her face flush, "Thank you. I hope you had a wonderful con this weekend."

"I did have a wonderful con. It's always great to meet fans such as yourself. You're worth the long hours and hard work."

Her eyes widened as he leaned forward holding his hand out to her, "Please remember that you're worth every minute we spend on set and getting to meet you at cons."

An electric current charged up his arm as her trembling hand touched his, "I'll remember that. Thank you again for an amazing weekend."

He watched her walk away as the next fan stepped up. Out of the corner of his eye, he watched as Clifford shook her hand and completed Austin's favor. Now it was all up to the universe if he would ever see Raelyn Burton again. There was a small spark of hope that was still burning deep within him that he would see her once more.

22
Twenty Two

Runaway
Chapter Seven – Healing
@PackNerd71

Hunter tilted his head slightly, "Have you ever manifested powers before? Even if you did not know it. Could have been something simple as moving an object or pushing someone out of the way of danger."

"No, I don't think so. Usually in moments like that I tend to coward away and go inside my own mind. The more he… he was in me the more I just blanked out." She explained as Hunter nodded.

He knelt next to her, "May I? I know you've been through a lot, but this may answer some questions about your powers."

Noelle nodded as he and Tiberius stood from the couch. Hunter was a special breed of werewolf that had telepathic powers. He had her lie on the couch and put her into a hypnotic state. The room was suddenly spinning, and she felt like Alice in Wonderland falling down the rabbit's hole. Flashes of everything that happened with Andrew passing by her and then Rhys's emerald eyes came into view.

Scenes from previous dreams she had of him since the moment she left Andrew. Moments of them together on hunts, late night drives in his car and nights snuggled together. Her body relaxed, and she could swear she was floating. Suddenly she was pulled from the moment, and she opened her eyes to see Tiberius and Rhys getting off the floor.

"Holy crap… What was that, Hunter?" Rhys asked brushing his hands over his jeans.

Hunter smiled slightly, "I think I have found what triggers her powers."

Tiberius scoffed as he picked up her chair sitting in it, "Okay I'll bite, what is it?"

Noelle looked up at Hunter silently pleading with him not to say Rhys's name out loud. He gave her a short nod.

"Love. Her powers are triggered when she feels immense love like that of her mate."

She felt her jaw drop slightly and her eyes snapped to Rhys who was giving Hunter a hard look. There was also a sadness in his eyes that she was not expecting.

"Mate? You can tell she's a wolf." Rhys asked.

Hunter nodded, "Yes. Like me, her psychic powers have prevented her omega from fully coming out, but the longer she's around us the stronger it will become. She'll need to be with her Alpha soon."

Rhys's head snapped up and for a moment she swore his eyes flashed red. The natural pull towards him tugged at her hard. The immense wave of heat spreading throughout her made sitting in his presence uncomfortable.

"I think I'm going to lay down for a little while. Suddenly, very tired." she muttered, heading towards her small bedroom.

She could hear them talking but decided it was best not to listen. Once inside, she leaned against the door taking a deep breath. A million thoughts were running laps inside her head, but one was standing centerstage.

Rhys Remington was her Alpha.

AUSTIN

The cool wind blew through his hair as Austin leaned over the balcony railing. He was looking out over downtown Kansas City thinking about everything that happened over the last few days. Picking up the glass tumbler next to him, he finished off the whiskey that was in it.

Austin had decided to skip going out with everyone and had been in his room since the convention had ended. He smiled looking at Calliope's text, always the worrier, he typed out a quick reply.

He walked back inside to place his phone on the charger when there was a knock on his door. Rolling his eyes, he walked over, flinging the door open.

"Cali, I said I was— "

Austin's breath caught in his throat seeing Raelyn standing there.

"Hi." She looked down at the piece of paper in her hands, "You don't play fair."

He stepped to the side, letting her in. Genuinely surprised to see her there and having his note in her hands. Raelyn looked around at the suite that looked identical to the one she was in.

"I only wanted you to know my intentions." He shut the door and suddenly the air in the room charged with raw energy, "Also, I never said I played fair."

His body desperately wanted to be next to her and it was hard to resist being alone with her. Austin motioned for her to sit on the couch as he walked towards a small cart with alcohol and glasses.

"Would you like a drink? I have whiskey and scotch or if you prefer, I have bottles of water."

He glanced over his shoulder to see her eyes drifting down his body. He cleared his throat, and she shook her head looking away.

"Um, water is fine."

Austin went to the mini fridge and grabbed two bottles for each of them. He already had a few whiskeys and wouldn't be able to uphold what little self-control he had left if he drank anymore.

"Was that all you came here for, Raelyn? To tell me I don't play fair."

"No. I feel like an ass for…" She paused looking down at the bottle in her lap, "For I guess breaking up with you in a letter. Not that we were dating, but we were more than friends. Hell, I don't know what we are. I just know we both deserve to discuss this like adults. Face to face."

Austin breath hitched as she brought the bottle up to her lips taking a long drink. A montage of images ran through his mind. One sexier than the previous and he adjusted his position in his chair.

"I'm all ears. I meant what I said in my note."

She picked up the piece of paper reading it out loud.

Raelyn,

I'm not giving up. I learned my lesson the first time when I messaged you all those months ago. You are worth every second I wait for you to be ready. I will patiently be here for you.

Love, Austin

"Here I am."

Raelyn sighed, bringing her legs underneath her on the couch, "This will never work out between us."

He leaned forward resting his elbows on his knees, "Tell me why you think that and don't say because I'm me and you're you. That's not a reason."

"But it is a reason. You're a world traveler, famous actor, male modeling son of a bitch."

He couldn't contain his laughter on the last one, "Now that one is a first for me. Still not a reason."

"Austin, you deserve to have someone who can walk down a red carpet with you and not be the laughingstock of Us Weekly. I would be an embarrassment for you. Not only in the looks department, but my baggage is large and heavy. The media would find out about it and start wildfires against you."

"That's why I have a publicist and a manager. They are paid to handle shit like that. You don't think Bernadette's mom isn't a big fucking piece of baggage in my closet?"

He closed his eyes taking a deep breath, "I'm sorry. That came out way harsher than I meant it too. All I meant is I have baggage as well and none of that should keep us from pursuing a relationship that could be good for both of us."

"I didn't mean to imply that you were without baggage. I know your team does an excellent job of keeping your personal life out of public eye." She started chewing on her bottom lip.

Austin moved over next to her, "Tell me what is really keeping you from being with me. I can tell there are some insecurities there and I'm sure they have to do with your ex. Be straight with me."

"I'm damaged, Austin. I'm damaged beyond all repair. Used up. A shell of the woman I once was. I'll only add more shit to your complicated life. I don't want to be a burden more than I already am. I learned my lesson the first time with my ex."

Hearing her talk so low about herself had Austin's blood boiling, "Did your ex put all of this in your head? If so, he deserves an ass kicking."

"He didn't put it there. It was already there." Her voice was barely above a whisper.

"Raelyn, listen to me." He took her hand and placed it on his chest over his racing heart, "You are not damaged. You've been hurt by at least two guys I know of and if I ever get the chance, they will get their teeth knocked in from me."

She scoffed trying to remove her hand. He held in place, and she looked up at him with tear filled eyes.

"The woman I fell for was not the woman you were. I fell for the woman right in front of me. The woman making my heart race. The woman who leaves me awestruck by her talent and brilliance. The woman who makes my knees weak with a simple glance or giggle."

He leaned in until his forehead nearly touched hers, "The woman that floods my body with desire and makes me feel like a teenage boy again. I don't see a damaged woman. All I see is a woman that has survived when all the odds were against her and came out the other side stronger."

"Austin…" Tears slipped down her cheeks, "If this doesn't work between us. I don't think my heart could take being broken again."

"I can't stay away from you, Raelyn. I'm not saying it will be perfect and that we won't be at each other's throats for one thing or another. My life is chaotic at best between my filming schedule, convention schedule and trying to fit time in to see my daughter. Let's not forget that most women run far from me once they interact with our very protective fans." They both chuckled.

He cradled either side of her face, swiping away the tears on her cheeks, "But you're worth it. Us, together, is worth fighting for. I don't think my heart can take losing you."

"What do you think all your fans will do when they find out you're dating one? They either hate it completely making your life hell or they will search out every little detail about me to critique and have an opinion on. Do you really want to deal with that at every convention?"

He let out a low growl growing more frustrated, "Do you want to be with me?"

"That's not the point." She pulled out of his grasp standing up.

"It's a simple question, Raelyn. Do you want to be with me?" He squared off, standing in front of her.

She let out a frustrated groan, "There's not a woman in this hotel that doesn't want to be with you."

"I don't care about them. All I care about is you. Do *YOU* want to be with me? Yes, or no?"

Austin closed what little distance there was between them. Immediately, Raelyn's hands pushed against his chest trying to keep him away.

"No, I don't want to be with you. I don't want to be with you because I know if I give in to my desire, you're going to break my heart. Everyone else I've ever let in has broken it why would the great Austin Jameson be any different." She yelled before covering her mouth.

He staggered back as if she had physically hit him. Finally, her truth was out, and it wasn't the fame, the fans or anything else he could control. He was going to lose her because every other person she ever let love her had taken advantage of her fragile heart.

"Raelyn, I— "

"I can't. I can't do this. I'm sorry."

He watched her walk out of his suite. His mind fighting with his heart rather to go after her. His heart telling him to run after her right now. His mind telling him to let her go and she would come back if they were meant to be.

"Fuck it." He growled running out of his suite and down the hallway.

She was pressing the elevator button repeatedly as he caught up to her. Austin grasped her arm, twirling her into his arms and kissing her.

Raelyn smacked her hands against his chest trying to push him away. He held her tighter against him.

"Come back." He murmured against her lips.

"Austin, please…"

He shook his head stubbornly, "I want this to work. Whatever this is between us. I want it. I want you, Raelyn."

Tears fell down her beautiful face, "Please don't say that. You're breaking my heart."

"Then come back with me. Let me show you that this is right between us. Everything that has been building these last few months is all real."

He placed his hands on either side of her face. Austin kissed away the tears on her cheeks.

"I want to take away all the insecurities."

He kissed her forehead and temple, feeling her let out a long, shaky breath against his neck.

"I want to erase all the doubts and worries."

She began to giggle softly as he peppered her lips and neck with kisses.

"All I want is you and it scares me shitless how badly I want you. I want us."

"I… Austin, I…"

He pressed his forehead against hers, "Please Raelyn, please come back with me. We've both been through so much shit, but I think that's why the universe put us together. Please, be mine. Let me be yours. Just come back with me…" His own tears now falling freely.

Austin looked down into her beautiful eyes fluttering open. His chest tightened around his pounding heart. This was the moment that could change everything. Either his heart would burst from absolute joy or break in complete agony.

He held his breath as her lips parted letting out two breathless words, "I'm yours."

RAELYN

"I'm yours."

Immediately, Austin's lips were pressed against hers. Raelyn had been fighting her body's demands from the moment she walked through his hotel door. Her mind being enveloped by a fog of desire from years of fangirling over the man currently leading her down the hotel hallway. His hands never leaving her body for any length of time.

The moment his door was shutting behind her, Austin had her pinned against it. His lips leaving a scorching trail of kisses down her neck. His hands squeezing her hips bringing her flesh against his body.

"Aus-Austin…" She breathed out, feeling the full affect she was having on him.

His hips pinning her in place and his mouth sealing over hers.

"You. All you." He smiled against her lips, "Now, you can feel what I've been dealing with the last few days."

Raelyn let out a strangled chuckle as his hands slid up her sides beneath her hoodie. He stopped the moment he felt her flinch. His hands pausing against one of her pudgy rolls. A chill shot down her spine, too afraid to look at his face to see how disgusted he was.

He tugged the hem of the hoodie up pulling it over her head. Beneath it was a simple black tank top that was a size too small for her. Daring to look up at him, she could not believe what she saw. Austin's wide eyes dark and traveling down the length of her chest and torso slowly. His lips parted and his tongue darted out over them.

"You're gorgeous." He whispered, leaning in to kiss her neck then down to her collarbone.

She gently pushed him back earning a small smirk from him. Her hands were trembling as she ran them down his chest and stomach. Watching as he closed his eyes leaning his head back.

"I lost a layer, only fair you do as well."

Raelyn pulled his t-shirt up over his head. Immediately her eyes went to the wolf paw print tattoo on his chest with a red moon in the center of it. Rarely did the fans get a peek of his famous ink he got for the show. Tracing her finger over the paw, she felt the rumble from his chest making her knees wobble.

He dipped down running his hands beneath her butt gripping her thighs and knew what he was trying to do. Instinctively, she backed out of his grasp.

"W-What?" His brows knitting together, "What did I do?"

"You won't… I mean…" She looked away from him embarrassed by her large form, "You won't be able to pick me up. I'm heavy and awkward."

He was nearly five inches over her as he stood in front of her, "You wanna bet?"

Before she could say anything, he was lifting her thick legs around his lean waist. Never had a man pick her up and carried her. She kissed him as he sat on the bed keeping her securely in place on his lap.

"Better get used to being picked up because I will definitely be using that to my advantage." He murmured against her neck.

"Never… will doubt your strength… again." Her words were coming out in large gusts of air.

Austin stood up with her long enough to gently lay her back against the mattress. Her legs dangled off the side as he stood in between them. He ran his hands along the side of her legs to the waistband of her leggings. Dragging them down her legs, Raelyn shut them quickly before he could see anything.

He tilted his head to one side, "Would you be more comfortable if I took my pants off as well?"

The smile spreading across her face earned a chuckle as she nodded. Everything around her stopped as he took one hand unfastening his belt and jeans. It had to be one of the simplest and sexiest things she had ever witnessed. Pushing his pants to the floor, he stepped out of them kicking them to the side.

"Better?"

It was and it wasn't. He was beyond human beauty, but a god among humans. His body was fine-tuned and toned in all the right places from years of training. Yet, his stomach was soft and cuddly looking. Her fingers were eager to touch him.

"Raelyn?"

"Sorry, taken back by how beautiful you truly are."

Austin laughed, "Stealing my lines, pretty girl."

He placed his hands on her knees, gently prying them apart and never breaking eye contact with her. She pushed herself further up the bed as he crawled over her kneeling back for him to lift her tank top over her head. Raelyn's arms wrapped around her bulging belly and the bed seemed to be extra creaky with every move they made.

"Why are you hiding? I've been dying to see every inch of you." Austin leaned down planting kissing along her arms locked around her.

"Decades of body issues won't magically vanish. Not even with your sweet endearments."

However, Raelyn found herself letting go of her stomach out of pure desire to run her fingers through Austin's soft hair. He made his way up her stomach, kissing and nipping at her skin until reaching her bra. He went for the front clasp, and she stopped him.

"Wait."

"Okay." He slowly let go of her garment decided to lie beside her, "What is it?"

She tried to keep from flinching when he wrapped his arms around her waist. If he noticed she couldn't tell as his fingers slowly drew circles against her ribs. She wanted to be confident and sexy with him, but every imperfection was screaming out to her in the brightness of his room.

"I've…" She let out a long breath, "I've never had sex with the lights on."

"What?"

Her face flooded with embarrassment, "I've never…"

"No, I heard you. I'm just trying to wrap my pea-brain around the fact that no man thought to shine a bright light on the stunning beauty that was before them." He scoffed, "Pretty girl, I'm so sorry for the fucksticks you were with before."

"Do you mind, maybe for now, could we…"

He rolled off the bed and hit the switch for the lights, but then turned them back on.

"Wait a moment, I have an idea."

Austin rummaged through his suitcase grabbing a few items. He shut the bedroom door blocking out the light from the living area. Then he went to the bedside lamps and covered them with his plaid and button-down shirts. Immediately the room darkened but she could still see Austin standing there.

"Is this, okay? I'm sorry for being slightly selfish but I want… I need to see you."

She nodded, as she took in Austin standing before her. His hands were on his narrow hips with his fingers sliding beneath the waistband of his black boxer-briefs.

"That makes two of us." She whispered.

His lips curled into a playful smirk as he pushed his boxers down his long legs. For a moment, Raelyn forgot how to breathe as Austin stood there in all his magnificent glory. In all the fanfiction she had read or written, could not have prepared her for how perfect he was in every way.

"Would you like to take a picture; it might last longer." He joked.

Raelyn giggled softly, "I'm sorry. Actually, I'm not sorry. I'm speechless. You're perfect."

He climbed over her, settling himself between her legs that now willingly accepted him. His lip pressed gently against hers. She felt her body submit to his will as he unclasped her bra letting it fall on either side of her. Austin slowly rolled his hips against her igniting a fire deep within her stomach.

He pushed himself up, his dark eyes shining with a passion she had never seen from a man. He kissed her once more.

"Are you sure? We can stop."

He was giving her an out if she wanted it or needed it. There was only one thing she needed and that was him.

"I want this. I want us. I want you."

That was all he had need to hear as they both fell into the depths of blissful oblivion together.

When Raelyn woke up, she found Austin staring down at her running his fingers down the side of her cheeks. She smiled, leaning into his touch, and giggled.

"What's so funny?"

"My first thought seeing your hand on my cheek was, oh my god I hope I'm not drooling."

He started chuckling but it didn't reach his eyes and panic-struck Raelyn. Pulling the sheet over her she mirrored his position on his side.

"What are you thinking?"

He scoffed, "What every guy thinks after sleeping with a woman he really wants to impress."

She tried to think of what he meant but came up empty, "You'll have to enlighten me. I've only been with two men in my life. First was my high school boyfriend and the other was my ex-husband. So, it's been a long time since I've done this."

She watched the shock filter through his green eyes, "Wait, you haven't been with anyone since your ex?"

"Nope. I told you; I took time for myself to work on me. I haven't dated anyone, kissed, had sex since months before my divorce."

"H-How? How did you ignore all the men that must have been throwing themselves at you?"

Now Raelyn busted out into a fit of laughter, "Yeah… right. No one was throwing themselves at me. I blended into the background where no one would notice me. That was until I started writing fanfiction for Red Moon, then I definitely caught the attention of someone."

She booped his nose making him smile, "That you did. My full and undivided attention."

"Now, back to my original question. What were you thinking?"

He leaned forward burying his head into her neck and shoulder. She felt him groan against her skin. Then he mumbled something into her neck, and she giggled pushing him back.

"What was that?"

"I said, I was worrying about if everything was good for you. If I… was good."

At that moment, she saw Austin, for the real man he was. Allowing himself to be vulnerable in front of her and concerned that he had made their first time together perfect. She leaned in pressing her lips to his and pushing him back against the mattress. His arms instantly wrapped around her, and his hand went up cradling her head.

"I take that as a yes, it was good for you." He laughed.

"I definitely would give you four and half stars across the board."

He pulled her lips to his, "Only four and half?"

She nodded, "Well yeah, I want see if you can make it a five-star round now."

Austin's jaw dropped dramatically, "Oh, a round two. I like the way your think, pretty girl."

Once more Raelyn was thrown into abyss of pleasure at the hands of the man who had stolen her whole heart and soul marking her as his forever.

The sun was shining bright through the curtains as Raelyn peeked open her eyes. Reaching behind her, she felt the cold sheets where Austin had previously been sleeping. She looked down at the floor grabbing her panties and his T-shirt. It was a little snug on her, but she decided to go with it having the little boost of confidence from their earlier activities.

Raelyn found Austin staring down at a brown envelope with a worried expression on his face. Clearing her throat, she stepped behind the couch not wanting to startle him too much.

"Everything okay?"

He tucked away whatever he was looking at back in the envelope tossing it on the small table. Turning around, she got her first look of him in only his boxers and knew the desire to be with him would never go away.

"Everything is great. How are you feeling this morning?" He walked up to her slipping his arms around her waist, "By the way, you look great in my shirt."

She felt her cheek flare, "Thank you. I'm starving…"

She looked up at him through her lashes chewing on her lip with all intentions of following through on what she was implying until her stomach growled loudly.

"That look and your stomach are sending me mix signals."

They both started laughing as Raelyn pressed her forehead against his chest, "I think my stomach will win this battle as much as I would like the other to win. I should probably let Maren know I'm alive."

Austin kissed the top of her head, "Tell you what. You go get Maren and we can all have brunch together before we leave."

Raelyn's heart dropped realizing she was driving back to Lawrence today and Austin was flying back to New Orleans. He cupped her face before kissing her lips.

"Don't think or worry about it. We'll talk and Facetime all the time. We can also plan out some dates you can come to visit me or vice versa. Eventually, I would like for you to meet Bernadette as well, but we can cross that bridge when you're ready."

She nodded, the sadness already burrowing into her chest. After a wildly emotional rollercoaster ride of a weekend, Raelyn was not quite ready to face reality again or to be away from the man who stole her heart.

Runaway
Chapter Eight – Alpha and Omega
@PacknerD71

Rhys placed his hand on her cheek before sliding it behind her neck. The next thing she knew his rough full lips were on hers hesitantly kissing her. Every nerve ending in her body fired as he kissed her. When he pulled away, he rested his forehead against hers. His breathing labored and a low rumble came from his chest.

"Are you sure?" He whispered his dark olive eyes staring into hers searching for the answer, "Once this happens there's no going back. You will be a part of our pack. I will be your Alpha and you, my Omega."

Without hesitation she nodded then bowed her head, "Yes, I'm yours."

He sat up his hands resting on her hips as his fingers hooked on either side of her panties. He drew them down her legs tossing them to the side and looking down at her.

"Last chance before I can't control my myself. Are you sure you want this?" he asked.

She nodded even though her body was trembling with fear and excitement. She watched as he stood up bringing his boxers down and kicking them off to the side. Noelle could not help the small gasp escaping her lips seeing him fully for the first time.

He gave her a wide smile, "I know, right? Impressive." He joked.

Noelle laughed thankful for the slight distraction. He leaned down kissing her lips again. His hand ran down her side to her leg. His mouth moved down her body until they hit her hip bone. Noelle's whole body was buzzing as she watched his head move between her legs.

"Rhys, please… no more waiting." She pleaded just before his lips touched hers.

She knew he was trying to pace themselves and move slow, but she needed to feel him. She needed him to replace the emptiness she felt as Andrew would push into her. She needed to feel loved. Rhys positioned himself right at her, looking down silently asking her one more time.

Nodding he slowly pushed inside of her, and her body arched off the bed. Suddenly everything started spinning and her body felt like it was on fire. The wolf inside of her finally clawed its way to the surface and a bright light flashed before her eyes.

"Calm. Steady. Breath Omega." Rhys's powerful voice echoed in her ears, "Breath, Omega."

Without hesitation or thought, she followed his command, taking a breath in and releasing it. Never had she felt this whole being connected with Rhys this way. His head dipped down into the crook of her neck, a low growl escaping his lips as he held still letting her get used to him. Noelle could now feel the difference between her and her Omega. Her wolf was born to obey her Alpha. Whereas she was meant to be Rhys's partner, the other half of his human soul that he had always been missing.

She wrapped her arms around his neck squeezing him to her, "Move, please. Rhys, please…"

The feeling of Rhys pulling out and thrusting back into her was indescribable. The way his body moved against hers and the strength within his body had her in awe. He moved at a slow pace the coil within her wounding tighter and tighter.

"Too much… have to hold back…" he mumbled into her shoulder.

She met each of his thrusts urging him to move a little faster. His body covering hers, his lips pressing against her racing heartbeat on her neck. His pace quickened as he was chasing his own release. Noelle squeezed her eyes shut feeling a familiar pressure within her body desperate to let go.

"So close… need to mark you… need you, Omega." He grunted as he lifted himself slightly.

Noelle could feel an odd sensation come over like lava flowing through her veins. She felt the coil snap as she called out Rhys's name. A wave of pleasure flooded her body followed by the piercing of Rhys' canines biting into her flesh. Suddenly everything went red leaving his Alpha bite on her shoulder.

AUSTIN

The week after the convention was one of the hardest to get through for Austin. Not since first having to leave his daughter to film had he ever felt so alone. He was sitting out on his back porch, watching the sun slip further down the sky. Raelyn was working a shift at the grocery store and as much as he wanted to text her. He resisted, not wanting to bother her at work.

"Hey daddy." Bernadette sat down next to him holding a notebook in her hand, "Are you okay?"

He smiled, "Yeah baby, why do you ask?"

She opened her book flipping to the middle where there was a page of her sketches. He took the book, looking down at his likeness, staring back up at him. One picture showed him mid laugh on the phone. His eyes seemingly shining and the creases around them deep from the joy on his face. The other one was of him sitting outside right now. His eyes heavy looking and his lips in a thin line.

"These are amazing." He whispered, his chest swelling with pride for the true talent his daughter was.

"Ever since you came back from your convention, you've either been super happy or sad. Did something happen?"

Austin was never good at hiding anything for her. He hadn't had a chance to talk to Raelyn about telling Bernadette about them. He wanted the decision to be made by both of them.

"Something did happen. I'm not quite sure I'm ready to talk about it yet, but soon. I promise."

Bernadette leaned her head on his shoulder while he wrapped his arm around her. They sat there for a few minutes watching the sky darken and the stars popping out for the night.

"Is it a good thing? Whatever happened." She asked.

He kissed the top of her head, "Yes, it is a good thing. Honestly, I can't wait to share it with you. I'm hoping it will be a good thing for you as well."

She wrapped her arms around his waist hugging him tightly. For a moment, everything was nearly perfect except for one important piece that was missing. Raelyn.

Austin still had another week before he was to fly back to Montana to finish filming Red Moon. He had enjoyed spending Christmas with his family but didn't know if he would make it another week sitting around the house without anything else to do.

With New Year's right around the corner, an idea popped into his head to visit Raelyn.

A picture of the two of them appeared instantly making his heart yearn to be there with her.

There was a long pause as he waited for her response. His stomach twisted after a couple of minutes. He tried not to panic that he had crossed a line or was too soon to see her again. Austin let out a sigh of relief seeing two rapid fire texts.

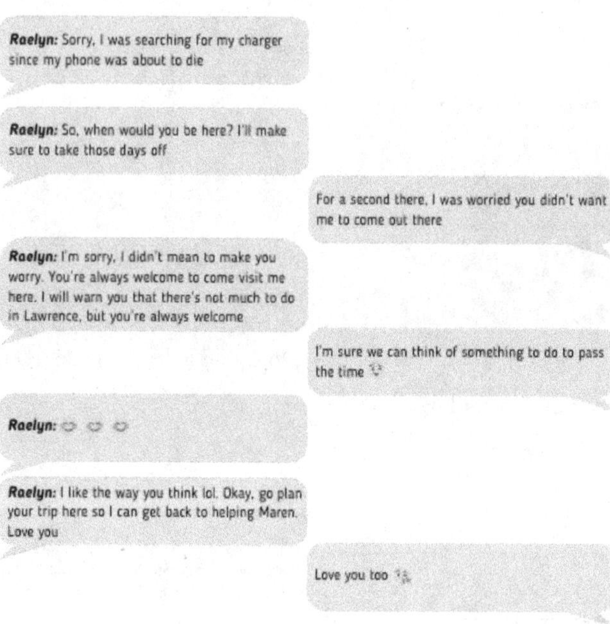

His cheeks ached from the smile on his face. He went up to his office and got on the phone with his manager to make the arrangements. Once again, she was not thrilled about the changes. By the end of their conversation, she helped him out. He would arrive in Kansas on December 29th and fly out to Montana on January 2nd. Now, all he had to do was tell his family about her.

The next night, Austin talked to Raelyn about telling Bernadette and his parents about them. Her response had taken him by surprise.

Austin, this is your family. You're the only one who can decide what's best for them. I would love for them to know about us and me, but if you think it's too soon then I'm okay with that. I trust you.

His love for her deepened, making a permanent mark on his soul. He had reassured her that he wanted nothing more than to scream out to the world he was in love with her. It was true.

If he had his way, he would have announced over his socials about finding the love of his life. He knew the pushback that came from that, and everything had to be strategically planned out to let the world know.

His eyes went to his side draw holding the envelope that had been slipped under his hotel door. He had Rachel and Clifford looking into who could have taken the photos from that night.

In the heat of the moment outside the elevators, Austin hadn't been thinking about anyone catching him and Raelyn making a public scene. Now, with those pictures burning a hole in his desk drawer, he was hyperaware of everything he may do or say to her.

And he hated it.

He went down to dinner, deciding there was no time like the present to tell his family. His stomach started to twist uneasily, not knowing how they would react to him having someone in his life. He wanted them to love Raelyn as much as he did, but previous experience told him it would take a while for them to warm up to her.

They were sitting around the table enjoying Bernadette's baked mostaccioli and garlic bread. Austin was pretty sure there was nothing his beautiful daughter couldn't do. When there was a lull in the conversation, he knew this was his moment.

"Hey, um… I wanted to tell y'all something."

Three sets of eyes turned his way, and his nerves twisted his stomach even more.

"What is it, son?" His dad sat across from him concern filtering through his eyes.

"I'm just gonna say it and then you guys can ask me any questions you want. A few months ago, I met someone on a fansite, and her name is Raelyn."

Even though his mom and Bernadette knew very little about him meeting Raelyn, they were still stunned after hearing the whole story.

"Now, Raelyn and I are attempting to have a relationship that is complicated. I want y'all to get to know her because she's special to me."

His dad had a small smirk on his face while his mom's eyes were on Bernadette. His daughter was looking down at her hands on the table. He could see her processing everything he said.

"Birdie?" He placed his hand on her shoulder, "If you need time to work out everything, that's fine."

"Is she nice?" She asked.

He smiled, "I think so. I know a lot of her students love her because she is kind to them."

Bernadette's forehead knitted together, "Is she nice to you?"

"Yes." He chuckled, "She's very nice to me."

"I only ask, because sometimes fans aren't nice. I've had some kids at school whose moms are fans. They don't say nice things about you or your character. Sometimes, they said gross things about you that I overhear. I don't want a fan to hurt you."

He pulled her to his side, kissing her temple, "I appreciate you being protective of me. I can't promise you that she may not hurt my feelings and vice versa. That kind of happens when you love someone. I don't think she would ever intentionally hurt me, and I know I wouldn't intentionally hurt her."

She looked up at him, the anxiety shining in her eyes from having a famous parent, "You love her?"

"Yeah, I do." He glanced up at his parents who were in the midst of a silent conversation, "I think you'll really like her. You two are a lot alike."

Bernadette hugged him around his waist, "I trust you, daddy. But if she hurts you then I'm going make sure all your fans hate her."

He squeezed her a little tighter, "Again, I appreciate that but please don't do that. It would really hurt me if you did."

"Deal. I'm going to go up to my room now. Goodnight."

They all said goodnight to her.

"All I will say is, be careful. We don't need another Britney on our hands even if it were to bring us another Birdie." His dad leaned forward patting his hand on the table, "I'm happy for you."

Austin watched him walk over to his mom and kiss her cheek before heading towards the kitchen. He moved over next to her and pulled out his phone. Pulling up the selfie he had taken of him and Raelyn at the convention, he handed it to her. He could tell she was fighting the smile trying to spread across her face.

"She's beautiful Austin."

"Yes, she is. She's smart and funny too." He took his phone back, taking one last look at the photo before putting it away.

"I want nothing more than for you to be happy. I'm sure whenever we meet her, we'll all love her as much as you do."

He wrapped his arms around her shoulder hugging her from behind, "I hope you do. I've really fallen for her and it kind of scares me."

His mom's laugh filled the room as she patted his arm, "Awe sweetie, it wouldn't be love if it didn't."

A few days later, Austin was staring out the window of an airplane. His favorite playlist flowing through his headphones, and he had his newest script in his lap. A little girl in front of him kept peeking over her seat at him. He waved as she giggled and sat back down. Memories of Bernadette being that little drifted into his mind making him smile.

He was thankful the flight wasn't that long, and no one seemed to recognize him. Once he landed in Kansas City, he grabbed his carry on and backpack heading towards the main entrance. He scanned over the large groups of people trying to find Raelyn. He noticed a woman with a chauffeur's hat on who looked familiar.

Once he could see her clearly, Austin stopped taking her in. She was wearing a black blazer with the sleeves rolled up to her elbows and a Red Moon graphic tee beneath it. Her beautiful legs were in black, skinny jeans that went down into a pair of black knee-high boots. Her black rimmed glasses were on the tip of her nose, and she held up a sign with the name Riley written on it.

Raelyn waved at him as their eyes connected and the tether tying them together tugged him forward.

"Hello, are you Riley?" she asked in her best professional voice.

"Yes, I am. Please lead the way, chauffeur."

She started walking and he took another moment to admire her as she did. The way her jacket and jeans showed off her gorgeous curves had his hands trembling to touch her.

"Are you coming?" She called out.

"God, I hope so soon…" He muttered to himself before catching up to her.

After an hour in the car driving to Lawrence, Austin's muscles were twisted into knots from holding himself back with her. His hand rested on her thigh as she drove, squeezing it ever so often. She would hum or sigh each time he did, truly testing his self-control.

"I know you're probably tired, but Maren insisted on being there when you arrived. Thankfully, she offered to bring dinner which is the only reason why I agreed to it."

Austin held in his groan and smiled, "Sounds great. It'll be nice to get to know her while I'm here. Have you told Katy or Zuhra?"

"No." Her smile faltered, "I trust them, but if I were a fan and another fan told me they were dating you. I'd think they lost their marbles even if I was good friends with them. I know Katy has a lot going on in her personal life right now and Zuhra is practically in her own world. They haven't been online to ask me about the convention and I haven't been online to talk about it."

"I'm sure you'll find the right time to tell them."

She glanced over at him, "You know I want to tell people. I just don't know how."

He slipped his hand behind her neck rubbing it, "I absolutely get what you're saying."

A soft moan slipped through her lips, "That feels good."

Austin let out a shaky breath as she turned down a little street. He watched as small ranch style houses passed by. They made another turn onto a cul-de-sac, and she pointed to a cute two-story home at the end of it.

"It's not much, but it's mine."

"I think it's perfect."

Before they walked up the path to her front door, Austin pulled Raelyn into his arms. He couldn't take another second without kissing her and didn't care if Maren saw them. He moaned into her kiss as she pushed him back against her car. He wanted more of her. Needed more of her, but a voice calling out to them snapped him back into reality.

"Get your horny asses inside and eat my delicious dinner!"

"Saved by the best friend." He chuckled.

A small growl came from her sending chills down his body, "More like rudely interrupted."

Austin kissed her temple whispering, "Plenty of time for that pretty girl."

The smile spreading across her face took his breath away. Grabbing his things, he followed her inside. Raelyn made her way down the small hall that led into her kitchen and dining area. Maren was pulling out foam trays of Chinese food and placing them buffet style on the kitchen island.

"Hello Austin, nice to see you again."

"Hey, smells good in here." His stomach growled as if on cue.

The girls giggled as Raelyn pointed to the next room, "You can set your stuff in there for now. Feel free to grab a plate and grab some food. I'll bring in some drinks."

Once they were settled in her living room, Austin was relieved to find the three of them falling into a comfortable conversation. At times, he would listen to the two of them tell stories from their wilder days or a funny story about one of their students. Seeing Raelyn relaxed and laughing brought a happiness into his heart he had no idea he was missing.

Not too long after dinner, Raelyn was walking Maren out to her car leaving Austin on the couch. The exhaustion from traveling hit him the more comfortable he became. He closed his eyes for a moment, figuring Raelyn would be back soon.

When he opened his eyes, Austin found himself still on the couch. Alone. Kicking the blanket off him, he went in search of Raelyn's room. Thankfully, there were little hall lights that lit his way up the stairs. Pictures of her with friends and students adorned the walls as he walked up to the second floor. He could see one room was her office and another a guest room.

The last door was cracked, and he pushed it open. He found his bags next to her dresser and he decided to discard his clothes there. Raelyn was sleeping peacefully curled up on her side. Carefully, he slid under the covers and curled up behind her. Wrapping his arms around her waist, he gently pulled her back against him, and she wiggled her butt into the perfect spot. He let out a soft groan trying not to wake her.

"I didn't have the heart to wake you." He heard her whisper, "I definitely couldn't carry you."

He chuckled, "I found my way. Now go back to sleep."

She turned facing him. Her fingers traced his jaw down to his chin and up to his lips. He watched her bottom lip disappear and her dark eyes shining in the moonlight coming through her window.

"I'm not tired."

"God I was hoping you'd say that."

Austin immediately lifted himself over her resting between her legs. This time there were no doubts between them. No hidden insecurities. No questions. There were only the sounds of two lovers reconnecting.

Austin felt the warmth of the sun shining on his face. Turning away from it, he heard soft giggles trying to be muffled.

"Mornin'" he said peeking one eye open.

Raelyn was propped up on her elbow looking down at him, "Good morning."

"What time is it?"

She looked over his shoulder teasingly pressing herself against him, "Almost nine. Would you like some breakfast? We'll have to go out to get your coffee."

Austin caught her wrists, pinning her to the mattress. He would never get enough of her laugh as he kissed his way down her body.

"Oh, I'm definitely hungry, but not for breakfast."

He kissed the inside of her thigh bringing out a long sigh from her. That's when they heard the front door close downstairs and a woman call out for her.

"Raelyn! Are you home?"

"Oh my god. Shit." She pushed him off her and scrambled towards her closet.

Austin admired her naked body as he chuckled, "Is that Maren?"

Raelyn poked her head out, "No. That's my mother."

Panic and fear sent Austin flying off the bed to his own bag to grab some clothes. He hadn't prepared to meet her mom especially after making love to her daughter only hours earlier.

Raelyn rushed out of her room as he stood near the door while getting dressed listening to their conversation.

"Mom, w-what are you doing here?"

He could hear now that she sounded like an older version of Raelyn, "I wanted to stop in and see you. I know we planned on seeing each other for my birthday, but…"

He stifled his laugh hearing Raelyn groan, "Maren told you I had someone here."

"Well, yeah, she did. Why haven't you told me about having a new boyfriend?"

"Emphasis on the word new, mom. I wanted to spend some time with him before introducing him to my family."

There was a long pause as the voices were further away, "Well… where is he?"

Ever the actor, Austin knew when to take a queue. He placed his baseball cap on backwards hiding the obvious sex hair he had going on and walked down the stairs.

"Mom, please don't embarrass me." Raelyn said as he walked into the living room.

Standing next to Raelyn was a petite woman a few inches shorter than her with long blond hair. She wore nice jeans and a simple blue blouse with a cream color peacoat. If he hadn't heard Raelyn address her as mom, he would have never thought they were related. The only thing similar between the two were their blue eyes. Which were both locked onto him.

He extended his hand out as Raelyn introduced them, "Austin, this is my mom, Faye Burton. Mom, this is…" Her eyes went wide with panic.

"I'm Raelyn's boyfriend, Austin." He shook her hand, "It's lovely to meet you."

Faye looked from him to her daughter and back, "You look familiar."

"Oh god…" Raelyn murmured.

"I'm an actor. I'm on a show called Red Moon."

Faye's eyes went wide, "Wait a second, you've been talking to a guy named Riley who took you to a convention for that show."

"Yes, mom. It's kind of a long story, but Austin was the Riley I was talking too."

He nodded, "Your daughter is a talented writer and caught my attention with one of her stories online. I use my middle name online to keep fans from finding out who I really am."

"Hmm." Faye's eyes scanned over him, and his muscles suddenly stiffened.

"Mom." Raelyn warned.

"Well, I think we should celebrate this new relationship. Let's grab some brunch together and get to know one another."

Austin nodded, "That sounds great."

"Yeah… sounds like a grand ole time." Raelyn scoffed as she turned towards Austin mouthing, *I'm sorry* to him.

Brunch with Raelyn and Faye turned into an afternoon of interrogation that Austin happily went through. He didn't blame Faye for being protective of her daughter. Especially knowing a little about her ex-husband, he felt like Faye went easy on him. Faye drove them back to Raelyn's house dropping them off. Before Austin got out of her car, she stopped him.

"Take care of my girl. Her heart is in the right place, but she hasn't always had the best taste in men. You seem different than the others. Don't break her heart."

He smiled, "Maren has already threatened to break my face if I ever thought about breaking Raelyn's heart. My intention is never to hurt her. I won't promise it because it will probably happen at some point. But know, it will never be intentional."

"An honest man. You are a rare creature Mr. Jameson."

"Mom, please release my boyfriend from captivity." Raelyn called out from her front porch.

Faye waved as she drove away, and Raelyn dropped her head against his chest.

"I am so sorry."

He wrapped his arms around her, "Don't be. I love meeting the people in your life. We all have something in common."

"Oh yeah?" She asked as they walked inside.

He leaned down kissing her briefly, "We all love you."

"Charmer." They both started laughing, walking further into the house and relaxing for the rest of the day.

AUSTIN

Before he knew it, Austin was back in Montana filming Red Moon once more. Being up there was surreal for him. Nothing had changed, the same crew, same sets, same everything. For him everything felt different, looked different. Calliope called it a love filter and made fun of him for it every time she caught him staring off in the distance.

His filming schedule was picking up as the end of the season was approaching. He and Raelyn talked every day with texts and Facetime calls whenever they could find time in both their hectic schedules. They were going into month three of not being able to see each other in person.

Austin was determined not to go another month without seeing her. While he was in his trailer for lunch, he was searching his calendar for a week where he could do just that. He knew she had spring break the same week Bernadette did, which would have been perfect if he wasn't filming a TV show.

In ten years of being the lead actor on the show, he never once asked for filming to be rearranged or pushed back. Until now. Walking into the studio offices in Montana, Austin was on mission to talk to Aaron the executive producer on site.

The penultimate episode did not have his character in it at all and was scheduled to film the week before Raelyn's spring break. He knew he was asking a lot, but he had to try.

"Hey Austin, what's going on that you had to meet with me right away?" Aaron stood, shaking his hand.

"Hey man, I'm sorry to barge in here but I wanted to see if there is any possible way to change the filming schedule slightly."

Aaron started laughing before looking up to see Austin was being serious, "Really? We only have three episodes left."

"I know and I normally wouldn't ask, but the week we shoot the finale is the only week I can get back home for an important family event. Bernadette will be on spring break from school, and we could all be in one spot."

Aaron was pulling something up on his computer, "So you want to see about switching episodes nineteen and twenty since Rhys is not in the episode nineteen."

Austin nodded, "Exactly. Like I said, I know it's a big ask. I figured it wouldn't hurt to come to you and see if it was even a possibility."

"Let me make some calls and I'll get back to you by the end of the day or tomorrow morning. It's not impossible since a lot of the sets will be the same. I'll try my best to make it happen."

He stood up shaking Aaron's hand again, "I appreciate it man. Thank you."

As Austin walked out of the offices, Calliope was waiting for him outside. He nearly jumped out of his skin when she sneaked up behind him.

"Jesus Cali, scare the shit out of me."

"That's my job. What were you doing?"

He headed towards the make-up trailer, "Scheduling. Seeing if we could switch some things around so I can see Raelyn during her spring break."

Calliope stopped him, "You've never asked for a scheduling change."

"I'm aware. I want to invite Raelyn down to New Orleans to meet Bernadette, but more importantly I'm tired of texts and video chats. I want to actually see her. In the flesh."

"I bet you do." She giggled.

Austin rolled his eyes, "I do. I miss her. A lot. We've been talking more about her meeting Bernadette. Two birds, one stone."

Calliope stopped him, "This is important, Austin. We'll make sure it happens. No matter what."

He pulled her into a hug, "I appreciate it. Now, let's go get all wolfed up."

The next morning, Aaron called him to let him know he was able to switch the two episodes around. He didn't miss the opportunity to tell him how the other execs did not like making special arrangements for actors. However, after they received emails from Calliope and Jackson, they were more apt to change things around.

The first chance he got, Austin called Raelyn and they planned her trip to New Orleans. After finalizing all her flights and pick up with Clifford, they both realized between her testing schedule and his filming schedule, they wouldn't get to talk until the day she would arrive in Louisiana. Which left Austin plenty of time to worry himself into a panic about telling his family.

During one of his weekends home, Austin sat with Bernadette and his parents letting them know about Raelyn coming to visit. Ever the protective daughter, Bernadette had asked to Facetime with Raelyn. After making the introductions, Austin paced outside his daughter's room trying to eavesdrop.

They ended up chatting for a couple of hours and he had to kick Bernadette off his phone in order to get some time with Raelyn. Bernadette ended up being more excited about seeing Raelyn than he was, but only by a little bit.

He arrived home on Sunday after spending all of Saturday cleaning his Montana apartment and packing it up for the summer hiatus. It felt weird to be wrapped on Red Moon before Jackson and Calliope. He promised that over summer, he would invite them all to New Orleans for a get together.

As he sat in his office Sunday afternoon going through his mail, he opened a large envelope filled with pictures of him and Raelyn over New Years. He looked at the handwriting and pulled out the other envelope in his desk.

The handwriting was the same from what he could tell. Looking through the photos, there were many of them out in Lawrence. Brunch with Faye, Christmas lights in the park, the afternoon he arrived in

Lawrence. The last few pictures were of him and Raelyn kissing outside her house and making love that night.

Austin pulled out his phone calling Clifford, "Hey. I have another envelope."

Clifford had come over as quickly as he could and was on the phone with Rachel. They were sitting at the kitchen table when his parents walked in with Bernadette. Thankfully, the pictures were safely enclosed within the envelope.

"Hey guys, how was the farmer's market?"

Bernadette wasn't fazed by Clifford being there and started telling them all about the different things she had found. Once she had gone upstairs, his parents began to ask questions.

"Austin has received some photos taken of him and Raelyn. We're looking into who they're from." Clifford explained.

"Is it something we need to worry about?" His mom asked, stepping beside him.

Austin shook his head, "I don't think so. They're threatening to send them to the press. Rachel has my legal team on it and Clifford is using his connections to find out who the person sending them are."

"And if they do get out?"

Austin chuckled, "Then the world will see a whole new side of me. I would be more worried about Bernadette ever seeing them or Raelyn. I'm going to tell her about it when she's here."

"Good idea. For now, business as usual." His dad smiled, leading his mom out back towards their home.

The next morning, Austin had pushed aside the photos and focused on the fact he would be seeing Raelyn for the first time in months. Bernadette had insisted she come with him to pick Raelyn up at the airport.

Out of precaution, Clifford also insisted on driving them. When they arrived, Austin pulled out Raelyn's chauffeur's hat placing it on his head. He put on his sunglasses and straightened his black, denim jacket.

"How do I look?"

Bernadette giggled, "Ridiculous."

"Perfect!" Austin grabbed the small sign Bernadette had made with Raelyn's name on it.

He watched the exit for the boarding area for Raelyn. He was hyper aware of any cameras that were remotely pointed in his direction. Finally, he spotted her walking towards the entrance. She was gorgeous in a pair of leggings and a simple blue sundress. Her hair was long enough now to braid down over one shoulder. She was carrying her backpack and looking down at her rolling suitcase.

"Miss Raelyn Burton?"

She stopped looking up at him and a grin spread across her face. Dropping all her things, she ran up to him and threw her arms around his neck hugging him tightly. His arms immediately wrapped around her, and he started peppering kisses over any inch of skin he could.

"I missed you so much." She mumbled into his shoulder.

"I missed you too, pretty girl. Come on, there's someone in the car waiting for you."

She didn't let go at first and when she did, he saw the tears rolling down her cheeks. He wiped them away and leaned in to kiss her.

"No tears. We have a whole week together. You'll be sick of me by the end of this trip."

She scoffed, "I doubt that."

His heart was pounding against his chest knowing she was right. He wanted her to stay forever, but knew it was still too soon for any talk like that.

Carrying her things out to the SUV, he heard her and Bernadette squealing as they hugged each other inside the car.

He jumped into the front seat and looked back, seeing them talking adamantly to one another. Seeing his two favorite girls together made his heart feel whole like it never had before. He even caught Clifford smiling at the whole moment.

"Good to see y'all happy." He murmured before driving away from the airport.

The first night was filled with good food and conversation. His mom was instantly smitten with Raelyn when she started helping her and Bernadette with dinner. Afterwards, they all went out on the back porch watching the sunset with drinks by the firepit.

Raelyn and Bernadette were talking about Bernadette's art projects and Raelyn's writing. Exchanging ideas and laughing whenever Bernadette had shown her the sketches of Austin. He never imagined life feeling as good as it did at that moment, and he knew this was all he ever wanted. The fame could disappear overnight, and he wouldn't care. As long as he had those two girls in his life, he was complete.

"Here you go."

Austin looked up seeing his dad handing him another beer, "Thanks pop."

He sat down next to Austin, point towards Raelyn, "Mighty good woman you found."

"Yeah, she really is." He watched as Bernadette wrote a note in Raelyn's notebook and she excitedly wrote a note right next to it.

"May I give you a piece of advice?"

"Of course, pop."

His dad looked over at Raelyn again before looking right at Austin. There was a seriousness in his eyes that made Austin sit a little straighter and listen closely.

"Son, she's a keeper." He smiled, "That woman is one you marry and treasure for the rest of your life."

Austin smiled, "I know pop."

His dad nodded, "Then you need to tell her everything. From the photos to Britney, everything. Secrets kill relationships. I hate to see you lose a good woman because you weren't honest with her."

He looked over to Raelyn who happened to turn and look at him at the same time. She smiled then waved at him. He smiled, waving back to her.

"I hear you pop. I won't lose her."

"Good because I like her and more importantly your momma likes her." He chuckled standing up, "Hey Birdie, go grab your overnight bag. Come have a sleepover with your pop."

His daughter looked up from her notebook, "Sure thing."

"You're welcome." His dad patted him on the shoulder laughing as he went inside to get his mom.

Raelyn walked over taking the chair his dad was in, "Bernadette doesn't have to leave."

Austin chuckled, "Pop is doing that more for me than anyone else."

He wiggled his eyebrows making Raelyn laugh, "Oh. Yeah, I guess that would be traumatizing. Seriously, I think we could behave ourselves."

"Speak for yourself. I, for one, know I can't. Not after months of not seeing you. I want you all to myself for at least one night." He slid his hand over her thigh gently digging the tip of his fingers into her soft skin.

He heard Raelyn suck in a breath making him chuckle when his parents and Bernadette came back out. After saying goodnight to them, Austin led Raelyn to his room.

Tonight, he took his time making sure the shades for the windows were closed and the door was shut. Once he felt assured no camera could take pictures, he spent the rest of the night showing Raelyn how much he had missed her.

The beginning of the week was some of the best days of his life. Raelyn fit into their little family perfectly and he could not imagine her not being there all the time. He had caught himself several times, almost asking her to move in and stay with them forever. Austin knew he needed to still tell her all the baggage that came with him. To make sure this was not just red, hot passion, but the solid foundation he had always been missing in his life.

His plan was to take Raelyn out for dinner on Wednesday and tell her everything. That afternoon, Raelyn was out with his mom and Bernadette so he could catch up on emails and a few requests for virtual interviews. Austin was wrapping up an interview with EW Online when he noticed several missed calls from Rachel.

"Austin, we have a major problem."

"Hello to you-" He was about to shut down his computer when she interrupted him.

"Go to your computer and search your name."

Austin thought that was strange but brought up Google search typing his name. Immediately news articles popped up with the headline *TV Actor Searches Fansites for Hook Up*.

"What the fuck is this?" He clicked on the article and a set of familiar photos popped up, "Oh shit."

"Yeah, oh shit is right. Now, we can get ahead of this. I already have legal working their way through taking down the photos and Patty is working on a statement to send out."

A text popped up on his phone from Clifford.

Clifford: Your mom just called. Picking up girls. Something happened at the mall.

"Rachel, I gotta call you back."

"Austin, we need to figure this out now. I told you dating a fan was risky. Now we're eyeballs deep into a shit show."

He let out a frustrated sigh, "I can't help who I fall in love with! Right now, something happened while my mom was out with Raelyn and Birdie. Clifford is going to get them, and I need to call him."

Rachel sighed, "It's all-over social media now."

"Do whatever you need to do to get it under control Rachel." He hung up before she could say anything else.

He walked out of his office and into his bedroom, "Damn it!"

Austin walked downstairs where his dad was walking in from the backyard on the phone, "Yeah. Yeah, I'm with him now."

"Is that mom? How are they? What happened?"

"Okay, I'll let him know. Thank you, Clifford." His dad ended the call, "Apparently some 'fans' came up to Raelyn and were harassing her. Your mom kindly asked them to leave, but they kept bothering her. When Raelyn tried to talk to them away from Birdie, they apparently dumped ice coffee all over her and a crowd formed around them."

His knees nearly gave out on him, having to brace himself against the counter, "A-Are they alright?"

"Yes. Security guards broke up the crowd and took your mom, Birdie, and Raelyn to a safe location. Clifford has them now and they should be here any moment." His dad grasped his shoulder, "What happened?"

"Those pictures were leaked to the media. It's all over the web and on social media. I was going to tell Raelyn tonight all about it."

One single thought entered his mind that had him grabbing hold of his dad's arms for strength.

"What if I lose her? I-I can't lose her because of this. Dad, I can't..."

The door to the garage opened as his mom walked inside, "Dear, grab some towels for us."

Bernadette walked in next helping Raelyn come in. His heart stopped and a cold chill shot down his body. Raelyn was covered in brown, sugary coffee. Her beautiful hair stuck to her face and neck. He could see a few red marks and scratches on her arms.

"Daddy!" Bernadette called out, snapping Austin back to reality.

He immediately went over to his daughter making sure she was alright, "Are you okay? Did they say or do anything to you?"

Bernadette shook her head and hugged Austin tight, "No, but Raelyn... they were awful to her, daddy."

"I'm so sorry Birdie. Everything will be okay." Austin squeezed Bernadette a little tighter, "Could you get me a pair of sweatpants and a hoodie out of my closet for Raelyn. Set them on my bed. I'm gonna help her get into the bath and then I'll be out to check on you. Is that okay?"

She nodded, heading off towards his room. Quickly, Austin went over to Raelyn and scooped her up into his arms. Once they were in his bathroom, he heard Bernadette telling his parents that he was helping Raelyn and shut his bedroom door. If he wasn't panicking about the woman in his arms he would have been beaming with pride for his daughter.

"Raelyn? I'm going to set you down and start a bath for you."

She nodded, not looking at him. She sat on the toilet completely silent as he started a bath for her. Once it was filled, he looked over to the shower and turned it on.

"Let's get this rinsed off you before you get into the bath." He helped her stand and started peeling her wet shirts from her body.

All her clothes were ruined by the coffee including her undergarments, "We'll go out and get new clothes."

Her eyes snapped up to his, "No. We…We can't go out. If they see us, then we'll get rushed again." Her hands were gripping his shirt as she spoke.

"Oh, pretty girl, I'm so sorry. This is all my fault. I'm so sorry." Austin wrapped his arms around her holding her trembling body, "Come on. The shower will warm you up."

She stepped inside, standing beneath the water. He heard her sniffle a few times and when he looked over, she was running her hands over the small cuts on her arm. It was when an agonizing sob came from her lips that he stripped out of his clothes and stepped in behind her. He ran his hands down her arms. When she flinched at his touch, his heart cracked into two.

"They called me fat, a cow, hippo, big Bertha. Nothing that I hadn't heard before."

His own tears were threatening to fall as she continued.

"They said why would a man like Austin Jameson ever sleep with a fat girl. One said it was out of pity. Another said maybe you wanted to see what it was like to fuck a fat person."

"Raelyn… you know…"

She turned around looking up at him and the tears began to fall down his cheeks. Her eyes were red, and he could see her own tears mixing with the water.

"I know, but… when you have people telling you the same thing over and over. You can't help but think that maybe they're right. Maybe I'm only attractive enough for guys to push past their disgust of my fat body to give it a go."

He placed his hands on either side of her face, "You know that's not true. You know how I feel for you. You know how much I love you, all of you."

He kissed her and she tried to pull away from him. He kissed her again and again until her hands went up into his hair pulling him closer to her. He carefully turned them around, so the water was beating down on him. Pressing her back against the wall as he trailed his hands down her body.

"All I see is a beautiful woman who has been beat down by so many in her life. All I see is a gorgeous body that I want to worship every day. All I see is the woman who holds my whole heart within her hands that I want to spend every moment loving and caring for."

She was panting as he touched her, "Austin, please… I need…"

His mouth covered hers as he showed her how he felt about her.

An hour later, once he knew Raelyn was asleep. Austin went out to the kitchen seeing his parents and Bernadette outside. Running his hand thought his hair, he walked out to make sure they were alright. Other than Bernadette being pissed off at the fans who hurt Raelyn, she was fine.

"You're one tough young woman, Birdie." He proudly said hugging her.

"I must get that from dad's side."

"Damn right." Pop called out.

Austin walked over to his mom and pulled her into a hug, "Thank you for taking care of my girls."

"You never have to thank me. I would do anything for them and you."

His body began to shake as he finally let out all the emotions he had been holding back. His mom rubbed his back then he felt Bernadette wrapped her arms around them.

"Come on pop, this is a family hug."

His dad came over hugging them almost completing their family circle. Only one person was missing.

His parents took Bernadette back to their place for the night. Austin heated up some leftovers and took them upstairs for Raelyn. When he walked inside his room, he found her sitting up and crying.

"What is it?"

"M-My blog." He feared he knew what she was going to say next, "They all found it. There were hundreds of DMs and posts from other fans. I…"

He set the food down and crawled into bed next to her. She sobbed into his chest setting her phone on his lap. He looked down seeing what she had done, and he held her tighter.

"I don't know what else to say other than I'm so sorry."

She sniffled, "It's not your fault. We knew eventually it would get out."

"Did Katy or Zuhra text you?"

She nodded, "They were a little upset I didn't tell them about you being Riley. Thankfully, they have my number and can talk to me that way. I told them I was deleting my blog."

His phone started ringing, "Rachel, it's not a good time."

"The press is outside of your house. I'm sending Clifford to come get you and your family. I think you need to head to your summer house early. You will need to contact Bernadette's school about online classes for the rest of the year."

"Raelyn is with us. Make sure she has ticket as well." He looked down at her as she sat up.

"She should head back to Kansas."

He slipped out of the bed, "I'm not sending her back to Kansas alone. She was nearly mobbed by fans while out with my mom and daughter earlier. She's coming with us."

"Fine. I'll make sure she has a ticket as well. I will email you all the information then I will fly out asap to meet with you."

"Thank you." He ended the call and got back into bed.

"Where are we going?"

He pulled her into his arms, "My family owns a residence in Aurora, Colorado. We usually go there in the summer for a few weeks. The press is outside, so Rachel is having Clifford take us all to the airport to go there."

"I'm sorry." She whispered.

He lifted her chin, "None of this is your fault. Now, let's lay here for a few more minutes before we have to gather everyone and pack."

She kissed him just beneath his chin making him smile. Even through all the crap, Raelyn could never fail in making him smile.

RAELYN

When they had flown out of New Orleans, the paparazzi swarmed them as soon as they were out of the house. In the airport, Clifford had led the charge using his large body to clear a path for them to a private waiting area.

Beyond the paparazzi, were the so-called fans. They were trying to get Austin's attention as he held on tightly to her and Bernadette's hands. When they didn't get a reaction out of him, they would start yelling out to Raelyn. In all the years she had been bullied and teased throughout school, none of that could have prepared her for this.

Hey fatty! Stop making him feel guilty for your insecurities! Stop blackmailing him in staying with you!

Austin doesn't like chubby chicks!

Free Austin! Save Austin from being squished!

"Don't listen to them." Clifford's gruff voice caught her attention, "Keep looking forward and walking."

She looked down to see she had let go of Austin's hand and stopped in the middle of the airport. Clifford's large hand was on her back gently pushing her to keep moving.

"I'm s-sorry." She whispered, feeling his hand pat her shoulder.

"Nothing to be sorry for. All these assholes… they should be sorry."

Clifford glared at the paparazzi extending his arm out to push them away from her. It had taken a few hours to get their plane ready and by the time they arrived in Colorado it was dark.

Now, Raelyn sat on the bay window, looking up at the twinkling stars and mountains bathed in moonlight. It would have been the perfect spot to write if she had felt inspired to. All she felt like doing was crawling into a deep, dark hole and being forgotten about.

"Hey."

She turned to see Austin leaning against the door frame. He was freshly out of a shower with a pair of dark gray sweatpants hanging low on his hips. Droplets of water rolled down from his broad shoulders over his chest.

Any other day, her mind would have swan dive into the gutter of desire. Tonight, all she could think was what her inner voice had been chanting the whole plane ride here.

He's better off without you and deserves better.

"Hi." She turned back looking out the window.

Seeing his perfection was too much for her fragile heart. When he walked over to her, wrapping his arms around her, tears slowly fell down her face.

"Pretty girl,"

She cringed hearing his nickname for her.

"Tell what you're thinking. I'm terrified I'm losing you within your own mind."

He never ceased to amaze her by seeing through her stone walls. It hadn't taken much for Austin to break them down when they first started talking. Now, as she scrambled to rebuild them, he was constantly making them crumble.

"Raelyn?"

She finally looked up at him. His eyes shining from the moonlight streaming in. His face scrunched together with worry as he sat down in front of her.

"You don't want to know what I'm thinking. You won't like it."

His hand covered hers, "I'm sure I won't and that's why I want you to tell me. So, we can work through it together."

She scoffed, "Together? Well, there's a point to start. We shouldn't be together. We should have never been together."

"Do you honestly believe this wouldn't happen even if I were with someone else?"

"If you were with someone equal to you— "

"Stop." He stood pacing next to the bed until sitting on the edge of it, "Just stop."

Raelyn stood up in front of him keeping out of arms reach, "What? Can you tell me that if you were dating Calliope or some other woman in the business who looked like her. That this would have happened?"

Austin was staring down at the carpet while gripping the edge of the bed tightly. Every muscle in his shoulders and arms rippling. She couldn't help the desire pooling in her stomach, but she did try to ignore it.

"Raelyn, some fans are never going to accept the fact that I'm going to date someone who isn't them. They will never like who I'm with. It doesn't matter if would be Cali or you."

"But they would be more accepting of Calliope." His eyes snapped up to hers, flashing with anger as she pushed further, "They would be. She looks like she belongs with you. I look like I belong behind my computer, writing dumb fanfics about falling in love with my favorite actor. That's just the cards that we were dealt."

Austin reached out suddenly grabbing her wrist and pulling her between his legs. He locked his hands behind her back keeping her in place.

"Haven't I shown you, told you, prove to you that I love you. You! From your mind."

He brought one hand up to her temple.

"To your heart."

His hand slid down over her chest.

"To your body."

His hands slipped down beneath her ass squeezing the round globes.

"All of you, Raelyn. What else do I have to do?"

Her eyes were bleary with tears, "That's the point, Austin. You don't have to do anything. You shouldn't ever have to prove why you love someone. Not to me. Not to the fans or the world. The fact that you have to justify being with me is why we shouldn't be together."

"Do you want to be with me?"

An exacerbated sigh escaped her lips, "Austin… that's…"

"What? It's what? You keep saying we shouldn't be together. I keep telling you I want to be with only you. What do you want? Do you want to be with me?" He stood, not letting her go, pressing every inch of his six-foot two body against her, "Tell me what you want, Raelyn."

"You know I want to be with you."

"Okay. That's all that matters then. Fuck the media. Fuck the fans that can't handle celebrities having a private life. Fuck anyone else who tells us who we should or should not love. Fuck 'em all!"

Raelyn could not help the chuckle that made it past her lips watching Austin ranting like a mad man. He pressed his forehead against hers. His warm breath came across her lips as he chuckled.

"I've lived nearly my entire adult life caring about what everyone around me thought. From the roles I picked, to how I look, to who was in my life as friends or more. I always felt like I had to live a secret life with my friends or women I wanted to be with. Eventually, I lost everyone but my family and those in my Red Moon family."

Raelyn could relate to that more than he could have possibly known. Shutting herself off from the world, people, life. All because she was too scared to ever let anyone close to her. Until she met Austin. He inspired her to want more out of life. To truly live it.

"I met you. I read your story and saw your picture. I knew deep down, in my soul, that I was meant to be with you. You were going to make me stronger. All those years of waiting were worth it because I finally found the one woman who was worth going against the world for."

His lips pressed hard against hers, "The one woman I wanted to kiss for the rest of my life."

Austin's hands were sliding up her shirt leaving a burning trail in their wake, "The one woman I wanted to love and be loved by and not give a fuck about what anyone else's opinions."

"A-Austin…" She moaned, as he backed her against the wall, "We can't… they'll hear…"

He scooped down pulling the sweatpants of his she had on down to the floor. They hadn't been able to get her any new undergarments as the cool air hit her burning skin. He lifted her up, wrapping her legs around his waist. His hot lips burning against the pulse in her neck as he pinned her to the wall.

"I don't care if God himself hears us. I need you. Like air to breathe or water to drink. I need you to keep my heart beating."

She wrapped her arms around his neck as he hastily pushed his own pants down and in one swift movement, they were one being. One soul. One heart in need of an all-consuming love to remind them that in the end all that matter was them. Together.

When Raelyn woke up the next morning, she found a note on the side table next to her.

Bernadette and I went to grab some new clothes for you while mom and pop went food shopping. Feel free to wear whatever of mine (or nothing) until I get back.

Love,
Austin

She laughed, putting on his sweatpants and hoodie she had on the night before making her way to the kitchen. She was surprised to see a woman sitting at the kitchen island.

"H-Hello."

She looked up from her phone, her dark brown eyes narrowing in on her, "You must be Raelyn. I'm Rachel, Austin's manager."

Raelyn shook the woman's hand, "Nice to meet you."

"I wish I could say the same." Rachel set her phone down, "You and I need to have… what I call a come to Jesus talk."

Her stomach churned, sitting across from the woman. She could tell Rachel was all business, which was probably what she was paid to do.

"I know all about you Raelyn. The moment Austin had me set up your little convention trip, I began looking into you. It's part of the job to keep my talent safe. I'll admit, I was skeptical at first about you."

Rachel took a long drink from her cup as Raelyn tried to keep the bile from coming up from her twisting stomach.

"I thought you were one of those fans who wanted Austin for his fame and good looks. Turns out, you're a good person. You had your heart broken pretty bad with a nasty divorce and you got your life back on track. I commend you."

"Thanks… I think." Raelyn wanted her to get to the point and fast.

"I have access to Austin's blog account and read most of what you two talked about over the months you thought he was 'Riley'. You actually fell in love with him as a person and not the actor. You truly care about him."

"I do. I love him. I'm in love with him. I could care less if he were famous or not."

Rachel smirked, "That's what makes you different and completely clueless."

"Excuse me?" Raelyn didn't like her tone.

"I'll be frank with you. What happened at the mall and airport. That is only the beginning if you keep pursuing this. Your entire life will be in the public eye of opinion. Every little flaw, skeleton, etc. Not only you, but your mom and friends will also be in the public eye. You don't seem like the type of girl who wants all her business out for the world to see."

She hated that Rachel was right, "That may be true, but I knew that going into a relationship with Austin."

"Yeah, but you didn't figure fans dumping ice coffee all over you or someone taking intimate photographs with a telephoto lens of you and Austin."

Her heart beat rapidly in her chest, "What?"

Rachel pulled out an envelope taking out the contents, "Here. Austin received these after the first time you slept together."

Raelyn gasped seeing Austin making love to her at the convention. Several pictures of them around Lawrence during New Year's including outside her house. More pictures of them making love. She swallowed the bile threatening to come out from her lips.

"See, Austin didn't tell you because we were trying to get out ahead of it. Paparazzi have been looking for dirt on him for years. He's never been impulsive enough to get caught. Apparently, you bring out the careless side of him."

Rachel took the photos back from her, "They're out there now. No putting the toothpaste back in the tube, but we can prevent anything like this from happening again."

"How?" Raelyn wanted to do anything she could in order not to have Austin's career ruined.

"You won't like it."

Raelyn leaned forward, "Tell me."

"You have to break up with him and never contact Austin again."

"You're right. I don't like it." Raelyn rubbed her hand over her heart as it throbbed within her chest, "Austin won't go for that."

"He doesn't have too. You'll be the one breaking up with him. He'll have no choice but to mope around for his summer hiatus and then move on to the next season of Red Moon."

Raelyn stood up, walking to the sink as Rachel's harsh truth unsettled her stomach. A quote her mom had always said ran through her mind.

If you love it, then you'll love it enough to let it go.

"This is the best option you have, Raelyn. I highly suggest you do what's best for Austin and yourself."

Rachel grabbed her things, "I have a driver waiting for you outside to take you to the airport. Here's your ticket and some cash to get yourself home."

Raelyn took the envelope, "You had this planned already."

"I always have a plan b and c and d in my back pocket. It's part of my job."

Raelyn hated everything about this. She loved Austin and Bernadette. She would do whatever was best for them. She didn't know if she could do this.

"I want to take some time to think about this."

"You have until tomorrow morning, but I'm betting I'll hear from you within a few hours." Rachel pulled out a card from her bag, "Again, you know this is the only choice… the right choice for you to make. For Austin, for his family and for you."

Raelyn clenched her jaw watching as Rachel stepped outside, "I look forward to hearing from you soon. Have a good day and I suggest you don't talk to Austin about this. Be the strong, independent woman you built yourself to be and make the decision on your own."

Without another look, Rachel let the door shut behind her, leaving Raelyn's mind reeling. She picked up the envelope with trembling hands and pushed away the desire to rip it to shreds. Heading back up to the master bedroom, Raelyn grabbed her phone and called the one person she knew could trust for clarity.

"It's about time you called me! I've been worried sick. Are you okay?"

Maren's concerned voice brought immediate tears down Raelyn's face, "I… I don't know what I am right now, Mare. I-I need your help."

"Raelyn, you're kind of scaring me. What's going on?"

She proceeded to tell Maren about everything including her conversation with Rachel. Saying the words out loud made Raelyn's stomach heave and it took everything in her to not run to the toilet to vomit. There was a long silence once Raelyn was done talking except for Maren murmuring expletives beneath her breath.

"You're not thinking about going through with it, are you?"

"How could I not think about it?" Raelyn looked down at the ticket taunting her.

Maren sighed, "Do you want my honest opinion?"

Raelyn scoffed softly, "That is why I called you."

"Rather you leave now or not, it won't change anything. It's all out there and you know there's no going back from that. The damage is already done. The only decision to be made is rather you face it together with Austin or by yourself with me always being by your side, of course. Only you can decide if you are ready to have a happy life in the public eye with the man you love or be miserable in private without him."

Raelyn let out a shaky breath, "Do you think it's worth it?"

Her friend's soft chuckle brought a smile to her face, "You know my answer."

Raelyn was sitting outside when Austin and Bernadette arrived home. His parents were inside making lunch while she sat writing in her journal. Austin sat down in front of her chair, between her legs and rested his head on her thigh. Instinctively, she began running her fingers through his long, silky hair bringing a long sigh from his lips. She had come to a firm decision and wanted to tell him about it before they went back inside with his family.

"Some fans approached Bernadette and me in the clothing store." He voice was agonizingly low as he continued, "They were super sweet asking for the normal picture with me and telling me how much they loved the show."

Her heart dropped as he looked up at her with shining eyes, "When I turned to see Bernadette, she was trembling. I walked her away from them and she told me how scared she was that they were going to attack us. I tried to explain that true fans of mine and the show would never do that and the fans that had come up to you were not true fans."

"Austin… I'm— "

He shook his head, "It's not your fault. It just breaks my heart that Bernadette and you had to experience the ugly side of fame. I've done everything in my power to protect her from that and now she's been right in the middle of it. I… I don't know how to fix it."

"I know of a way…" Raelyn said as Austin's eyes hardened staring up into hers.

"No." He shook his head, standing, "Don't even say it, Raelyn."

She stood in front of him, "You know it would help calm things down for the show, the fandom, you and Bernadette."

"You leaving and us breaking up won't fix a damn thing. It will only make things worse. I'm not talking about this anymore." Austin took off towards the wooded area on the edge of the property.

Raelyn watched him until he disappeared into the tree line then turned around seeing his mom comforting Bernadette at the kitchen table. Whatever decision she had made an hour earlier was now out the window. She pulled out her phone and texted her answer to Rachel before she could lose her nerve.

Raelyn was sitting outside the airport entrance watching as people walked in and out. She looked down at her phone that was shut off. By now, Austin would notice her not being in bed beside him, finding her note. Calls and texts would be rushing to her phone, and she wouldn't be able to resist not talking to him. A single tear dropped down on the black screen before she got up, walking inside to head back to her normal, miserable life.

She tried to keep herself busy making lists of what she would need to do once she was home. Raelyn knew Austin would come looking for her. She needed a plan to cut all ties with him, the show and the fandom.

On the plane, she pulled out her tablet and logged into her personal account. She still had quite a few chapters of Runaway that were never posted. She decided to reread her own work since she was unable to go back to Tumblr for the foreseeable future. For many people who had been following Rhys and Noelle's story, Raelyn and Austin's story had come to a halt with a permanent *to be continued...* at the end of it.

Runaway
CHAPTER NINE – THE PLAN
@PACKNERD71

"Come again?" Noelle asked, trying to process what Hunter said.

He placed his hand on her shoulder, "Noelle, you're pregnant."

She backed away from them shaking her head, "That's not possible, Hunter. I can't be pregnant… the doctor told me there was no way for me to become pregnant."

She was breathing heavily, trying to keep what little she had in her stomach down. She knew she had been feeling a little under the weather since her night with Rhys. She figured it was some kind of weird, wolf, mating thing. The possibility of being pregnant hadn't even crossed her mind.

"Hunter, are you sure?" Rhys asked.

Noelle placed her hands over her stomach, "This can't be… I can't be…"

"Yes, I'm sure. All her tests were normal. Our doc ran a pregnancy test not knowing her history."

She looked up to see Hunter and Rhys smiling and couldn't understand why they were happy.

"H-How far along?" She asked even if she already knew the answer.

"Almost ten weeks." He looked to Rhys before giving a short nod, "I'll schedule a time for the doc to come check on you in a few weeks. I'm sure you two have a lot to discuss."

Once the door shut behind Hunter, Noelle grabbed Rhys' hand, "What's going on between us?"

"What do you mean?" he asked, tilting his head slightly.

"I mean we slept together which was great. I know I'm your Omega and part of the pack but what does that exactly mean? How does this work with a child? Are you even interested in having a relationship or is this some kind of pack arranged marriage."

Noelle didn't mean it as harshly as it had come out but nonetheless it was exactly what she had been thinking for the last few weeks. She had truly fallen in love with Rhys and didn't know if her heart could take him not feeling the same.

Rhys brought his hand up to her cheek, his fingers going into her hair as she leaned into his touch. Leaning down he placed his lips on hers, bringing about a small fire in the pit of her stomach that traveled throughout her body.

"I love you. I'm in love with you." He whispered against her lips, "I love you. I love our child. I can't wait to have a future with both of you. I never thought I would have this type of life, but I realize that I just hadn't met the person I was meant to have that life with."

Noelle was speechless as he kissed her cheek. She wrapped her arms around his neck as the tears fell down her face. She didn't know what she did to deserve such a wonderful man, but she would do anything to thank the universe for putting him in her life.

"I love you too." She felt him smile against her cheek.

AUSTIN

It had been nearly a week since Raelyn had left. Seven days since she left a note on his pillow that flipped his world upside down.

"This is bullshit, Rachel and you know it."

She shrugged, "All I know, is Raelyn reached out to me for a plane ticket home. All I did was respect her wish to go back home."

"You should have called me. You should have let me talk her out of this."

"Should I have, though?" She leaned forward, "This saved your family from embarrassment. This saved your career."

"I lost her! I lost the woman I love. Who cares about my fucking career if I don't have anyone to share it with."

"There will be other women, not fans, but women equal to you."

Austin stood, walking out of his kitchen unable to hear someone else utter the same godforsaken words Raelyn had. Every word out of Rachel's mouth was pissing him off. He headed off towards the woods lining the edge of his Colorado property needing to clear his head. Raelyn's letter playing in his head like a teleprompter.

Austin,

I would do anything for you. No matter what the risk or cost, I would do anything to protect you. I love you enough to know I have to let you go. Don't try to contact me. I'm doing this because I love you. Please tell Bernadette that I'm sorry.

Austin, please don't let this change who you are. Your fans, the Red Moon pack, they need you. Keep inspiring them. Keep teaching them how to protect fiercely against monsters. Keep loving them. Goodbye.

Raelyn

He had reached the edge of the woods and slumped to the ground, resting against a tree. The ache in his chest made it impossible to breathe. His heart one crack away from shattering into a million pieces. He bent over, placing his head between his knees, willing his lungs to take in the air they needed.

"Austin?"

His best friend's voice was his tipping point. Calliope and Jackson had flown into Colorado as soon as they could. Suddenly, his chest burned as the fiery sob ripped through his mouth. He felt Calliope's arms wrap around him as she rocked him like a mother holding her child.

"Shhh. Let it out. Don't hold it in."

Another wave of agony flowed out him as he gripped her arms like a life preserver. Austin could no longer see anything through the tears and squeezed his eyes shut. His mind screaming at his heart.

Stop crying! STOP crying! STOP CRYING!

His chest felt like it would collapse in and crush his lungs. Red flags were flying in mind as he grasped at his chest taking in tiny gulps of air.

"Austin, calm down. Breath with me, buddy."

Calliope took his hand, placing it on her chest and taking a deep breath in. He tried to mirror her, but the panic was too overwhelming. The edges of his vision were getting darker and all he wanted to do was fall back into the oblivion of his misery.

"Oh no. Austin… you have to stay with me."

Calliope sounded far off as he felt a pair of arms wrap around his neck and legs squeeze around his waist, "Open your eyes and look at me."

A million stinging pinpricks spread over his cheek making his eyes snap open. He stared into his best friend's bright olive eyes. Her forehead pressed to his as she took a deep breath in smashing her chest against him. She blew the breath out and took another in.

"That's good. Breath."

Austin felt his lungs burning from the cool air hitting them. He let out a shaky breath before taking in another too quickly. His lungs jerking in his chest as he hiccupped. Calliope's body began shaking with laughter as he held onto her.

"You know, if I didn't know Cali was in love with me, I might have an issue with this."

He looked up to see Jackson standing in front of them with his arms crossed over his chest. Calliope placed her hands on either side of his face.

"Are you okay?"

He nodded as she unwrapped herself from his body and sat beside him.

"We were having a moment of panic." She explained as Jackson sat down on the other side of him.

"Does this have to do with the break-up spreading like wildfire over the fansites?"

"It's already on the fansites?" Austin looked at his friend curiously, "What were you doing on the fansites?"

Jackson rolled his eyes, "I have a few fans I'm friends with that send me links. Fan drama is entertaining. Better than any daytime soap operas."

Everything over the last week flooded his mind once more. The photos being leaked. The fans mobbing her. Her letter. His heart ached more for her than himself.

"I want to know she's okay. I need to know if she's okay."

"Have you tried calling or texting her?" Jackson asked.

He nodded, "Her number is out of service, and she deleted her blog. I've tried messaging her friends online, but none of them will talk to me. I never thought to get Maren's information."

Calliope stood from her spot, "I have Maren's email. I'll reach out to see if Raelyn is okay."

"Maybe she couldn't handle everything and needed the break."

Austin narrowed his eyes at Jackson, "Look I know you were never a fan of us dating, but you can't really believe that?"

Jackson let out a long breath, "I think Raelyn was already thinking about breaking things off with you and Rachel saw an easy way out. I'm sure she was getting pressured to make everything that happened go away and she does what she does best."

Austin had been thinking the same thing which was why he couldn't listen to her lies anymore. He leaned over to Jackson as Calliope was typing an email to Maren on her phone.

"Are you still friends with the private investigator that helped you with your stalker fan?"

Jackson nodded, "Yes and because you're my brother from another mother, I already called her to look into everything."

Austin was surprised since Jackson had been so against him dating Raelyn, "Thank you."

"I may think you're insane for dating a fan, but I can't deny how happy she makes you. You were a completely different man, and I really liked that guy. Anything I can do to help I will…"

"But?"

Jackson chuckled, "But, I want you to be real about the fact that Raelyn may have left on her own."

The thought had crossed his mind more times than he liked to admit. He knew that scenario was more likely than any other.

"Trust me, I know that's a possibility. Either way, I want to hear it from Raelyn in person and not from a letter."

Jackson stood, stretching his hand out to help him out. He grabbed his hand and Jackson pulled him into a tight hug.

"I'm also on Team Auslyn, but don't tell Cali." His friend whispered.

He hugged Jackson a little tighter, "Your secret is safe and thank you, brother."

When he got back to the house, he found Bernadette sitting on the back porch with her sketch book. Jackson and Calliope headed inside while he went over to her. His chest tightened as he watched her wipe away tears from her face. As much pain as he was in from Raelyn leaving, his daughter was equally hurting.

"Hey baby, whatcha doing?"

Bernadette looked up with a soft smile that didn't meet her tearful eyes, "Drawing. Processing."

He sat down on the ground beside her chair and leaned his back against it, "Do you wanna talk about it?"

She didn't answer but held her book in front of him. Taking it from her, Austin was met with a beautiful picture that had him grasping his chest above his heart. He found himself and Raelyn cuddled on the couch laughing.

Next was Bernadette and Raelyn making silly faces on the swing in the backyard. The last one brought tears rolling down his cheeks. It was Raelyn sitting on the bay window looking out to the mountains. She was in his sweats and hoodie with her hair down in natural waves. Her glasses at the end of her nose and the moon reflecting in her eyes.

"These are beautiful Birdie."

"Thanks." She whispered then sniffled, "I miss her daddy. I didn't know her well, but I felt close to her. I'm so confused."

Austin looked up at her, "I am too. I promise, I'm going to find out what happened."

Bernadette leaned over the side of the chair and hugged him, "I hope she'll come back."

They sat there for a little while longer before Bernadette went inside. Austin took her spot and stared up at the stars in the night sky.

A bright star shot across the dark expanse, and he closed his eyes making a wish. He repeated the wish over and over until it was imprinted in his mind. When he opened his eyes again, he could feel that wish seeping into his heart. Making him more determined to find Raelyn and find out what happened the day she left.

Then his phone rang, pulling it out he could not believe whose number was flashing on his screen. He knew if he didn't answer it, she would call Bernadette and bother her.

"Hey Britney."

Both of his best friends shot looks his way as they walked through the door. He shrugged as Britney's high-pitched voice filled his ears.

"Hi Austin, how are you? I saw what happened and wanted to make sure you were alright."

He groaned, "I'm fine Britney. Nothing to worry about."

"I thought maybe we could grab a drink and talk about some stuff."

"I don't think that's a good idea. Plus, I'm filming currently." He lied hoping she would buy it.

She cut in, "I know you're in Colorado. Rachel let me know when I emailed her about talking with you. I happened to be in Colorado for work and thought it would be a good opportunity for us to catch up. Talk about the upcoming summer and Bernadette visiting with me."

Austin knew there was more to it than that. It always was with his ex, but he also knew if he didn't meet with her then she would make his life hell. More so than it already was, and he didn't need that.

"I can meet you at the Rocky Clubhouse around seven, is that okay?"

He heard her sigh, "That's works for me. Thank you, Austin."

"Yeah, no problem. See you then."

He ended the call and immediately laid into him agreeing to meet with her.

"Austin Jameson, don't you dare rebound with your ex!"

"Haven't you learned your lesson that fangirls be cray-cray?"

Austin held his hand up at them, "Trust me, I have no intentions or desire to get back with her. She Birdie's mom and if I don't play nice occasionally, then she makes my life and Birdie's hell."

Calliope patted his leg, "I get that, but don't fall for whatever games she's going to play. I'm still holding out hope for Auslyn."

Austin nodded, as the wish he had made earlier filled his mind once more.

I wish for Raelyn to be happy even if that means she's not with me.

There were several times Austin wanted to turn around and not go to the Colorado Club. Sitting in the parking lot, he was still debating if he should go in or not. After a few minutes, he finally got out of his car and walked up to the entrance. He found Britney waiting for him at the bar flirting with the bartender.

It had been almost five years since the last time he had seen her. He almost couldn't believe it was the same woman he watched get carried away by court officers as she screamed and cried losing her custody rights of their daughter. Seeing her now reminded Austin of the first time he met her, and it was comforting in a way.

"Hey Brit." He sat down next to her giving a quick glance to the bartender.

"Austin, how are you?" She hugged him and he hesitantly wrapped his arms around her waist.

He let go of her quickly when she looked like she was leaning in to kiss him, "I'm doing fine. What kind of work are you doing in Colorado?"

She smiled sitting back in her seat, "I'm doing some modeling up here for online catalogs. I was waitressing for a while back in Los Angeles and was signed to a new modeling agency."

"Congratulations. I guess that means you might have to cut your plans with Bernadette."

If there was anything good Austin could say about his ex was, she truly loved their daughter. Any time he had talked to her, Britney would light up when talking about Bernadette.

"Actually, quite the opposite. I'm going to be moving permanently to Louisiana in May. The agency is opening an office in Baton Rouge. They want me to model a little and run the office area."

A current of cold spread over his body freezing his muscles and heart. Having Britney living an hour away from them was a horrifying thought. He knew Bernadette would hate knowing her mom could show up at any time. Austin turned towards the bartender catching his attention by placing his card on the bar.

"Scotch neat and refill of whatever she's drinking."

Britney smiled, "My usual, whiskey and cola."

Raelyn popped into his mind and a tearing pain ripped up the middle of his heart. The bartender slid a glass to him which he down it in one gulp. It burned down his throat until dive bombing in his empty stomach. Tapping the glass against the bar, the bartender refilled it and this time he sipped it.

"You don't like that I'll be so close." She pulled the straw to her cherry-colored lips taking a long drink.

"It never works out when you live close by. That's why you stayed in Los Angeles, and I moved back to my hometown. It's the routine we're all used too."

"I know, but I want to be more apart of Bernadette's life. She in seventh grade now, a teenage girl who will need her mother." She leaned forward, her fingers brushing against his arm, "She's going to need a strong family front to make it through high school."

Austin turned towards the bar clenching his fist, "She has a strong family. I'm there, her grandparents, Jax and Cali are all there for her."

Britney scoffed, "Austin, she needs her parents. She needs her family together."

He gawked at her for a solid minute letting her implications settle in his mind. That's when he knew this had bad idea.

"Goodbye Britney." He looked to the bartender giving him the signal to pay his balance.

She grabbed his arm, "Please wait and hear me out."

Once he had his card in his hand, Austin snatched his arm out of her grasp, "No thank you. I know what you're trying to suggest and there is no way in hell."

He started walking towards the entrance and made it as far as the first row in the parking lot. Britney was hot on his trail. Her hand grasped his elbow, and he whipped around towering over her.

"What do you want from me? More money? Do you need a treatment center again? What?"

Wrapping her arms around her waist, Britney looked away from him, "I want my family. I want my daughter. I want you."

He scoffed, "No you don't. You never wanted me. You wanted my character and everything my fame has brought me. You never once wanted me."

"I've changed, Austin. I've been in therapy for years now and work on my struggles every day. All I'm asking for is a second chance. A second chance for us to be a true family."

The next thing Austin knew, Britney had pushed herself against him and her lips were on his. The taste of cheap lipstick and flavored lip gloss made him push her back and wipe his mouth.

"What are you doing?"

She took his hands and placed them on her hips, "I'm reminding you of the good times. The times we were in love and had fun. I promise you I'm the girl you fell in love with all those years ago."

He stepped away from her, his heart aching for the woman he truly loved, and his body starve for the attention of a woman to take the edge off. He turned away from her and ran his hand through his hair.

Britney's small hand pressed against his back, and he spun around pinning her to the nearest car. His lips crashing to hers and his hands running down her sides. Her hands immediately slid up beneath his shirt and her long nails clawed down his back.

"Austin…" She breathed out, "Please take me back…"

Something in his mind snapped him back to reality and sent him back far away from her. His stomach twisted into a tight knot pushing what little was in stomach up to his throat.

"W-What's wrong?" she asked, wrapping her arms around his waist.

"You're right. You are the same girl that I fell in love with all those years ago." He looked down at her smiling happily, "But, I'm not that same man. I fell in love with a woman who made me want to be a better man. Who made life easy and comfortable. She made me want to move mountains for her."

Britney backed away from him this time, "You mean fatty-mcgee who seduced you into being with her? Austin, you didn't love her. She made you believe you did. You could never love a woman like that."

Rage flowed down his veins. He imagined for a moment, this being the moment he would phase into a werewolf like Rhys.

"Don't ever talk about her like that. She is a better person than you or me or anyone in this world. She could flawlessly love Rhys and myself, never confusing the two. What no one gets, I had to convince her to go out with me. I'm the one who begged her to stay with me that first night. She didn't want to pursue me. I…"

He was breathing heavily as Britney stared at him dumbfounded, "I'm the one who pursued her. She's the only one I want to be with."

"Austin," Britney called out as he started to walk to his car, "I will be a part of my daughter's life. If I have to hire a new lawyer and take you back to court. I will."

He turned around, trying to keep his anger under control, "You do what you have too. Maybe, just maybe, you should talk to your daughter about what she wants. I think the answer will surprise you."

Austin took off towards his car never looking back. When he reached it, his stomach finally heaved, and everything came out onto the ground. There wasn't much to empty from his stomach. For once he was thankful for the acidic taste in his mouth for getting rid of Britney's lipstick and gloss on his lips.

Arriving back at his house, he sat in the drive for a long time replaying the last couple of weeks in his head. How fucked up everything was and how determined he was now to find Raelyn and find out what happened the day she left.

RAELYN

The movers brought in the last of Raelyn's boxes. She thanked them as she shut the door, leaning against it. The last month had been a whirlwind as she decided what she needed to do for herself. She needed out of Lawrence, at least for the time being. She knew eventually Austin would come to find her and her will power would fail her. Raelyn hated leaving Lawrence, she loved her jobs, her family, her friends… Austin.

His handsome face was constantly at the forefront of her mind. The crinkles that fanned out from his beautiful eyes. The way he would laugh with his whole body. His smile that could brighten the darkest days.

At night, when she was lying in bed, were the moments she thought about him most. The way his hands engulfed hers. How his arms fit perfectly around her plump waist. How their bodies molded together making love. Then one night crying in the darkness of her room, Raelyn made the decision she could not live life like this.

That moment sent her moving an hour away from the only home she had ever known. Now, she was the proud and terrified owner of a humble home in a small town outside of Kansas City, Missouri.

"What have I done?" she muttered, looking at her entire life packed within boxes.

Cordy meowed loudly from the bathroom he was being held captive in. Raelyn opened the door, and he zoomed past her.

"I'm sorry!" She called out going to his box of things, "Let's get you settled first then I'll tackle my stuff."

For the next several hours, Raelyn set her office up after making sure Cordy had all his necessities in place. The lower level of her house was a finished open space that was perfect for her dream office.

Thankfully, the guys from Ikea were sweet enough to build her desk and bookshelves the day before. She organized all her books, sitting back and admiring them when she was done. She had dreamed of having a library and office someday. Now she did, but she couldn't help thinking about what it had cost her to get it.

She dedicated a section of the downstairs for Cordy's new cat mansion along with tracks running along the walls where he could walk around the whole lower level. His approval was given when he laid down in the little hammock and went right to sleep.

"Cordy, I think we need a drink and set up our bed for the night." Raelyn ran her hand along his fur as she walked up the stairs to the kitchen.

She looked through a couple of boxes before finally finding a glass to wash out. She had gone to the store the night before to grab some essentials and food. She pulled the bottle of whiskey out of the cabinet and poured herself a small drink to down immediately. The amber liquor sent waves of warmth throughout her body. Pouring a larger drink, she made her way to the second-floor master bedroom.

The second floor had three bedrooms, two of which she had no idea what she would do with. For now, they would be storage if needed, but eventually she would set one up for Maren to visit.

"Shit." Raelyn hurried to her bedroom remembering that she was supposed to call Maren.

When she picked up her phone, she cringed at the sight of three missed calls and several texts from her.

Raelyn sighed Facetiming her best friend. Maren's glare sent chills down her spine.

"I'm sorry. I left my phone upstairs and went to work in my office. I'm a horrible best friend."

Maren scoffed, "You're lucky I love you. Now show me around your new house."

Raelyn took her on a little virtual tour. She let Maren pick out her guest room and sent her links of how to decorate it. When she went back down to her office, Maren had nearly fallen out of her chair seeing her library.

"Looks like you got your dream house. I'm proud of you. Even if I hate that you're so far away, I'm still proud of you."

Raelyn sat at her desk, "Thank Mare, that means a lot to me. So, tell me what's going on at school and in Lawrence."

Maren told her all about the new teacher assistant that replaced her. A lot of her students had emailed her asking where Raelyn was. Hearing that added another crack to her fragile heart.

"I, uh… I got an email from Cali."

Raelyn's eyes snapped to Maren's, "What did she want?"

"What do you think? She wants what everyone else wants. The truth about what the hell happened."

Raelyn felt another brick of guilt being added to her shoulders, "What did you tell her?"

Maren sat back in her bed, "I told her nothing. I haven't replied to her. What am I supposed to say? Raelyn upped and moved all because her boyfriend's manager bullied her into breaking up with him."

"I wasn't bullied…"

"Bullshit! But I don't want to talk about that. What do you want me to say to Cali?"

Raelyn thought long and hard about that question, "Tell her I'm moving on and so should she."

Maren's jaw slacked, "You can't be serious?"

"I am. I moved away to start a new life… minus you, of course. She should move on as well."

"Damn right. You can't get rid of me that easily. Raelyn, are you sure— "

She shook her head already feeling the tears welling up beneath her eyes, "Please Maren… don't. I-I can't."

Maren nodded, "Okay. Let's talk about when I can come out and visit you."

Raelyn smiled, "Now that I would love to talk about."

They ended up talking for another hour before Maren needed to get some sleep. Raelyn finished off her drink feeling the numbing effect kicking in. She looked at the stairs knowing she should go up to her room and get it put together. Instead, she walked over to the round oversized chair curling up with her favorite fuzzy blanket and turning on a sleep mix from her phone.

***

Raelyn peeked open her eyes feeling the warmth from the early morning sun shining in from her window. She glanced at her phone seeing it was still too early to be awake. When she went to turn over her back collided with something firm and warm.

"Five more minutes, darlin'" Austin raspy voice mumbled into her shoulder as his arm pulled her back against his body.

She ran her fingers down his arm, lacing their hands together, "Maybe we should stay here all day."

A low chuckle rumbled against her skin, "Now that's a great idea. However, I think Birdie had her heart set on going to our spot by the lake. I heard her last night hit a breakthrough on her new project."

Raelyn's chest swelled with pride, "That daughter of yours is one smart and creative young woman. Wonder where she gets that from."

Austin moved back from her, rolling her back against the mattress, "First, she's, our daughter. She's not only mine, but ours. Second, she gets that from her daddy, but it's nurtured by her loving momma." He leaned down kissing her lips gently.

Tears blurred her vision with the reminder that Bernadette was her daughter now. They were a happy family. Together.

***

Raelyn's eyes snapped opened bleary from the tears slipping down the side of her face. Her chest aching badly enough she sat up to rub the pain from it. No matter how long she massaged the spot above her heart, this was a pain that would not go away. Laying back down, she pulled one of her pillows into her arms and let the grief of losing the family she wanted flow freely down her face.

Over the next few weeks, Raelyn settled into her new home and city. She had applied to a few remote publishing positions and would be starting an entry level editing job. While getting to know her new city, she found a local bakery that served lunch that she would visit often to get out of the house.

Sometimes she would take her laptop with the hopes that inspiration would strike. Many times, sitting in the little bakery, Raelyn would have an idea for a new fanfic story when she began to write down the idea, Austin would pop up in her mind. Suddenly all her inspiration would vanish.

She often found herself in the same predicament staring at a blank document while moments with Austin would play like a movie in her head. She decided if she couldn't write then she would try to read the books on her to be read list.

Picking up a popular book on her new social media accounts, she only read a few chapters before putting it down in frustration. Cordy meowed at her from the floor as she laid on the chair in her office.

"I know, I know. I'm pathetic. Everything reminds me of him even when I'm trying to forget about him."

She looked down at Cordy as he tilted it to one side meowing again.

"Don't judge me. If I could forget about him like this," She snapped her fingers, "Then I would be out trying to find you a nice and normal dad."

Cordy huffed before trotting over to his hammock as if giving up on her for good.

"See… like I told Austin, everyone eventually leaves." She sighed, "I really miss him."

Raelyn decided to go upstairs to make herself some dinner as she hit the landing, her doorbell rang. Peeking through the window, she found a delivery man hold a large bouquet of flowers.

"May I help you?" she asked, opening the door.

"Miss Raelyn Burton?" She nodded as he handed over the flowers, "These are for you. Have a good evening."

"Thanks." She took the large vase into the kitchen and opened the bag covering the flowers.

All her favorites were in the bouquet. Red roses, pink tulips, and sunflowers. She found a note figuring it was from her mom or Maren since they were the only ones who knew her address. When she saw who the bouquet was from her blood went cold.

She picked up the vase and walked out to her garage tossing the note and the flowers in her garbage bin. It was a switch turned on, as her shoulders relaxed and a weight was lifted from them. She went back down to her office opening the blank document once more. Her fingers began to dance over her keyboard as a new idea rooted itself within her mind. Before Raelyn knew it, she had the outline of an original story. A new spark of inspiration igniting within her mind and heart.

Since she could devote a lot of her time to writing, Raelyn planned out a schedule for her editorial work while treating her writing like a second job. She couldn't remember the last time she lost herself on a new project or enjoyed her days working.

The cool spring months were starting to give way to the warmer summer months. On her trips into the city, she saw more kids riding their bikes, hanging out at the local coffee shop, and starting to enjoy their summer break from school.

During the Fourth of July weekend, Maren came out for her first visit to spend a week with Raelyn. While Raelyn waited for her to arrive, she was hit with a wave of overwhelming sadness.

She could imagine Austin walking in through the front door with his baseball hat pulled down and dark sunglasses over his recognizable green eyes. Her chest throbbed suddenly as the void within it spread a little deeper.

The doorbell rang and she could hear Maren's booming voice through the door, "Raelyn!"

She opened the door pushing a wide smile on her face and keeping the tears welling up beneath her eyes at bay. Her best friend dropped her bags and threw her arms around her. She could no longer hold back the tears as she hugged Maren.

"I missed you, Mare." She whispered.

Maren held her at arm's length, "I missed you too, but you look like hell. We need a girls' night in with all the junk food and whiskey we can get."

"That sounds amazing, and I know the perfect spot to grab dinner from."

Everything in the world felt almost perfect as she walked arm in arm with her best friend out to her car.

Almost perfect.

Raelyn drove to her new favorite Chinese restaurant to pick up their order she called in. Maren was in awe of her new hometown with its small town feel to a major metropolitan. Raelyn pointed out the park she would regularly sit at to write, and people watch. When they were near the bakery, Maren made her stop to get one of their famous gooey butter cakes.

Once they were sitting on her couch in the living room, Raelyn began to flip through her TV choices for something to watch. She flipped to the next channel when Austin's face came on the screen. It was an episode she had never seen from the latest season of Red Moon. She quickly skipped to the next channel resisting every instinct in her body to keep watching it.

"You okay?"

Raelyn shrugged deciding to put some music on for background noise, "I'm fine."

"Bullshit." Maren reached over placing her hand over hers, "Tell me the truth."

"I'm a fucking mess."

Maren patted her hand before sitting back into seat, "Go on."

"I feel like I lost everything and being in this house reminds me every day of what I gave up. Did I tell you that Austin's manager sent me flowers when I first moved in?"

Her friend shook her head taking a bite of her dinner.

"Yeah. My favorite flowers, signed from *Rachel Foster and The Red Moon Family*. Needless to say, I threw them in the trash."

"What a bitch move." Maren took a drink of her wine, "Let's not dwell on that. Tell me more about your editing job and writing.

Raelyn and Maren sat up talking for most of the night about her new project, editing assignments, how she had been dealing with the break-up, moving, and missing her online friends. Raelyn was showing Maren her room when her friend blurted out something she had not quite been prepared for.

"Austin came out to Lawrence to see me."

"W-What? When? Why?" Raelyn leaned her shoulder against the door frame to keep her knees from giving out.

"A little over a month after you had moved here. He got my email from Cali and asked if we could meet somewhere in Lawrence. He…" She bit her lip having an inner struggle of some sorts.

Raelyn went over to sit next to her on the bed, "He what?"

"He was a mess as well. Unshaven, hair shaggy and frown lines, Raelyn. The man had literal frown lines on his face. I felt bad for him."

What little of her heart Raelyn had been able to piece back together shattered once more. The dark hole swallowing the pieces into the abyss residing in her.

"What did you tell him?" She asked.

"Nothing. He didn't ask me too." She chuckled, "He knew I would never betray you. I have to respect the fact that he didn't even try. All he asked is if you were happy and doing well."

She tried to push the lump in her throat down, "Your answer?"

"I said you were content where you were at, but happy wasn't the word I would use to describe you. He said he could relate. He gave me his phone number to reach out if I ever needed him for anything or to keep in touch. Then he left."

Raelyn looked down at her hands twisting the blanket on her lap. There had been quite a few whiskey induced nights where she had typed out a long text to Austin but never having enough liquid courage to hit send.

"What am I supposed to do, Mare?"

Maren wrapped her arm around her, "For once, I don't have an answer for you."

That night Raelyn hardly slept. Tossing and turning as Austin filled her mind. Finally, around 4:00 am she went down to her office and found Cordy sleeping on her desk chair.

"I guess I'm writing from my reading chair tonight." She whispered, grabbing her laptop.

Recently she had created a new website for herself that she was considering posting her fanfiction on. She opened the folder with 'Runaway' looking through her aesthetic covers and chapters. Pulling up Canva, Raelyn spent the next few hours redesigning her covers and reformatting her document. By the time Maren had come downstairs around nine o'clock Raelyn was getting ready to post her story to her website.

"Raelyn…" Maren was looking down at her phone with wide eyes, "Look at this."

She took the phone from her reading the text notification on the screen.

> **(310) 555-0583:** This is Jax. Have Raelyn call me at this number. It's important. I know what's really going on

She looked up from the phone, "Do you think…"

Maren nodded, "Make the call."

RAELYN

Raelyn stared down at the phone, still unable to process Jackson's text. What did he mean, *he knew what was really going on*? Her stomach churned as she handed the phone back to Maren.

"You call him."

Maren shook her head, "Oh no, you need to do this. Call him from my phone if you don't want him to have your number and put it on speaker so I can hear everything."

Her hands were trembling as they listened to the phone ringing and prayed, he wouldn't answer. Apparently, the universe had other plans. On the third ring a deep voice came through the speaker.

"Raelyn?"

"H-Hi Jax, I have you on speaker with Maren." Her friend smacked her arm, "What is it that you need to tell me?"

"Hold on."

They could hear him moving about as part of her was hoping he was going to Austin so she could hear his voice. Deep down, she was terrified that was exactly what he was doing.

"Sorry, had to walk down the street. Cali and I are staying with Austin in New Orleans while the rest of the Jameson family stayed in Colorado. First, I want you to know that when you left, Austin had me hire my P.I. friend to track down the real reason why you left. He was determined that you did not leave on your own."

"I'm sure you thought I might have. He must have been really convincing to get you to help..." She paused taking a breath, "I'm sorry. That was mean of me to assume."

Jackson chuckled, "You're right, I didn't know for sure, and that helped push my decision towards helping Austin. Plus, he's a hot mess and I hate seeing my brother hurting."

Raelyn inhaled a shaky breath, "I guess your P.I. friend must have found something or are you calling on…"

"No, Austin has no idea I'm talking to you or that I have this information. I wanted to talk to you first."

"You have my undivided attention."

There was nothing that could have prepared her for when Jackson began to tell her. Everything his P.I. had found out sounded like she was staring in her own romance suspense novel. Her heartbeat was echoing in her ears as Maren spoke.

"I can't believe this! How in the world was his ex able to do all of this?"

Raelyn's mind was reeling, "Wait… this was all Britney and Rachel's doing?"

"Yeah. Apparently, Rachel has been trying to get some press drummed up on Austin to get him noticed by other studios. When Britney reached out to her about reconnecting with him, they had this little reunion planned out until he started dating you."

Jackson paused for a moment before continuing, "Rachel hired a sleazy paparazzi to photograph you guy when the right moment arrived, he was to leak them. Britney planned out the ambush on you in the mall with a few of the younger models at her agency."

"Why? All because she didn't like me or what?" This bothered her more than she expected it too, "I'm literally nothing. Why go through all this trouble?"

Maren smacked her arm hard this time, "You're a catch, Raelyn. I wish you would see that in yourself."

"I have to say, I agree with Maren. Women throw themselves at Austin all the time and never once have I seen him fall as hard and fast as he did for you. You're special. To Britney and Rachel that means you are a threat to their happy family reunion."

There was a spark heating within her chest as everything became crystal clear. A spark that had her heart beating at double speed pumping petrifying fear throughout her body.

"You have to tell Austin. He needs to know about Rachel not having his best interest and working with Britney." She paced in front of her desk.

"I've already told Clifford to keep watch on him and Cali hasn't let him out of her sight. I plan on telling him after you tell me what's going to happen next."

She scoffed, "What do you mean? You're going to tell Austin everything that is what happens next?"

"And after that?"

"What are you getting at, Jax? Say whatever is on your mind."

His voice was firm as he spoke, "Are you going to be with Austin? Taking care of Rachel and Britney and the mess they created is only part of the problem. I want to know before I tell Austin all of this that you're coming back to him. I'm pretty sure he will start a man hunt for you and he's already teetering on the edge."

Maren glanced at her, raising an eyebrow at her. Raelyn didn't know how to answer that question. Her first instinct was to immediately say yes, but there was one nagging question that kept her silent.

"Raelyn?" Maren asked.

"I can't answer that because that decision is for Austin. If you're asking me if I still have feelings for him then yes, I do…"

"But?" Jackson and Maren asked in unison.

"However, Austin may not be able to forgive my actions or… want to be with me."

Her chest tightened. She desperately wanted to be with him but knew there was a greater possibility that he wouldn't want to be with her anymore.

"I think you underestimate his feelings for you." Jackson let out a breath, "Austin and Cali are going to be here soon. Cali and I are leaving at the end of the week to get our place settled in Montana for the new season. Will you text me your number so we can call you then. Take this time to think about if you really want to be with Austin and everything that comes with him. Until then, I'll keep this info between us."

"Alright." She paused, "Thank you for being there for Austin. Not only for all the crap going on with me. I know you never liked the idea of him dating a fan. Also, with everything else going on. I appreciate everything you're doing for him and us."

His soft laughter made her smile, "No need to thank me. I would do anything for Austin and Birdie including swallowing my pride and admitting that I was wrong about you and him. Talk soon."

The call ended and Raelyn went to sit down in her chair again. Her muscles throbbing as the tension slowly eased out of them. The spark of hope still smoldering within the vast void within her chest.

"Now what?" Maren asked.

"I honestly have no idea."

Maren walked over rolling Raelyn's chair away from her desk and kneeling in front of her computer. Raelyn laughed as she pushed her chair back over for Maren to use.

"What are you doing?"

Maren's fingers were flying over her keyboard, "We need to come up with a plan for an epic reunion."

"Mare…" She began but her friend held up her hand.

"You haven't seen him. He's miserable without you. I don't see any possible outcome where he doesn't immediately forgive you and take you back. Now, I think it's only fitting that a reunion of this sort would take place at a convention."

Raelyn shook her head in disbelief, "Maren Gilmore, have you become a fangirl?"

Maren's eyes slowly looked up from the computer, "It's all your fault. Not only am I committed to finish watching the series but I'm also a hopeless Team Auslyn shipper."

"Oh my god, seriously? Team Auslyn?" Raelyn could barely contain her laughter.

Maren's laugh joined hers, "Blame Cali, she is the one who labeled you relationship. Now, let's pick out a convention to go to."

While Maren planned out the perfect convention reunion, Raelyn sat on her reading chair scrolling through her social media until curiosity got the best of her. More than a few times she had thought about reading through Red Moon fansites to see how Austin was doing. Fear of what she would find about herself there kept her far away from them, especially Tumblr. Now, she pulled up her app and created a new blog to see what fans were saying about Austin.

Immediately tears pooled beneath her eyes seeing photos from conventions of Austin. He was standing with a fan for their op with a wide smile spread across his face. His hair and beard were not as well kept as normal, and his eyes were not as bright. From anyone who didn't know him, he looked like a normal actor smiling for the fan with her arms around his waist.

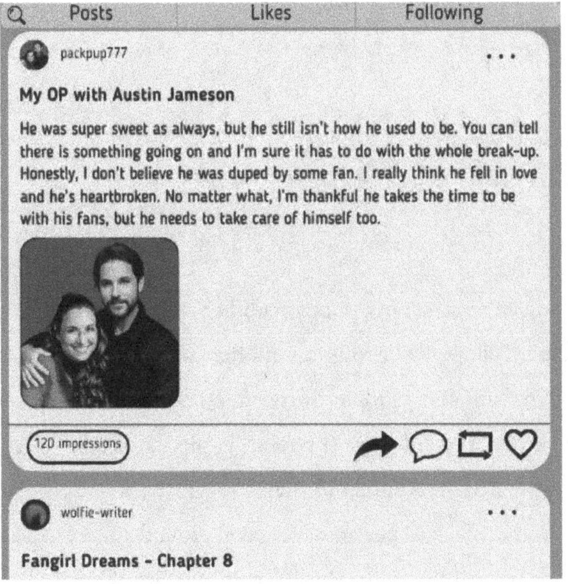

Raelyn kept scrolling through blog post after blog post of encounters with Austin. Almost all of them were concerned about his broken heart. She had been surprised to see some of them mentioning her old blog and how they were rooting for them to get back together. There were hardly any fans spreading hate about their relationship or her specifically. Whenever someone did decide to throw out their nastiness, the fans would unite like a wolf pack to defend Austin and her.

However, it was the amount of fanfiction she saw inspired by her and Austin that blew her mind. Story after story with Austin falling in love with a fan and having a happily-ever-after filled the Red Moon hashtag. Raelyn could feel that small spark of hope growing bigger and spreading out from her chest.

She picked up her phone sending Jackson and Calliope a text from her phone. It immediately buzzed with a reply from Calliope.

Raelyn watched her phone with her stomach churning waiting for whatever Calliope was going to send her. When her text appeared, there was a picture that had Raelyn trying to catch the gasp escaping her lips. Tears began to fall down her cheeks as she stared at the picture.

Bernadette was sitting in a chair on the back deck of Austin's Colorado home. She had her arms wrapped around Austin's neck hugging him over the arm of the chair. She enlarged the picture to see Austin's face. He was staring down at Bernadette's sketchbook with a sad smile and sagging shoulders. His jaw was set in a hard line.

As Raelyn was lying in bed that night, she reflected on the encouragement from her friends. All the love and acceptance from the fans online about her and Austin being together. She felt the flame within her burning brighter with hope that soon her heart would be whole once more.

Over the next few weeks, Raelyn was constantly texting with Maren, Jackson, and Calliope in a group chat. Jackson was waiting to tell Austin about everything until the next convention in New Orleans where the great convention reunion would take place. Jackson and Calliope placed Raelyn and Maren on the special guests list so they could move about the convention with ease.

Raelyn arranged for her neighbor to come check on Cordy while she was gone to New Orleans. Cordy had voiced his discontent with her leaving by placing himself in the center of her suitcase.

"I know you're not happy about this but in the end, it will be worth it… I hope."

Cordy laid down with a huff. Raelyn sat beside her suitcase petting him.

"I'm going to make amends with Austin. Do you think he'll forgive me?"

There were moments Raelyn felt her cat knew exactly what she was thinking and feeling. Cordy stood and stepped out of her suitcase pressing his head against her hand. He chirped his approval before walking over to her side of the bed and curling up on her pillow. Maren had arrived the day before so they could fly out together. They were sitting in the living room eating dinner and flipping through channels when they landed on a Red Moon marathon.

"I could try and find a movie." Maren mentioned, as Austin came on the screen.

Rhys stepped in front of the young twins, "You were reckless. You could have exposed the entire pack to hunters or worse the civilians. What were you thinking?"

Raelyn shook her head, "I don't mind watching Red Moon."

She tried to pay attention to the episode for Maren's sake, but her mind was playing an all too familiar game of *'what if*. She was nervous about seeing Austin again even with his friends reassuring her there was nothing for her to be nervous about. Raelyn was also terrified to confront Rachel. Terrified of the hell she could make Austin's life and the anger that was simmering beneath the surface in herself.

"Raelyn, spill it." Maren's voice snapped her back seeing the credits rolling on the episode, "You're lost inside your head."

She smiled, "I'm trying to think of every possible scenario that could happen when confronting Rachel. What if she tries to ruin Austin's career? What if Britney tries to use all this publicity against Austin? What if…"

"Stop Raelyn." Maren moved over next to her, "You'll drive yourself even more crazy than you already are. You won't be alone facing Rachel or anyone else. We all have your back. All you need to focus on is Austin."

Her smile fell slightly, "What if he can't forgive me?"

Maren chuckled, "Then I guess I get to break his pretty little face for breaking your heart."

They both laughed as Maren continued, "Seriously, I don't think you have anything to worry about. That man is madly in love with you. Once he hears about the shady shit his manager was pulling with his baby momma, he'll have no choice to forgive you."

"I'm glad you're so sure about that." Raelyn leaned her head on her friend's shoulder as they continued to watch Red Moon.

Runaway
Chapter Ten – All Things End
@PackNerd71

Rhys looked over to Hunter and Tiberius who was holding Noelle's lifeless body in his arms. His chest tightened as his heart dropped to the pit of his stomach.

"No…" he choked, his legs moving on their own towards them.

Tiberius was cradling her body as tears streamed down his face. Hunter stepped back as Rhys took Noelle from him.

Looking down at her, she seemed to be asleep. Her lips were pale, and her eyes closed. Suddenly, the emotions burning in his chest erupted from his mouth. His Alpha roared deep within him as he crumbled to the ground clenching her to his chest. Rhys could not stop the tears from cascading down his cheeks.

He felt Tiberius's hand gently squeezing his shoulder as Hunter knelt next to him. They helped Rhys carry Noelle's body to the Chevelle making the trip back to the Red Moon Compound.

The next few days were the toughest he had ever experienced. The pack held a traditional burial ceremony for Noelle. Watching his Omega, his mate, the love he didn't deserve but needed burning in the pyre. Tiberius and Hunter were standing on either side of him as they all silently said goodbye to Noelle.

As they walked back towards the center of the compound, they walked to the café where everyone in Red Moon was milling around and preparing for a pack feast.

"What now?" Tiberius asked.

Rhys pulled out three glass tumblers along with a bottle of whiskey, "We go on."

He poured each of them a drink, "To Noelle." he said as they tapped their glasses together.

"To Noelle." Tiberius and Hunter repeated all three of them downing their drinks quickly.

AUSTIN

Austin stared out the car window as the city he loved passed him by. This was the one convention he loved the most since it was in New Orleans, and he could be home with his family. This year, he was particularly grateful to be close to home and to have his friends already there with him. Jackson and Calliope were already at the convention hotel, allowing Austin to take his time to get there.

Ever since the photos of him and Raelyn were leaked, conventions had become a minefield for him. Most of the fans were respectful to not ask about his personal life. There were still a few who reminded him of his ex when he first met her, that felt entitled to knowing everything about him.

His phone started to ring, seeing it was Rachel he let out a long sigh, "Hey. I'm almost there."

"It's fine, Jax and Cali are holding down the fort. I wanted to check on you. Are you doing alright?"

He rolled his eyes tired of people asking him that, "I'm fine and I'll be better once everyone stops asking me."

His manager's voice was noticeably timid as she spoke, "We ask because we care."

"Wow, so you do have a soft side." He chuckled.

"Don't tell anyone about this. I have an intimidating rep to protect." She laughed.

"Your secret is safe with me. See you in a bit." There was a pause long enough to make Austin check if the call dropped.

"I have someone special coming to the convention to meet with you. I hope that is alright."

He was glad she couldn't see him rolling his eyes. The last thing he wanted to do was network, but he would since Rachel always had his best interest.

"Sounds great. I will be on my best behavior."

She laughed, "Now that would be a first. I'll see you soon."

Austin took a deep breath as they approached the side entrance to the hotel, "You got this. Put on that happy mask and take it one step at a time."

Conventions were always busy, but this convention was one of their larger ones. Fans were walking around the entrance normally blocked off for the actors. He noticed Jackson waiting for him as he got out of the car.

"Is there another convention happening alongside ours?"

Jackson chuckled, "Nope this is all for us. I guess they knew you needed cheering up and my endless GIFs of Tibs mannerisms is no longer working."

"I hate to break this to you, but your GIFs never worked," he laughed, "but it's the thought that counts, I guess."

They headed towards the green room where all the cast was milling around. Austin noticed Rachel off in a corner on her phone. Her familiar scowl told him not to bother her. Austin headed towards the couch where Cali was engrossed in reading something on her tablet.

"Stop reading fanfiction." Austin said startling her.

"Damn it, Austin! Don't do that."

It felt good to let out a genuine laugh, "Couldn't resist. How was your panel?"

She rolled her eyes, which meant she had to moderate through questions about him. Another brick of guilt stacked on top of his shoulders. By now his wall of guilt was starting to resemble the Great Wall of China.

"I'm sorry."

"You have nothing to be sorry for. The fans who have the balls to ask such questions should be apologizing." Cali gave his arm a little squeeze looking past him towards Rachel, "What's up with her?"

He chuckled, "I don't know. She called me on my way in to check in on me. Surprisingly, she seems to have developed a heart recently. She also has someone coming to meet with me... so yay."

She started to laugh as she glanced down at her phone then her eyes widened, "I, uh, I need to go find Jax really quick. I just remember something I was supposed to tell him before his panel."

She ran out from the green room leaving Austin confused, "O-Okay…"

He chatted with a few of the other guest actors before deciding to take a walk around the backstage area and listen to some of the other panels. Ben and Tricia were on stage answering a question about their characters getting together. Austin peeked out from the side curtain looking at the crowd.

His eyes scanned over the first few rows until his heart stopped and every muscle in his body seized. There was a woman sitting in the crowd that looked exactly like Maren. He stared at her a little longer, trying to see if it was truly her. Suddenly a set of small arms wrapped around his waist.

"Hi daddy." Bernadette whispered.

Austin looked down at her before looking back up trying to find the woman again.

"H-Hi baby."

When he looked down at her again a set of bright green eyes were curiously looking up at him, "What's wrong?"

"Nothing." He wanted to look one last time but decided to walk Bernadette further behind the stage so no one would notice them, "I thought I saw someone I knew in the crowd."

"Oh okay. Did you decide if you were singing tonight?"

He cursed at himself silently. If he had arrived earlier, he could have done soundcheck with the band, but he had been throwing himself a sizable pity party before the convention.

"I'm sorry baby, I was hoping to chill backstage tonight. Is that alright?"

Bernadette nodded, "Of course. We can still watch, right? I was hoping Clifford, and I could sit on the side to watch."

The fact that his teenage daughter wanted to hang out at a convention to watch his friends perform amazed him. He was truly thankful for the universe giving him Bernadette.

"Whatever you want. As long as Clifford is okay with it then I'm fine. Just make sure you stay with him the entire time."

She clapped excitedly then gave him a quick peck on the cheek, "Thanks daddy. I'm going to go find him now. Love you!"

"Love you too." He called out as she went back towards the green room area.

Austin was going to peek out the curtain again when he heard Ben ending their panel. He could hear the crowd moving about and knew there would be no way for him to spot the woman again. The chances of Maren being at a convention were as unlikely as hell freezing over.

"Get your shit together Austin." He muttered to himself heading off towards the ops room.

Austin had his first group of solo ops and Jackson duo ops done when the main ballroom was cleared for the concert. He and Jackson headed backstage where Calliope was chatting with Bernadette. Clifford walked up whispering something to Jackson then smiling down at Bernadette.

"You ready kiddo?"

She nodded eagerly, "Thanks again Cliffy for hanging out with me."

Austin couldn't love his little girl any more than in that moment. He watched as Clifford melted into a pile of goo next to her.

"Anything for you kid."

Bernadette hugged Austin as they walked out from behind the curtain. He stopped Clifford as he walked by.

"Thank you. I appreciate you staying with her." Clifford patted him on the shoulder with a nod and followed Bernadette through the curtain.

As he sat backstage with his best friends, he allowed himself to relax for a moment. Enjoying the first few songs played by the band and the laughs shared with his friends. The way the night would have been perfect is if Raelyn had been there. Jackson had gone to get another round of drinks when he returned, he sat beside him.

"There's someone in the green room waiting for you."

Austin's shoulders tensed, "Do you know who it is?"

Jackson shook his head, "No. The convention staff said they're on the special guests list."

Downing the last of his drink Austin headed back towards the green room. He stopped outside the door taking a deep breath before opening it. Immediately he was hit with a wave of berries and flowers filling his nose and he froze. His rapid heartbeat drowning out all the noise from the concert as he let the door shut behind him.

In the middle of the room stood Raelyn with her back to him. Waves of copper hair fell down past her shoulders. Her beautiful, curvy body was covered by a simple pair of dark jeans, Red Moon graphic tee and her Chucks. His hands began to tremble as she turned around. Behind dark rimmed glasses were the soft blue eyes of the woman his heart and body ached for.

"Hi Austin."

Her voice barely above a whisper but rang clear as a bell in his ears. His body snapped into action, closing the distance between them as he pulled her into his arms. He felt her body begin to shake as she cried into his chest.

"I'm so sorry. I-I didn't know what to do and I'm so, so sorry." She began to ramble until he cut her off, sealing his lips over hers.

Her hands were gripping his shirt as he pushed her back against the wall. He nipped at her bottom lip as she granted him permission to deepen the kiss. Austin's mind was filled with a dense fog of desire as his hands touched every single part of her he could. When he pulled away from her to catch his breath, his mind clear enough to slow things down.

"I'm sorry, I didn't mean…" He cupped her face allowing the tears to flow down his face, "I missed you so much… fuck I thought I would never see you again."

Her hands covered over his, "I know. I didn't think I would see you either."

Austin took a deep breath stepping back to give her some space and was surprised when her hands immediately reached out for him. Wrapping his arms around her, they both went over to the couch to sit. He couldn't believe she was there and, in his arms, again. His whole world had been in a state of chaos since she had left, and he didn't even know it until that moment when everything felt right again.

"Raelyn, what the hell happened? One moment, you were lying next to me in bed and the next you were gone."

She buried her head in his chest as another wave of tears fell down her face. He wiped them away before kissing her temple.

"Take your time. When you're ready then tell me." He whispered.

It took a few minutes for her to tell him what had happened. The anger that ran through his body had his hands trembling. He knew

Rachel was involved in some way, but the full gravity of her involvement didn't hit him until hearing it from Raelyn.

The door opened as Jackson and Calliope walked into the room. The smile on his friends' faces filled his chest with joy.

"Sorry to interrupt the happy reunion but I think you need to see this." Jackson handed him a manilla folder.

Flipping through the file Jackson's P.I. friend had compiled made Austin dangerously close to losing it.

"She seriously did all of this to drum up more press for me and get me back with Britney?"

Jackson nodded, "Yeah. Apparently, she has been trying to leak stories about you for years, but you've always been careful not to do anything press worthy. I'm pretty sure she saw an even bigger opportunity when Britney reached out to her about reconnecting with you and Bernadette."

Austin stood unable to keep his rage still, "That's it, I'm handling this now."

"Hold on cowboy, a screaming match with your manager in the middle of a convention is not the brightest idea." Calliope had her arm hooked with Raelyn's holding her hand, "Plus if you interrupt the concert while Maren is out watching her newest Red Moon crush perform. She will definitely murder you."

Raelyn was first to crack with a soft giggle, "I guess since Jax is a taken man, she focused on the single member of the pack. Ben."

A knock on the door silenced their laughter as Rachel walked inside. Tension filled the room as Austin, Jackson and Calliope surrounded Raelyn.

"What the hell is she doing here?" Rachel narrowed her eyes.

"Rachel, so glad you happened to come in here. Maybe you could clear up a few things for all of us." Jackson stepped in front of Austin.

Rachel slammed the door, "Not until this psycho fan is escorted out of the building. Austin, I think we'll have to get a restraining order against her."

He walked over to Raelyn, pulling her to his side, "No. No, I think you need to explain why you hired someone to follow me and Raelyn around and take intimate, private photos of us. Or explain why bribed some of our fans to attack her and my family in order to get more press coverage for me."

At that moment, the door opened again revealing Britney, "Rachel? Is Austin here..."

Rachel stood her ground as Britney stepped next to her, "Is that what she told you? Austin, you know me better than that. She's obviously lying unless she has any kind of proof. I think we all know she obsessed with you and can't handle that you're going to be getting back with Britney."

Austin was seeing red as every word Rachel spoke fed the raging fire inside him. His momma brought him up to respect women no matter what, but right now he wanted nothing more than to knock the daylights out of his manager.

"She's doesn't." Jackson chimed in as Rachel smiled, "But I do."

Jackson handed her the file folder with all the proof his friend had gathered. Including financial statements from an account Austin had no idea she had opened with part of his earnings.

There was also a record of text messages between her and the fans discussing her plans for them to attack Raelyn. Finally, the texts messages between her and Britney were the icing on the cake.

"This is ridiculous. I told you she would be trouble and now she is affecting your career, your safety and your family's safety…"

sure,'t you dare talk about my family and that includes Raelyn," Austin felt Jackson's hand gripping his shoulder, "Needlessly to say you're fired, and I will make sure you never have another client ever again. Be thankful I don't press any charges against you."

Rachel pushed one of her fingers into his chest, "You'll regret this, Austin Jameson."

"I promise you, I won't. Now get out of here before I have security escort you out."

Rachel opened the door to walk out, bumping into Clifford, "Right this way, Miss Foster."

Austin turned his gaze to Britney who had been unusually quiet during the whole exchange. Her eyes were on Raelyn, sizing her up.

"Do have anything to say or should I have Clifford escort you out as well?" Austin stepped in between Britney and Raelyn.

"I can't believe you want her. You could have the family you always wanted us to be now. You, me, Bernadette… all of us together. Traveling together. Building memories and seeing the world. You choose her? Her?!" She pointed at Raelyn, "Over me?"

Austin felt the bile raising in his throat, "No, if you remember I chose to be alone over having you in our lives. I chose my daughter, MY daughter over you. You only ever loved one person in your life and that was you."

"She's my daughter too, Austin! She needs her mother and not some fat slut in her life." Britney yelled.

Austin was about to throw her out when Raelyn stepped up beside him.

"Britney, you will always be her mother. You will always be a part of her no matter what is going on between you and Austin."

Britney smiled, "Well at least she has common sense if she can't have looks."

"However, it takes a hell of a lot more to be a mom. You have to sacrifice, choose everything that's good for her over your own needs or wants. Honestly, I don't think you know the first thing about loving another person let alone a beautiful young woman you barely know."

Austin smiled, lacing his fingers with Raelyn's, "I think you so go now before you give me any more reason to have your custody fully taken away."

"You can't do that, and I want to see my daughter now."

Clifford walked in with a couple of other security members, "Bernadette is enjoying the concert right now, but I'll make sure to let her know you said hello. Now, you need to go with these gentlemen before we call the cops."

Britney narrowed her eyes at Austin then Raelyn, "I will make sure you are never a part of my daughter's life. You just wait until my lawyers hear about this."

Raelyn smiled stepping up to his ex, "I can promise you that I will love and care for Bernadette as if she were my own. Which is way more than you have ever done for her. Now leave."

Clifford ushered Britney out and once the door closed, the exhaustion of everything hit Austin. Walking over to Raelyn, he wrapped his arms around her and pulled her down onto the couch.

"Are you both alright?" Jackson asked with a small smile on his face.

Raelyn chuckled, "I think so, for now."

"We're going to go find Maren and Birdie. You two take all the time you need in here." Jackson slipped his arm around Calliope left the room.

"Are you okay?"

He looked down at Raelyn seeing her forehead furrowed with worry. Her cheeks flushed and her tongue darted out over her lips. The remaining anger that was burning in his chest turned into a raging desire and he lifted Raelyn's leg over his lap.

She let out a surprise yelp straddling his hips. His lips captured hers while his hands snaked up her back holding her in place to grind himself against her.

"I need you…" He whispered breathlessly.

Raelyn kissed him then whispered back, "I'm yours."

RAELYN

Raelyn couldn't believe how in twelve hours her whole life could change. She was lying next to Austin watching him sleep. She ran her fingertips down the side of his rosy cheek to his full lips brushing her thumb against them. A small hum rumbling in his chest as she traced up his jaw into his soft hair. Raelyn brushed the few wayward strands from his face watching a slow, sleepy smile spread across his face.

"Mornin'"

"Good morning." She whispered before kissing him.

His arm slipped around her waist pulling her flesh against him, "I really wish I didn't have to work."

She giggled as his lips trailed down her neck, "You don't want to disappoint the fans. Plus, I'm pretty sure if I don't go then Maren will be pissed at missing a possible opportunity to see Ben."

"She does know I could introduce them, right?" He chuckled.

Raelyn nodded, "Oh she knows. She wants it to happen organically. You know like in the movies when the celebrity meets a normal person then falls in love."

Austin laughed, "No, I have no idea what you're talking about." He pressed his forehead against hers.

After months of talking, dancing around each other and being together, Raelyn no longer saw him as the famous actor she once dreamed of meeting. Now, he was simply Austin to her. Loving father, boyfriend, and a good man.

Raelyn had decided to stay at Austin's until Bernadette was ready to leave. It gave her time to hang out with Bernadette and have a good cry over everything that had happened. They were sitting out on the porch waiting for Clifford to return to take them to the convention. Bernadette pulled out a notebook and handed it to her.

"I finish part of my story. I… I was hoping you could read it."

Raelyn flipped through the book filled with Bernadette's words, "Birdie this is amazing. It would be my honor to read it."

"Raelyn, may I ask you a question?"

She nodded, looking over at Bernadette. She was fidgeting with the hem of her shirt, obviously having a battle in her mind.

"Sweetie, whatever you want to ask it's okay. It will stay between us unless it's something that your dad should be a part of. Take your time and let the words come to you."

Raelyn texted Clifford to take his time and make a lap around their street if needed. After a few minutes, Bernadette wiped away the few tears running down her face and asked her question.

"Is it okay for me to love my mom, but not like her? I know you told me about you and your dad. How you guys always butted heads. I feel like if I love her but don't like her then I'm a bad daughter."

Her heart broke for the young girl beside her, "The people that we are supposed to love are sometimes the people hardest to like. It is perfectly okay to love your mom but not like her. You have to do what is best for you and take care of yourself. Sometimes that means not staying up all night writing so your body can rest."

Bernadette laughed as she continued, "Other times that means putting distance between those you love in order to create boundaries for yourself. Taking care of yourself will never make you a bad daughter. It makes you a responsible human being. No matter what, your dad and I will support you in whatever decisions you make."

"I'll remember that when I want to get a piercing or tattoo."

Raelyn pulled her into her side hugging her tightly, "Maybe come to me whenever you get that urge and I'll help you convince your dad."

Clifford pulled into the driveway as Bernadette was showing Raelyn designs of tattoos she would want once she was old enough. When they arrived at the convention, Calliope was waiting for them with a couple of extra security guards.

"Is this because of everything from yesterday?" Bernadette asked, taking hold of Raelyn's hand.

She shook her head, "No. You don't have to worry about that. Let's go inside and find your dad."

When they walked into the green room, Austin was waiting for them with Jackson. Bernadette ran up to him hugging him tightly while Raelyn stuck back with Calliope.

"What's going on?"

"Extra precaution. Rachel had a lot of access to Austin, and he wanted to be prepared if she tried anything stupid."

Raelyn nodded as her eyes connected with his. Her heart fluttered as his face lit up with a smile. Walking over, he pulled her into the opposite side of Bernadette and kissed her.

"You look beautiful." He whispered.

"Not too bad yourself, handsome."

Raelyn and Bernadette spent a lot of their day backstage or sitting on the side of the stage listening to panels. Maren had been overjoyed when she saw Raelyn, talking excitedly about how she got to talk to Ben after his panel.

"Seriously Raelyn, I think I'm in love."

Raelyn rolled her eyes, "I think you mean lust."

"How dare you? I take offense." A sly grin slid across her face, "However, from what I can tell I'm sure he's one hell of a— "

Raelyn covered her mouth gesturing down to Bernadette, "We're in the company of an innocent."

"I probably know more about sex than anyone in this place. I'm a teenager." Bernadette chuckled before quickly following her comment, "Not that I'm interested at all in it. Ew. Gross."

"Please stay that way for a long time. It's truly overrated." Raelyn joked.

Maren gave her a pointed look before whispering, "I'll make sure to mention that to Austin."

She walked away before Raelyn could say anything to her, which was good since Clifford was coming to get them for the main panel. Calliope, Jackson, and Austin were by the stairs when they came through the curtains. Austin ran up pulling both of them into his arms. Bernadette pulled away first giving Raelyn the opportunity to kiss Austin quickly.

"Break a leg."

His smile made her heart flutter again as he ran up the stairs and on stage with his best friends. She wondered if that feeling would ever go away being with him, praying it never did.

"Hey kiddo, why don't we go watch the panel out in the audience." Clifford said, offering his arm out to her.

Bernadette looked at Raelyn who nodded, "Go on. Make sure to heckle your dad for me."

"Will do!"

Raelyn watched them walk back out through the curtain and turned her eyes to the screen projecting the panel.

"Mr. Tardy-To-The-Party." Jackson joked.

Calliope laughed, "Leave him be he was getting some smooches."

Raelyn's body seized with terror, "Oh no…"

The crowd was going nuts yelling out to Austin about who it was. She prayed he would play it off and that he was getting a good luck kiss from Bernadette. The universe of course never worked in her favor in moments like this.

"Alright, alright. You know what, we're going to nip this in the butt right now. Hold on a second."

Raelyn watched in horror as Austin ran off stage and appeared on the stairs. She immediately began shaking her head.

"No. Austin, they will riot if they see me."

He held his hand out to her, "They're going to find out one way or another. Might as well do it on our terms and no one else's."

She walked over placing her shaking hand into his, "I hate it when you're right. This is going to be bad."

"We'll get through it together." He kissed her cheek before leading her out on stage.

The room was silent as they walked to the middle of the stage. Thousands of eyes staring up at them in shock. Then a roar of boos and insults hit Raelyn like a tidal wave. Her grip on Austin's hand tightened and she tried to pull away from him.

There you go, putting yourself in situations that prove you're an idiot.

Her inner voice sounded off.

Austin slipped his arm around her shoulders tucking her safely into his side. Her mind absorbing every insult thrown at her and every glare snared her way. She could feel the tears threatening to fall.

"A-Austin, please…" she said softly, looking up at him.

He pulled the mic up to his mouth, "I know y'all have a lot of opinions, thoughts, feelings about the woman beside me. There have been a lot of rumors and lies flying around about her. About us. I'm here to be open and honest with all of you. To set the record straight on everything that has happen."

The crowd quieted and Calliope stepped up beside her taking her hand.

"I think everyone should listen to what they have to say. So shut it!"

There was a low rumble of laughter as Jackson came up beside Calliope.

"Nearly six months ago, I logged onto my Tumblr account in search of fanfiction to read. From time to time, I will go on there and see what y'all are creating. I found Raelyn's blog and loved her stories. The depths and layers she saw within Rhys were awe inspiring. I don't normally interact with fans online, but I had to message her."

Austin looked down at her smiling, "After a few bumps in the road, messages back and forth, we became friends. Right before the convention in Kansas City, I knew I didn't want to only be friends. I fell in love with her, and it terrified me."

Raelyn felt the tension in her muscles slowly easing out the more she focused on Austin.

"After Raelyn found out who I was. By the way, I had lied and told her I was a fan named Riley. Fellas, not a smart way to try and get a girl to date you."

The crowd chuckled as he continued, "I had to beg her to have dinner with me that night. The next day, she told me there was no way this would work out. Even though, she had feelings for me, Raelyn knew how problematic it would be for me to date a fan."

Jackson let out a fake cough, "No shit."

"I told her I wasn't giving up. Once again, I found myself outside the hotel elevators begging her to stay with me. She must have had pity for me because she did stay."

Raelyn rolled her eyes playfully smacking his chest as he laughed. He winked at her before looking out over the crowd. Raelyn gathered what little courage she had to glance out in the same direction. A lot of fans were listening intently while others were sighing like it was the most romantic story they ever heard.

"My former manager took advantage of some of our fans and created a plan to get my name in the press."

He paused, "Part of the reason our fans are amazing is because they fiercely protect us. Y'all are our pack and when you go against another member of the pack it gets ugly."

There were a few howls from the audience and cheers.

"That was all Raelyn was trying to do. She sacrificed her own happiness, her home, her entire normal life to protect me. Now, we've sorted through all the drama that has happened and we want our pack to be happy for us. To welcome her with open arms and love her, but not as much as I do."

I don't think that's even possible. Way to go, you finally found a good one.

Raelyn was surprised by her inner voice compliment and realized it was because she truly believed that too. There was no one in this world who loved her as much as Austin did.

"And I do. I love this woman with all my heart and soul. I truly want all the fans to be a part of our lives. You're so important to us and we want to share our lives with all of you. What do you say? Can we all get along and accept that I'm a normal dude who fell in love with an extraordinary woman."

The silence was deafening until two people in the middle of the crowd stood up. Raelyn squinted immediately recognizing them. They began clapping as Maren stood next to them clapping as well. Soon the whole room echoed with applause as every fan stood. Off to the side, Raelyn caught a glimpse of Bernadette running up the side ramp towards them. She hugged Raelyn with tears falling down her face.

"Now y'all know if Birdie loves her then she's good people." Jackson said wrapping his long arms around them all, "Alright enough with the lovey-dovey crap. Let's take some questions from these awesome fans."

Raelyn felt Austin kiss her temple, "Thank you for being strong and braving the masses."

"Anything for you." She whispered back before hugging Bernadette to her side and walking backstage.

Raelyn stopped at the bottom of the stairs when she saw Katy and Zuhra standing next to Maren. They ran up to Raelyn engulfing her into a group hug. She could no longer hold back the tears from falling having her three closest friends with her.

"Girl, next time you want to run away from us. Don't." Zuhra said.

Katy nodded in agreement, "We would have had your back online. You didn't have to delete your blog and yourself out of our lives."

"I'm so sorry. I couldn't deal with everyone coming at me and I didn't want to be a burden on you guys."

"Raelyn Burton, when will you learn that you're not a burden. We love ya." Maren shook her gently making them all laugh.

After the panel were autographs for the main cast. Clifford hung out with Bernadette in the green room while Raelyn and her friends went to each cast member's tables. She practically had to drag Maren away from Ben's table as he laughed pocketing her number she slipped him on a piece of paper. When they approached Austin's table, Raelyn pulled out the item she wanted him to sign.

"Hi, how…" He stopped seeing it was her and grinned, "How are you, darlin'?"

"I'm doing well. How are you?"

"Better now that I'm seeing you." He chuckled.

She set her item on the table, "I bet you say that to all the girls."

Austin shook his head, "I really don't. What am I signing for you?"

She watched as his eyes read the cover then snapped up at her.

"I recently was able to focus solely on my writing career. I had this little story on Tumblr called Runaway and it was a favorite of someone's that is special to me. I was hoping you could sign the first finished manuscript of it."

"You turned Runaway into a book?"

She nodded.

"You wrote a book?"

She started laughing while nodding again.

Austin walked around his table, picking her up and twirling Raelyn around. All around them were fans cheering and clapping for them. He sat her down with his arms still wrapped around her.

"Congratulations pretty girl! I'm so proud of you." He kissed her in front of everyone causing louder cheers, "I can't believe you wrote a book!"

She placed her hands on his chest, "All because of you. All of it was inspired by you and Rhys. That book would not exist without you. Thank you for being in my life."

Raelyn could see the tears shining in his eyes as he leaned on and kissed her again, "Thank you for being in mine."

36

RUNAWAY
EPILOGUE
@PACKNERD71

"Rhys." she said just barely above a whisper.

The sob burning in his chest escaped his lips as he made his way over to the side of her bed. He leaned his head down onto her chest letting out a year's worth of despair. He felt her fingers threading through his long hair as her cheek pressed against the top of his head.

Lifting his head with tears streaming down his cheeks he pressed his lips against hers, no longer being able to hold back. At that moment everything was right in Rhys's world. Everything in his past that brought him to this moment made sense to him and his life was completely perfect.

His Alpha and her Omega together once more bring a balance to his soul that he didn't realize he needed. The how and the why of how Noelle was back would be explained later. Right now, all Rhys wanted to do was enjoy the fleeting moment where he had everything he wanted.

The End.

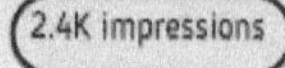 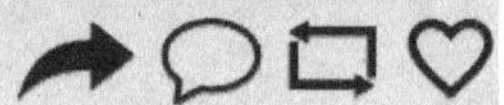

If you enjoyed this story, then check out my ***Masterlist***!

My Nerd Pack: @rhys-remingtons-beta @wolfpackbaby @ladyremington1972 @idreamofwolves @carryonmywolfpackalpha @justaustinandrhys @ajameson-remington @rhys-remington-is-a-warrior @pupperofdoom @rhysrandthepack @redmoon-austin @PackLeaderAlpha

2.4K impressions

RAELYN

Two Years Later

The fall leaves painted the landscape in oranges and reds as Raelyn sat in her office staring out the window. She could not believe where her life was now compared to when she met and fell in love with Austin Jameson. They had many, *many* bumps in the road that led them to where they were now. Every bump was worth it to have the family she always dreamed of.

Raelyn looked back to the stairs hearing the soft thuds of her daughter coming down them. Bernadette was now a sophomore in high school and thriving. She was working with Raelyn on writing and illustrating a graphic novel to be published with her publisher. Yet another thing that had Raelyn constantly pinching herself.

Runaway had been picked up by one of the big four publishing companies and today was her release party for it. She should have been getting ready, but she couldn't pull herself away from her newest project.

"Mom, you have to get ready. Seriously, I feel like the parent in this house between you and dad. I got him in the shower and now I need you to go get dressed."

Raelyn smiled waving for Bernadette to come over to her computer, "I will if you read these couple of pages for me. Please?"

Bernadette rolled her eyes, "Go, go. I'll read."

Raelyn kissed the top of her head and walked up to the master suite. Austin and Bernadette had decided they wanted to move into the house Raelyn had purchased. The first time they visited her, they both had fallen in love with it.

Raelyn walked into their suite hearing the shower shut off. She walked into the large closet pulling out the outfit Maren had picked out for her while video chatting from Montana.

Austin joked that he saw more of Maren than her while they filmed the last season of Red Moon. She walked back out in time to see Austin walking out of the bathroom with a towel wrapped around his waist.

Her breath caught in her throat as her eyes traveled down his body. Droplets of water were running down his broad chest and his hair was sticking up in every direction, being the longest it had ever been. When her eyes finally met his, she could see the same desire pooling shining within them. Even after two years of being together, he still made her heart flutter and body yearn for him. As he slowly walked towards her, Raelyn knew she was in trouble.

"Austin, we can't be late."

"Mmhmm." He hummed still coming towards her, "We could be quick."

Raelyn laughed, "We're a lot of things together. Passionate. Loving. Sweaty."

He laughed as she continued, "Quick, is never something we are together."

The distance closed between them as Austin had backed her up against a wall. They both knew she would never say no because as much as he wanted her, she wanted him. He took her hands dragging them down his chest to his stomach feeling every ab he worked hard for. He stopped when they touched his towel, and she could feel him pressing against her thigh.

"This is your day pretty girl. It's your decision what happens next." He bent his head down brushing his lips against her ear, "You can feel what my vote is."

Raelyn was about to unwrap his towel for his waist when Bernadette knocked on the door.

"You two better be decent in there and getting ready. I swear you guys are worse than the horny kids at school."

Raelyn stifled her laughter as Austin growled in frustration, "Saved by the daughter."

"We'll be down in ten minutes. If we're not then you have every right to come barging in here." Raelyn called out over Austin's shoulder.

"Ten minutes then I get Clifford."

They listened to her footsteps fade as Austin rolled his eyes, "Cock blocked by my own kid. Damn."

Raelyn ran her hand behind his neck pulling his lips to hers and tugging at his hair. He groaned into her kiss and pressed himself firmly against her thigh again.

"You're killing me…"

"Remember, Bernadette is staying over at a friend's house after the party. We have a whole night in the house by ourselves."

Austin's face lit up, "I love the sounds of that."

Raelyn slid her hand over him unable to resist touching the gorgeous man in front of her, "I promise if you're on your best behavior all night then I'll make our private after party worth your suffering now."

She kept stroking him slowly as his head rested on her shoulder, "Hmmm, deal, but you gotta stop touching me or the warden will punish us."

Raelyn withdrew her hand and kissed Austin again, "Couldn't resist. Now get dressed while I get ready in the bathroom."

They were downstairs and ready by the time Bernadette had walked into the living room with Clifford. They started laughing when she handed him a twenty-dollar bill.

"I thought for sure you were going to have to pull them off of each other."

Austin rolled his eyes, "Alright, let's get this show on the road."

Clifford drove them to the Civic Center where Raelyn's literary agent, Leigh Meyer, and Austin's new manager coordinated with the convention company to hold her book release party. They decided to sell a small number of tickets for the event the proceeds going to a local shelter for women and children.

A lot of the cast from Red Moon, their families and friends were in attendance along with about a hundred and fifty fans who would all receive a copy of her book and autographs from her and the Red Moon cast.

People were mingling as they walked inside the main ballroom. Bernadette rushed off finding her core group of friends that she had invited. Including the boy who currently held her heart. Raelyn elbowed Austin in his side gently.

"Stop glaring at the poor boy. He's already terrified of you."

He growled, "He better be terrified of me. He breaks her heart, I'm gonna break his legs."

Raelyn chuckled pulling him towards their group of friends. Jackson and Calliope were talking with Maren and Ben. The three couples had become a small family over the last couple of years. Jackson and Calliope had recently gotten engaged while on vacation after the show had finished filming.

While Maren had recently moved into a bigger home so Ben could be there in Lawrence. Since he could travel for his job, it made sense to them for him to move to her. It wouldn't surprise Raelyn if they were engaged soon, as well. Leaving her and Austin still only dating.

Must be something wrong with you. Not like you're both busy with careers and anything.

Her inner voice piped in as she finished off her champagne to quiet her. Maren hooked her arm with Raelyn's pointing to Austin.

"What's with the mountain man look? It wasn't that long ago I saw you in Montana looking more like a man and not Bigfoot."

The group laughed as Raelyn brushed a strand of his hair back behind his ear, "I like it. Well, the hair at least. The beard could be trimmed up."

Austin looked over at her, his bottom lip disappearing beneath his teeth and his eyebrow arching. She narrowed her eyes at him with a silent warning. She had recently confessed a few days earlier how his beard had inspired a whole new series of sexy one-shots on her blog. The memory made her shiver as he leaned in, pressing his lips to her ear.

"You were loving my beard earlier this morning."

Raelyn let out a shaky breath as he chuckled.

Leigh walked up, leading her backstage to get the event started. Raelyn looked over the schedule feeling her chest tightening. Public speaking was never something she wanted to do. That's why she was a writer.

Now, she was positive if she were to open her mouth the only thing that would follow was vomit. She was about to run to the trash can when she spotted Austin walking behind the stage.

Raelyn ran up to him, burying her face into the crook of his neck trying to push the panic back down into the void which it came from. He held her tightly rocking her back and forth.

"You got this, pretty girl. All the people out there love you and are so proud of you. The fans have said nothing but good things about it. You have nothing to worry about."

She nodded, "You're right. You're right. I... I just can't shake the nerves away."

Austin looked around them before placing his hand on the back of her neck and crashing his lips to hers. Her hands went up into his silky hair pulling at it. His chest rumbled with a groan as hands traveled down the curves of her body. She no longer flinched when his hands went over the speed bumps of her body. She didn't shy away when his hands slid over her butt and pushed her against him. No longer did she ask for the lights to be turned off or to hide from everyone when he showed some PDA. Her confidence soared when she was with Austin because she knew in his eyes, she was beautiful and that was all that mattered.

"Better?" He asked, resting his forehead on hers.

Her knees were jello, her body filled with desire and her mind cleared of all panic.

"Much. Thank you and I hate you."

He started laughing, "W-Why?"

She smiled up at him, "Because now I have to go out there and speak to people with ruined panties."

"Well at least you can hide yours. Pretty sure the show I'm giving right now will be all over the fansites later tonight."

Raelyn glanced down seeing how worked up he truly was, and another wave of yearning washed over her. Looking back up, she watched his eyes darken as she chewed on her bottom lip.

"Only a few hours then we can screw each other silly. Promise."

"Oh, I plan on making you keep that promise. Now, I'm going to go out there and do my thing." He kissed her once more, "You'll be great. I love you and incredibly proud of you."

He kissed her quickly, heading towards the side stage. She giggled watching him adjust himself then walking out with a microphone.

Everything went as smooth as it could. Raelyn made it through reading the first chapter and the fan questions. When Calliope came out on stage, she was surprised since the signing portion was supposed to start.

"Hello everyone. For those who don't know me, I'm Calliope Melton and I played the adorable omega, Ash, on Red Moon. We have a little surprise video for our number one Red Moon fan, Miss Raelyn Burton."

The room went dark as a video started to play. Calliope wrapped her arms around Raelyn as they watched the video. Raelyn could hardly hold back the tears as bloggers from Red Moon read their comments from her original fanfiction story. There must have been twenty or thirty people including Katy and Zuhra who couldn't be at the release party.

The video ended with a frame of text saying, *And from her biggest fan...*

Austin appeared on stage reading the comments he had posted.

Intriguing... I can't wait for the first chapter.

Let the slow burn begin! Rhys is going to have his hands full with her. My favorite part was this: "She leaned against it taking a deep breath now trying to calm her body once more as it was buzzing with new emotions. Excitement and hope were running through her veins followed quickly by doubt and guilt." I can relate... oh, how I can relate.

Man, oh man, things are certainly building between those two. Rhys needs to hurry up and just kiss her! Another amazing chapter.

NOOOOOOO!!!!!! @packnerd71 Why?!?!? Oh, you know Rhys is going to rush there and kick some major Alpha ass! He has to get to her in time... please tell me he gets to her in time! Ahhh! I need the next chapter!

I was scared Rhys wasn't going to make it in time, but I should have never doubted him. I really wish he could have taken a chunk out of Andrew. I hope he'll be able to help Noelle through this. Can't wait to see how their relationship changes after this. Loving this series @packnerd71

"Playing Rhys Remington for thirteen years gave me insight of how his mind worked, his feelings and struggles. Raelyn was able to write more layers and more depth to a character I felt was living inside of me. There is no one who gets Rhys like I do except for Raelyn Burton. I knew she would be the only one who could continue the Red Moon pack stories."

Austin laced their hands together as he continued, "She's a weaver of tales and builds a story that will comfort readers then leave them needing more. I could not be prouder of her than achieving her goal of being a published author and inspiring young writers all over the world. Including our daughter, Birdie."

She glanced down to see Bernadette wiping away tears tucked under her boyfriend's arm.

"Here's to the first book in the Red Moon Pack series, Runaway and the beautiful, talented, inspiring Raelyn Burton."

Everyone in the room began cheering as Austin pulled her into his arms, "Congratulations pretty girl. I love you."

"I love you too." She kissed him, not caring if everyone saw them.

Her favorite part of the night, after Austin's speech, was being able to talk with fans about her book. She tried to spend as much time as possible with each of them and ended up going late into the evening. She had one book left to sign and looking up she giggled seeing Austin standing there.

"How the tables have turned." He laughed sliding his book in front of her.

"Who should I make this out to?" she asked before looking down to the open book.

A small gasp escaped her lips as she watched him place a small velvet box on top of her book. Within it sat a beautiful shining diamond ring and suddenly Austin was eye level with her sitting in a chair. Their friends and family were surrounding them all with big smiles on their faces.

"Raelyn, I fell in love with you from the moment I saw your picture and read your stories online. For a time, I had to imagine what my life would look without you in it, and I hated it. I never want to imagine my life without you again. Raelyn Burton, will you be a part of my life forever as my wife and marry me?"

She picked up her marker and opened his book. Her hand was shaking as she wrote out his name then her answer signing her name beneath it.

"Yes. Yes!" She walked around the table and kissed him.

He slipped the ring on her finger then turned around revealing Bernadette behind him. She had tears running down her face holding onto a packet of papers.

"A month ago, my dad received a letter from the family courts in Louisiana stating my mother had given up her parental rights to me."

Raelyn's jaw dropped as she looked from Austin to Bernadette, "Oh sweetie…"

"It's fine. I'm fine because my mom made a great sacrifice in order to do what was best for me. Even though I will be eighteen in a couple of years, I still want to do what is best for me. You told me that when you came back into my life. I always have to take care of me first."

Raelyn wiped away the tears on her cheeks, "Yes I did."

"I ask dad to help me start a process that can be finished once you two are married." Bernadette handed her the papers in her hands, "Raelyn, will you officially become my mom and legally adopt me?"

She felt Austin's arm wrap around her as she stared down at the adoption papers. Looking up at him, she could see the pride in his eyes that were focused on his little girl.

"Bernadette, it would be my honor to be your mom." She hugged her whispering, "No matter what these papers say. You were always my daughter and I love you so much."

"I know mom. I love you too and that's why I want it to be official."

Austin came up behind them wrapping his arms around them and then everyone around them followed suit.

Once Raelyn was home, the exhaustion from the night took over the moment she laid down on their bed. When she woke up a few hours later, Austin was sitting up beside her on his tablet. She laughed softly seeing him reading fanfiction.

"Hey sleepyhead."

"Sorry handsome, I know we were supposed to have this wild, sexy night and I passed out on you." She pushed herself up enough to kiss his cheek then snuggled into his side.

Austin kissed her head, "It's okay. I think you agreeing to marry me and to be Birdie's mom made up for it. We will have plenty of time for wild and sexy times."

"Looks like you're still getting your sexy times with that fanfic. Whew."

Raelyn had read a little of the smut scene happening between Rhys and female main character. Austin set his tablet down and laid down beside her.

"Promise me, you won't stop writing fanfiction. It's such a vital part of the fandom and I would hate for ours to lose your stories."

Raelyn ran her fingers through his hair, "I promise I won't stop writing fanfiction. Actually, come with me. I want to show you something."

They walked down to her office, and she pulled up a folder for her newest manuscript that wasn't a Red Moon novel. She opened the outline she had finished a few days earlier. Austin sat in her chair, while she sat on his lap letting him read her next project.

"So, you've created a whole fake fandom and fake fanfiction for that fandom to insert into a book about a man meeting his favorite actress and falling in love?"

"Yep." She answered simply.

Austin chuckled, "That's brilliant. What's the title?"

She opened the manuscript to show him the working title.

"I love it. This book is going to be very meta for you." Austin hugged her tightly before kissing her cheek and making her laugh.

Raelyn read the title one last time before shutting down her computer and following Austin back up to their room.

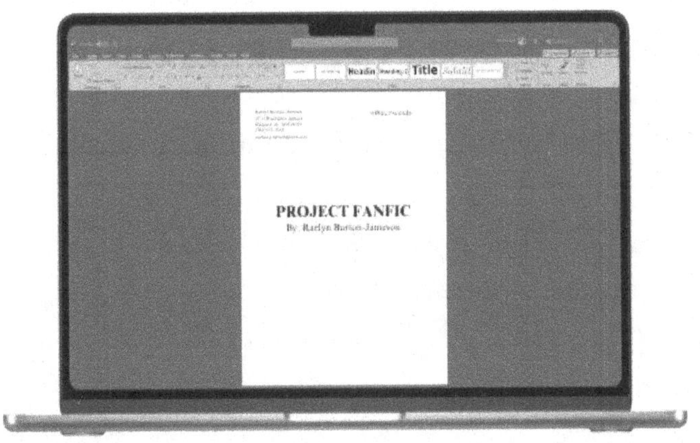
PROJECT FANFIC
By: Raelyn Burton-Jameson

THE
End

SNEAK PEEK

Book 2 in the Fangirl Series coming out early 2025

Buzzworthy Mention! Author Laurel Adler's debut novel, Tethered Souls, is a whirlwind paranormal romance that will keep you on the edge of your seat while asking yourself will they or won't they. Following our wayward heroine, Scarlet, on an adventure to find the witch that cursed her from birth. Her path leads her to find a rough around the edges hunter of monsters, Justin. When the curse latches onto Justin, they both come to find their destinies were always tied together. If you love a world filled with supernatural creatures, a knight in a shining classic car and twist ends then you should absolutely check out Tethered Souls.

Laurel leaned back in her office chair rereading the blurb about her debut novel. It was still surreal that her book was out in the world for people to read. Her agent, Leigh Meyer, had sent her the link to Buzzfeed's article that also featured another one of her clients' books. Leigh had a lot of buzz going for her three newest clients that all had debut or sophomore titles releasing.

Laurel's phone buzzed with a new text from her debut authors group thread.

Raelyn: Did you see?! buzzfeed.com/books/mostanticipatedreleases Emerson: Look at you guys getting all the hype! Congrats!

Me: Leigh just sent it to me. Pretty cool.

Laurel wasn't good at handling praise rather it was from friends or the press. It was moments like this she wished her best friend, Thomas Reed, was around. He would have had some kind of wisdom to bestow onto her about accepting the good and pushing the doubt aside. For a split moment, she thought about calling him, but knew he was busy and didn't want to bother him over something so little.

Emerson: Pretty cool? Girl, this is awesome! For a debut to get a mention on that list is amazing

Me: I know… I guess I'm not used to people knowing about my book

Emerson: Well you better get used to it!

She rolled her eyes thankful that neither of her friends could see her. Raelyn Jameson and Emerson Holbrook both had books releasing but had been in the literary world one way or another beforehand. Raelyn had a successful series of novellas based off her husband's TV show. Raelyn's first standalone book, Project Fanfic, was inspired by how she met her husband. Similarly, Emerson's debut book was about the same. She was a social media manager who after much encouragement from her boyfriend decided to write her book.

Laurel was the oddball of the group. Her debut novel was inspired by pure imagination and the desperate hope that there was someone out there for everyone. It was only dumb luck that she had submitted her book to Leigh on accident. She had meant to send it to another literary agent with a similar name at the same agency. The universe took pity on her and Leigh ended up loving her book. In a complete whirlwind of a year and half, Laurel's life changed when they sold her book to the same publishing house as Raelyn's. Now, her book was out there, and her publishers were waiting for her next book. Which was what Laurel was trying to work on when Leigh had sent her the link from Buzzfeed.

For the last three weeks, she had been sitting in her office staring at a blank document and blinking cursor. She had an outline for a sequel to Tethered Souls, but the words were not coming out. The floodgates of doubt and self-loathing had busted wide open.

Raelyn: Hey Laurel, isn't this your best friend?

Raelyn: news.google.com/entertainment/heartstrings/zeppelinfoster

She clicked on the article. Her heart dropped seeing the photo attached and skimming the article.

Rockstar Gone Wild. Zeppelin Foster, lead vocals for the rock band, Heartstrings, held a wild after party in celebration for his band's album reaching platinum status. They were at, Envy, a local club in Los Angeles, where it is reported Foster was buying drinks for everyone. When the club closed at 2AM, Foster is seen here leaving with no shirt on, drinking from a bottle of whiskey and two young ladies beside him.

Me: Crap... I need to go. I'll talk to you guys later

Her stomach churning from seeing her other best friend drunk and leaving with two girls, he could easily be their father.

Me: I'm sure you've seen the news about Zepp. Is he okay?

She sent her text to Thomas, who happen to be Zeppelin's manager. The three of them had been friends since grade school. When Zeppelin had decided to pursue being a rockstar, Thomas had insisted on being his manager. They had been by each other's sides navigating fame and fortune leaving Laurel to her books and modest life. It was moments like this that she was thankful Thomas was there for Zeppelin. His wild spirit was one of the many things that attracted her to him, but he needed someone to be a voice of reason in his life. *Thomas: I don't know yet. I'm on my way to him now. I'll let you know*

Me: Please do and smack him upside his head for me

Thomas: LOL! With pleasure

Looking at the picture of them on her desk, the familiar ache from deep in her chest throbbed. Most days, Laurel preferred the solitude of writing full time. She was uncomfortable socializing or speaking in front of people. She hated large crowds and always found ways to seemingly disappear into the background. The only time she ever wanted to talk or hang out with anyone was with her boys or new author friends. Right now, she was missing her boys a lot.

REBLOGS & HEARTS PLAYLIST

TOP 10 SONGS

1. All Our Own - Radio Company

2. Fictional - Khloe Rose

3. Rewrite the Stars - Zac Efron, Zendaya

4. Slow Burn - Kacey Musgraves

5. Yeah Boy - Kelsea Ballerini

6. Chasing After You - Ryan Hurd, Maren Morris

7. Rush Rush - Paula Abdul

8. Worth It - Danielle Bradbery

9. I'll Remember - Madonna

10. Rock Song (Acoustic) - Louden Swain

Check out the full playlist by scanning the QR below!

ACKNOWLEDGEMENTS

I would like to thank my Supernatural fandom family for being one of the main inspirations for this story. I particularly want to thank Kat, Zee, Jen, Jordan, and Kelly for all your love and support. I would not be the writer or woman today without all of you in my life.

I want to thank my best friends for always putting up with my crazy writer ways and for being the first people to read my drafts. Paul, Megan, and Morgan, I love you all.

To J.A. the man who inspired Austin Jameson, the constant joy and light you give to the world through the roles you play is immeasurable. Thank you for all the blood, sweat, tears and time you put into your craft.

Finally, to my Mumsie… I would not be the woman I am today without you. Thank you for always listening to my ramblings about my characters, my writing, and my favorite actor. You have always been my greatest inspiration and role model. I love you.

ABOUT THE AUTHOR

Nikki Rae was born and raised in Saint Louis, Missouri, being an only child with her imagination to entertain her most days. As a child, she discovered her love for writing that continued throughout her childhood and teens.

Experiencing her own heartache as an adult led her to finding her favorite TV show, actor, and fandom family. That moment would be the inspiration for her novel, Reblogs & Hearts.

Still residing in Missouri, Nikki spends her days working as an Assistant Deli Manager at a local grocery store. She loves to read, attend concerts, travel to fan conventions and snuggle with any one of her three cats that deem her worthy of their time.